Best Wishes

Tony Award

Revenge
In the Motor City

Tony Aued

ISBN:-10-1539102580
ISBN-13:978-1539102588

This book is dedicated to my wife and best friend, Kathy.

Tony Aued

Cover is courtesy of Virgilio Art. Special thanks to Carl for all his hard work.

Other Novels by Tony Aued

FBI Thrillers

Blair Adams, The Package

The Abduction

The Vegas Connection

The Blame Game

Murder Mysteries

Murder In Greektown

Greektown Conspiracy

Motor City Justice

ONE

John Franklin couldn't believe that it was two in the morning as he stumbled while searching for his car in the parking lot of the Gentlemen's Club on Eight Mile Road. He wasn't sure where he parked. The flashing yellow lights behind him announced the evening's entertainment with a ten-foot-high silhouette of a beautiful blonde woman dancing across a stage. Searching through his pockets, Franklin's fingers fumbled while trying to grip his car keys. It was close to closing time and he had had more than one too many. Holding onto cars to steady himself, he hit the alarm on the key fob. It sent out a screeching sound telling Franklin that his car was around the corner. He took a deep breath hoping to gather his composure. Opening the door, he slumped behind the steering wheel just as he was about to heave out everything he'd spent hundreds on. Before he could react up it came. "Shit," he yelled, although no one was anywhere near to hear him. It hit the inside of the glass, spraying back all over him. Franklin's breathing was rapid; everything outside was spinning and he had trouble focusing. *Oh my God, I can't drive like this.* So many drunks think that they are okay to drive, although they often have an inner struggle, knowing better, but not listening to the voice of reason. He thought, *Can't get a DUI, it would be all over the front page.* He bent forward, his head resting on the steering wheel.

A harsh voice outside startled him, "Hey buddy, you okay?" Franklin looked out the driver's window splattered with the evening's fare, attempting to focus on the man standing next to the side of his car. Trying to wave the guy off, he slumped back in the seat, hoping to steady himself. Pressing the window button to lower it a few inches, he felt the rush of fresh air. It was cool outside, and his breathing caused the windshield to fog up, so much so that Franklin couldn't see anything. He again closed his eyes. John Franklin's life was spiraling out of control; he was going through an ugly divorce from his high school sweetheart. He came from a prominent family that put him in a position to be appointed by the mayor to a special commission. Now as the deputy mayor, he was investigating corruption in the Detroit Public Schools, a job that he excelled at. In the first year alone, he uncovered many schools receiving less-than-standard equipment from suppliers, although they were paying for a quality product. As the mayor's right-hand-man, Franklin was a key person on the mayor's staff, but the divorce was taking its toll. Drinking and hanging out in strip joints would finally catch up with him. John was like many forty-year-old men who become disappointed with their marriage, lose interest in their job and turn to alcohol. There wasn't any winner in that game, just a life headed for disaster.

The loud sound of someone rapping on the driver's side window startled Franklin from his drunken stupor. He saw a giant man outside. The guy was yelling, "You can't sleep here, this ain't a hotel; pull your car out of here, now." Franklin tried wiping the inside of the driver's side window that was crusted with drying pieces of food and slime. He was trying to see who in the hell was shouting at him. Lowering the window a little more, he saw a tall man standing next to his car. The guy was huge, maybe six foot four or five, holding a club in his right hand. The guy again yelled, "You heard me, you can't stay here; pull your car out now!" This time the man rapped his club against the side of Franklin's Ford. "I said go!" Franklin tried waving him off as he started the car. He searched the entertainment system of his white Ford SUV, "Where is the button for the defroster?" he said aloud. Franklin could see the man still standing next to his car as he rolled the puke splattered window all the way down.

John figured he needed to say something. "Sorry, I'm just tired, give me a minute."

The big man waited but didn't look very friendly. Not sure if the guy behind the steering wheel could drive, he continued to watch Franklin who had been slumped in the driver's seat just seconds earlier. Sticking his club in the car's open window, in a gruff voice he said, "Pal, you don't look good, let me call you a cab."

"No, I'm fine." He put the gearshift in reverse and slowly backed up. Thankfully there weren't any cars directly behind him. *Stroke of luck*, he thought. Looking at the screen on his dash that showed parked cars in the row behind his, he was glad that he had the rear camera to help with the task. Exiting the parking lot, he could see that traffic on Eight Mile Road appeared clear. He now was talking to himself, "Only a couple miles from here, I'll be fine." Turning right onto Eight Mile he headed east to I-94. He was startled when another car seemingly coming out from nowhere blew its horn at him. His response wasn't exactly friendly as he stuck his finger out of the window. The air rushing in felt good and helped keep him alert, as much as you could be after a dozen shots and stuffing singles into your favorite strippers outfit, or lack thereof. Although he was swerving, there wasn't a cop car in sight, so maybe this was his lucky day.

He turned onto the ramp to I-94 and headed downtown toward his condo off of Jefferson. Trying to steer the vehicle and stay in the far right lane was quite a task but Franklin made it to his exit and headed south. Once he reached Jefferson, he went west to Joseph Campau and turned into the parking lot of the Stroh River Place condos. Pulling down the long street past the Atwater Brewery into the condo parking lot he stopped, pissed that someone was parked in his spot. "Damn, this is crap," he yelled out the window. Franklin saw several openings near the river bank that were marked

"Management Only." He accelerated into one of the spots, squealing tires and slamming the car into park. He slid out from behind the wheel, seeing that he had taken at least two spots. Shaking his head, he stumbled to his lower level condo door. Struggling to unlock the door, he dropped the keys twice finally got the front door open. Once he was inside, he tossed his stained jacket and pants on the floor, walked to the bedroom and fell onto the king-size bed, alone again. John Franklin passed out, happy to have made it home without incident.

***

The red and blue flashing lights from the police car in the parking lot brought residents out of their apartments, some with cups of coffee, others dressed and ready for work. 911 calls to the police came in from one of the managers who spotted the body in the parking lot. The caller was still in the state of shock when the officers arrived. It was just after six in the morning and traffic hadn't started building up downtown. The Stroh River Place was in the shadows of the Renaissance Center along the renovated Riverwalk. "What's going on down there?" a resident asked her husband as she stood looking out through their French doors. They saw the rental manager standing with two officers, both pointing to the vehicle in the lot.

"I'm not sure except that guy from downstairs parked his car across at least two spots." Her husband was shaking his head, "Not sure what's going on but it looks like it has something to do with the white Ford Explorer."

"I thought you sent a complaint to the management company about that vehicle parked all over the place."

"I did. They promised that they'd do something but it looks like it didn't do any good. They continued watching as an EMS vehicle pulled in and stopped next to the police car. He stepped outside for a better view and called back to his wife, "Must be someone hurt, there's an emergency vehicle out there now." She moved next to him and watched two people in uniform standing at the front of the Ford SUV.

Neighbors were gathered outside around the scene while an officer kept them back with his arms opened wide. "You got to stay back folks, we've got to secure the area." Thirty minutes had passed when an unmarked car arrived. It pulled to the other side of the black and white, blocking the view people might have had of the front of the Ford. Detective Jim Sampson stepped out of the arriving vehicle and moved next to the cop standing near the Ford. Sampson was a veteran of the force and involved in many important cases. He asked, "Have you been able to contact the person who owns that vehicle?'

"No. We ran the plate and the owner lives in the building across the way, name's John Franklin. Not sure why but that name sounds familiar. We knocked several times but no one answered."

A young lady dressed in a business suit who was standing close overhead them. She interrupted, "Officer, the car belongs to the guy that lives in that lower condo." She pointed directly to Franklin's place. The high-end condo units were located just off of East Jefferson and St. Aubin Street and ran in a semi-circle around a small pond. The parking lot was in the outer rim and buffered up to tall grass and cattails that were common to land that bordered the Detroit River.

The officer moved closer to her. "Do you know the guy?"

"No, not really. Only thing I know for sure is he works downtown. I met his wife once and I know they'd been having problems and I heard she left him a while back. Seems they had been arguing a lot. I guess that it was pretty ugly near the end."

"Thanks." Sampson, a tall dark haired man turned to the other detective who rode with him. The second detective, a much shorter man nodded as Sampson told him what the officer's said. There were close to twenty residents now in the driveway where the officers were roping off the area around at least three parking spots, with Franklin's car in the center. The two detectives headed back to the first floor condo with an officer. Knocking on the door, there still wasn't a response. The officer pounded harder and called out, "Police!" They stood there for a few minutes waiting for an answer. Sampson asked, "Are we sure he's in there?" The officer answered, "Residents said he's been known to drink heavily and his car is out there. I'd say he's in."

The officer rapped his club on the front window frame. This was the second time Franklin heard knocking outside, but this time it startled him. He opened his eyes but the room was spinning and he wasn't in any condition to walk let alone see who was there. The knocking was unbearable. *What the hell!* The noise got louder. Finally Franklin yelled out, "I'm coming, keep your shirt on." He stumbled out of the bed, still feeling dizzy, into the living room. He again called out, "I'm coming." There were clothes strewn across the floor. Franklin moved to the door and opened it a few inches. Standing in his boxer shorts he yelled, "What do you want?"

Detective Sampson displayed his badge, stating again, "Detroit Police!" As the door opened a little, Sampson saw the man, quickly recognizing him. "Mr. Franklin, you need to let us in."

"Police?" Keeping his hand on the door, Franklin peeked through the opening, only to see the other two officers standing outside. "What do you want?"

"You need to let us in."

Franklin moved closer looking out at the man through the slight opening and as he did that, Sampson slipped his foot into the gap. Franklin had no choice and allowed them to enter. They noted the clothes tossed on the floor, dirty dishes and empty beer bottles on the coffee table. Sampson stared at the man in front of them; he looked pretty rough. "Are you John Franklin?" He nodded. "Do you own a white Ford Explorer?" Franklin wondered what the hell was going on, but again nodded.

Moving further back into the room, Franklin asked, "What's this all about?"

"Better put a pair of pants on Mr. Franklin, you'll need to come downtown with us."

Franklin was trying to gather his senses, "I'm not going anywhere until you tell me what this is about."

"Get dressed Mr. Franklin; we'll tell you once we're outside. It would be best for you to follow our orders."

Franklin turned toward the bedroom then stopped. "You need to tell me what's going on now. I'm not going anywhere with you." He became indignant, "Do you know who I am? I work for the mayor; you can call him." He plopped down in a large chair.

"Not a good move Mr. Franklin. We know who you are, and it's not going to help you right now." Sampson approached, "Please stand up." Franklin resisted, but an officer moved in grabbing his right arm. "Stand up, now." Once Franklin stood, the officer said, "Turn around." Grabbing handcuffs from his belt, he cuffed Franklin, much to the man's sudden shock."

"Hey, what the hell! Didn't you hear me? I work for the mayor. I'm not going anywhere with you!"

Sampson quickly jumped in, "Officer, Mr. Franklin is the deputy mayor. We'll take him downtown but let's do it with a little care."

The officer nodded, removing the cuffs, "Okay. Mr. Franklin, you need to come with us." Putting his hand on Franklin's back and moving him to the bedroom, "You'll need to put some clothes on, you're going downtown." Franklin wanted to resist but was having trouble walking and wasn't in any condition to argue with the officers but he asked, "What's going on?"

The officer turned to Sampson, Jim said, "Let me handle this. John, we've found a dead body under your truck. If you've run someone over you'll be charged with vehicular homicide."

John Franklin was stunned; *I didn't hit anyone, did I?* His mind replayed everything from the previous night. Too many Jack Daniels shots; it was all so murky. He was still dazed; there was no way to gather any details from last night. "Let's get dressed Mr. Franklin, you can make your call when we get downtown."

***

Outside paramedics were hard at work under the front of the white Explorer, kneeling on the grass with a stretcher nearby, while an officer was taking photos of the scene. Another strung yellow tape around the area as the crowd was being moved further back. "Officer, you'll want to document this, bring your camera," the paramedic called out. A second medic slid under the bumper as they tried to free the body. Although badly mangled, the only thing they were sure of was that it was a female. Her legs were crushed and the skirt was caught under the front of the vehicle. One of them called to the officer, "We've got a problem."

"What kind of problem?"

"The lady's body is tangled in the frame. We need to lift this vehicle to get her out."

"On the frame?" The officer moved closer, ducking further down to see what they were talking about. "Oh shit, she's mangled." He quickly pushed back from under the vehicle, feeling sick at the sight. "I'll get the detective. What do you need us to do?"

"You'll need to get a tow truck to lift the vehicle up so we can get her out." The officer made a call as the two medics slid out from under the Ford.

Onlookers peered around to see what they were doing. One lady turned to the crowd, "I think there's a body under that car." A voice behind her asked, "Can you see who it is?" She shook her head. Someone behind was heard asking, "Is it Franklin's wife, Misty?" They watched with anticipation. What could Franklin have done? People were buzzing as the paramedics continued to move along the front of the vehicle. Another person in the crowd yelled, "Hey, look," pointing to where Franklin was being escorted in cuffs to a police car, "they're taking him in." People could see the officer who had his hand on Franklin's back. The man was cuffed and they were putting him in the back seat of a squad car. Franklin sat in the vehicle, still dazed, trying to figure out how this happened. He shook his head, trying to remember the events of last night. He knew that he was wasted leaving the parking lot of the strip club on Eight Mile, but he didn't remember anything that would cause him to be arrested. "Hey, Officer, I never hit anyone with my car, why in the heck are you taking me in?" The two men in the front never turned to acknowledge his question. Now Franklin was yelling, "I'm innocent, you need to take me back home, now!"

One of the officers in the front turned around, "Mr. Franklin, you have the right to remain silent, anything you say…"

"Okay, I got it, you're reading me my rights. I need to talk to your superior."

"You've met Detective Sampson, he's handling the case and will go over everything with you at the precinct." Staring at Franklin, waiting for a response, the officer finally turned back around when the rider in the back didn't have anything more to say. The ride from Stroh Place condos on Jefferson to the Second Precinct was short. The squad car pulled up to the front of the building and one of the officers got out and opened the back door. "This is where you get out." Franklin slid his feet out the opening and started to stand as the officer put his hand on Franklin's head so that he didn't hit it on the door frame.

They escorted the suspect into the building and were met by the desk sergeant. "Who you got there, Bill?"

"John Franklin, the suspect in the incident at Stroh Place."

"Put him in interview room two, Detective Sampson is still at the scene. I'll let him know where his suspect is." The desk sergeant looked as the two men headed toward the hallway, thinking, *He looks familiar.*

Franklin started to walk with the officer, and then stopped. The drunken stupor was wearing off, "I demand to know what in the hell this is all about!"

The officer gripped Franklin by the handcuffs and continued directing him toward the short hallway, as he explained, "Listen, walk with me, we're going to the interview room." Franklin was shaking, but did as he was told. "I want my lawyer; I demand to get my phone call!"

They continued down the hall and once he was inside the interview room another officer entered, "Mr. Franklin, I'll need to do a breathalyzer test."

"Not until I talk to my attorney!"

"That's not a good idea, Mr. Franklin. We know you've had a few drinks and I'm guessing you've slept much of it off. It isn't going to look good if you refuse the test."

He thought about it for a minute. *Maybe they're right*, "Okay, but I want it noted that I requested my attorney." The officer administered the test twice. Franklin asked, "So, what's the verdict?"

"Looks like you blew a 0.08."

"Hey, that's under .10, I'm in the clear."

"No, in Michigan you register impaired. Our laws are the same as everywhere else in the U.S. and your numbers are over the limit; you're still drunk this morning."

"I want my attorney, now!"

"Take that up with Detective Sampson when he gets here. Until then, the only thing I can offer you is a cup of coffee. You don't look so good."

Franklin knew it was over. "At least call the mayor's office and give them a message for me."

The officer figured that he would take the number to quiet Franklin down. "Give me a phone number, I'll ask the captain but no promises."

Once the officer left Franklin he gave the information to his captain. The captain looked at the note. "It's the mayor's office number. I'll make the call, he'll want to know where his deputy is, and more importantly, why. Is he still cuffed to the table?"

"Yes, sir."

"Under these circumstances let's put someone in there with him, tell them to remove the cuffs. I don't want someone coming back and saying we abused the suspect or tried to coerce a confession."

TWO

The early morning call to the Special Investigative Unit from Chief Mathews was unusual. Mindy, the teams secretary, turned to Don, "Detective Frederickson, it's the chief, he's on line one."

He looked at his watch surprised, grabbing the phone and turning to Mindy, "Christ it's only seven-thirty, wonder what's up!" He answered the call, "Yes, Chief, what can I do for you?"

"Don, I hoped you were in. Hate to do this, but the mayor called, looks like a member of his staff is in some kind of a mess. Seems that the guy has been having problems and was arrested this morning. Don, it doesn't look good. The information we have is he's suspected of possible vehicular homicide."

Frederickson raised his eyebrows, "Vehicular homicide?" He took a breath, "Okay, Chief, who is it?"

"The deputy mayor, John Franklin."

The detective was shocked, surprised it hadn't hit the news yet. "I understand Chief, this is big and it could be front page news."

The chief continued, "Don, I wouldn't want to get us involved but the mayor is concerned. This is an election year and this will have obvious repercussions along with everything else the mayor's been dealing with."

Frederickson got it-- political fallout. The deputy mayor has been arrested and it will reflect on the administration. "Sure Chief, what do you want us to do?"

"Don, check it out, get the details, I want it off the record. I'll get back with the mayor."

"Okay, I'll put Detectives Spano and Harper on it right away." He got up from his desk moving slowly, still having some problems with his left knee from the accident the previous year. He'd been back to work for only a few weeks but insisted that he was ready to return to the force. Walking toward Harper's desk, he stated, "The chief wants us to check out an arrest for him." She looked up as he waved to Detective Spano who had just come into the room. Joe Spano moved next to Amy Harper's desk as Frederickson detailed their assignment.

Amy was the first to speak, "So who's been arrested?"

Frederickson sat down. "The deputy mayor. May be involved in a possible vehicular homicide. So far the police haven't released Franklin's name or details until they are sure that he is responsible for the accident. That gives us little time to gather whatever we can." Both Spano and Harper listened, knowing that this was a bit unusual but with it being a high profile suspect, it was understandable. "The chief wants us to gather details on the incident right now and report back to him."

Amy Harper asked, making sure she understood, "If we're only to get the details, couldn't the precinct involved do that and relay it back to the chief?" This didn't make much sense to her.

"Listen, we're doing this as a favor to the mayor; he wants us to help so he's not involved. Right now that's our only assignment. Like I said, the guy works for the mayor. I'm sure he wants to know what the facts are before it hits the papers."

Spano chuckled, "Figures, some big shot runs someone down and we're supposed to keep it quiet."

Frederickson stood, "No, Joe, you don't have it. The chief wants us involved, but right now just behind the scene. We have to keep the chief and mayor in the background for now; it's not a cover-up. Now just get us the details." Spano looked down at the floor. "I want Amy to head to the Second Precinct and see what this case is about. Vehicular homicide is going to be big news; not sure if it's a hit-

and-run situation." Turning back to Spano, "Joe, how about you heading to Stroh's River Place condos. Maybe you can get a look at the accident scene."

The two detectives headed out and Frederickson moved back to his desk. It had been eight months since the crash on I-94. He was glad to be back at work at downtown headquarters. The team of course was keeping an eye on him but he kept telling them, "I'm okay, 100%. I don't want any of you showing me extra care." The SIU team had always been close, but after the events last year, they were even closer.

Detectives Harper and Spano walked to their squad cars in the garage. "Spano, don't worry, Frederickson understood what you meant." He nodded, but felt bad that he said what he had. "Joe, call me from the scene, I'll do the same from the Second." The ride from downtown to the Second Precinct only took Harper a few minutes. She pulled to the far end of the officer's lot and walked to the front door.

The desk sergeant looked up and chuckled, "Detective Harper. You slumming?"

She laughed, "Hi, Bob, how's Julie and the kids?"

"Good, thanks for asking." He glanced at the single gold bar on her lapel. "Congrats are in order, Lieutenant. How can we help you?"

"The chief needs some details on a suspect that you're holding."

"Must be the guy who keeps yelling that he works for the mayor. We've got him in interview room two. I'll show you the way."

"Thanks, but right now I just need to talk to the arresting officers or the detective handling the case."

The sergeant looked at the sheet on his desk, "The case is being handled by Jim Sampson." Turning he pointed to two men standing in the precinct captain's office. "Sampson's the tall guy."

"Thanks." He buzzed her in and she walked toward the captain's office. Watching Amy walk past he smiled, like many of the men that met her, she always got smiles. Why not, Amy Harper was beautiful, tall with short dark hair that highlighted the curve of her face. Harper always got second looks from the guys. Standing outside the room, she watched as the two men seemed to be having a disagreement. The tall guy, Sampson, was leading the conversation. Harper wondered what the issue was.

The man behind the desk looked up and saw her standing outside, and the meeting quickly broke up. The captain stood, saying something to the officer who turned and walked out. The captain followed him. "Lieutenant, what brings you down to the Second Precinct?"

Harper smiled, "Captain, I'm not trying to interfere with your investigation. We were called by the chief to get some details on the John Franklin arrest. We're just on a fact-finding mission." She noticed that he took a step back when she mentioned Chief Mathews. "Our team was directed to get details for the mayor before this all hit the press."

"I understand. We haven't all the details yet, but I'll give you everything we've got so far." They both walked into his office and he motioned for Harper to sit. Grabbing his phone he called Detective Sampson, "You need to get in here and bring the details on the Franklin case." The captain had been on the job for over twenty years, and he always remembered the commandment that his first partner taught him: You work with what you've got. Yes, Franklin was the deputy mayor, however, it's his car that was on top of a female's body in the parking lot and he was stone drunk with no recollection of the events of last night. If Franklin didn't kill the lady, maybe questioning him might lead them to the killer, but until then, it was Franklin's ass in the sling for it.

***

Driving to the condos along the Detroit River, Detective Spano wished that he hadn't spouted off about a potential cover-up. Lieutenant Frederickson put him in his place right away about the assignment on the mayor's staff. *Got to learn to keep my big mouth shut.* Arriving at the parking lot at Stroh River Place, he saw the wrecker loading the suspect's Ford Explorer onto the flatbed. He turned on his flashers, and blocked it from leaving the scene. Getting out of his vehicle, he called out, "Is this the vehicle involved in the vehicular homicide?"

"Yeah, we was called to bring it to the impound lot."

"I need you to wait here a few minutes before taking it anywhere. Just pull over and I promise it will only be a couple minutes." Spano was surprised that there wasn't anyone around. Usually these sorts of things drew a crowd of people wanting to know what happened. Spano heard the tow truck driver mumbling under his breath, then the guy nodded, "Okay, I'll do what you want but whose going to pay for my time while I wait?"

Spano looked back at the driver. "It's simple, either you unload the vehicle and head back to your dispatch office, or wait like I said." The driver put both hands up in front of him giving in to the request. Two officers headed toward where the wrecker driver was stopped. Spano turned around, holding his badge in his right hand, "Detective Spano, I need some information before this wrecker can leave the scene."

Looking at each other, the first officer approached and offered, "Detective Sampson from our precinct is handling the case, and you'll need to talk to him."

"Yeah, I know, my partner is meeting with him right now. What I'll need from you is to fill me in on what happened." Spano held his ground as they seemed puzzled. Aggravated, Spano stated, "Hey, this should be a quick explanation; what happened and how does this Ford fit in?"

Both officers looked at Spano, then one of them explained, "The guy who owns that Ford was taken in. Looks like he may have run over and killed an as-yet-unidentified woman." The other guy jumped in, "They said the guy was still high or drunk when they questioned him. He kept saying he worked for the mayor. Detective Sampson kept us back to witness the emergency techs pull the body out from under the car and then we got the Ford loaded on the wrecker."

"Did it look like the guy ran her over, here, in the parking lot?"

"Not sure but we heard that the body was pretty mangled."

"Thanks." Spano moved closer to the front of the Ford and climbed up on the wrecker's flat bed. One officer followed him. Kneeling down, Spano looked under the front fascia, surprised that it wasn't caved in, yet the frame was covered in blood. Pointing to the front of the Explorer, he asked, "Doesn't this seem a little odd to you."

"What?"

"There's no visible damage to the front or the bumper, and all the blood is under the vehicle."

One of the officers asked "What's odd about that?"

"Well if this guy hit the woman, wouldn't there be some damage to the front of the vehicle? Shouldn't there be blood all over the pavement, or was she lying on the ground when she was run over?" Neither officer had any information nor suggested that they knew anything to add. "Did either of you look under the Ford?"

"No, the two responding officers and Detective Sampson handled that. We were just here to make sure the vehicle got loaded onto the flatbed and taken to the impound lot."

Spano grabbed his cell phone and started taking pictures of the front end and undercarriage. "Shit, that's a lot of blood under there," he said aloud. The officer standing next to the vehicle nodded. He continued taking pictures then jumped down. Pointing to the wrecker driver, "You're free to take it to the impound lot."

He watched the wrecker pull off as one of the officers asked, "Do you want to see where it happened?"

"Yeah." He followed both men to the line of parking spots. They pointed to the two last ones marked "Management Only." "Is this guy also the manager of the place?"

"No, from what we were told, it's suspected that he came home drunk and parked across two open spaces marked for managers."

Spano knelt down as he glanced back at the officers that were watching him. He again asked, "Didn't it seem odd to you that with all the blood on the bottom of the Ford, there isn't drag marks, just blood on the pavement under where the Ford was parked?" Both men shrugged. The sun had just crested over the condo complex and the glare made it hard to see. Spano put his sunglasses on and walked around the taped-off area. The sound of waves crashing on the shore caught his attention as a freighter passed. The ship must have been a thousand feet long and carried Canadian flags. He could see the huge freighter sliding past, sitting low in the water, thinking its belly filled with steel or iron ore. He wondered to himself where it was headed. *Some days it would be nice to just sit on the shoreline and watch them go by,* he thought. It had been a tough year for the SIU team. Last year Amy Harper's apartment had been broken into and she was attacked, then Detective Frederickson was ambushed by a garbage truck on the interstate. Spano continued to stare out at the water. The bright glaze from the sun on the water caused shimmering lights to dance off the surface.

The two officers looked at each other, not sure if the detective wanted them for anything else. One of them called out, "Detective, do you need us anymore?"

Spano looked back, almost forgetting that they were there. He shook his head, "I'm good for now, thanks." They shrugged and headed back to their squad car. He continued to stare off, not sure why, but the water had him in a trance. It was soon over when the sound of his cell phone broke into his thoughts.

THREE

John Franklin felt like crap. With less than four hours of sleep after a major binge, and no memory of the night before, he knew he was in deep trouble. Although he had been uncuffed and an officer sat in the corner of the room, he felt a rush of terror in his heart. Although it was hours since he left the strip club, he still blew high enough on the breathalyzer to be charged for drunk driving. He was seated in a chair at a metal table. Tears welled up in the corners of his eyes as he wished he could think clearly back to last night. *What happened?* He was searching for answers. He knew he was at the Gentlemen's Club on Eight Mile, but he was sure he drove back home without incident. *Could I have hit someone? Surely I'd have noticed if I did, wouldn't I?* He ran everything over again and again in his mind, trying to erase the cloud of alcohol that hung over him. He hadn't talked to anyone for a while and the officer standing guard wouldn't answer any of his questions. Since an officer had administered the drunk driving test, he was left in the room without any update to his request for an attorney. The interrogation room was bleak, nothing on the metal walls, just a large mirror on one side, probably one way glass, he figured. He was sure that someone was on the other side watching his every move. He was startled when the door opened. To his surprise, a female officer walked in and brought him a tall paper cup steaming with black coffee. John Franklin looked up at her. His eyes opened wide, "Mary?"

The officer put the coffee in front of him. She had a sneer on her face, "I knew you'd end up here one day after all the drinking your wife said you've been doing." She turned to leave the room.

"Wait, Mary, you've got to help me."

She shook her head, "Help you, after all that shit you put Misty through? A detective will be with you soon," then she walked out slamming the interview room door.

Franklin was stunned; he didn't know that his wife's friend was a cop. Why didn't Misty ever tell him that Mary was a cop? He was sure that his wife's friend would call Misty right away and tell her everything. Just one more thing to add to their issues. He slumped back in the chair looking at the cup of coffee wondering how all of this transpired. He couldn't remember any details after leaving the strip club on Eight Mile. What could have happened? He wished he could put it together but it was all cloudy to him. Too many drinks and now fear gripped his every thought. Franklin had been in the Second Precinct interview room for over two hours and no one had come in to interview him since they brought him that first cup of coffee. Now one of his wife's best friends shows up and she's a cop. How much worse could this get? He hadn't gotten his phone call and wanted to see his attorney. Did they even call the mayor like he asked? He put his head down on the table and started to sob. His life had taken a horrible turn and he didn't know what was next.

***

The gruff voice on the phone was quick to question his man on how the plan was proceeding. He wasn't happy and the tone of his inquiry was clear, "Gino, where in the hell are you?"

Gino Rossi was hoping that he'd have a better answer before his boss called. "Boss, I've got it all handled."

"Don't peddle that shit to me, Gino. The guy was supposed to be dead! Is he dead? Hell no. To the contrary, he's in the hands of the cops. How do you think you'll get to him there?" Before Gino could answer, he fired off more questions. "Did you forget the plan we decided? Did they find his body? Everything was clear; do you remember us talking about it?" There was silence for a second, and then Tony continued yelling, "Once he gets to talk to the cops it will go bad pretty quick!"

Gino had to say something. "Tony, I know, but I have a back-up plan." He could hear the man in the background pounding on the desk.

"You wouldn't need a backup plan if you had handled the damn thing right in the first place! Where are you?" Antonio Virgilio, known to his men as Tony, was an aggressive individual who demanded only perfection. They knew, if you didn't perform, he was quick to admonish them at the least, or as many heard, terminate them.

Gino Rossi had been with Tony only a short time; however, this went sideways. Tony had other plans for Gino, wanting revenge since his uncle, Vinnie La Russo, was brought down last year, hurting their drug empire. Gino, like everyone else, knew that Tony wouldn't accept failure from anyone, and after the problems last year, his mind ran with panic at the thought that he didn't accomplish his assignment. He wanted to assure Tony that he'd handle this. "Tony, we've got a man in the Second Precinct right now; he's got connections. We're gonna get the guy."

The line was silent, this time for several seconds. "Gino, I want you to report to me pretty soon that it's been handled." With that final statement the phone went dead. Gino took a deep breath, knowing he'd better get the job handled or he'd be the one swimming with the fish.

Tony wasn't a patient man. He already had a major setback last year; another mistake wouldn't be received very well. His drug connections in Canada were dismantled by the police; he wanted to build it back up. He made a promise that he'd retaliate against the cops that destroyed their business. He needed to avenge his partner's capture, and somehow get the team of detectives who handled it, and do it soon. Tony headed back into his business in St. Clair Shores, upset that Gino killed the stripper but failed to accomplish the other part by killing Franklin and making it look like Franklin committed suicide. Since that didn't happen, Tony planned to make a call hoping to accomplish the other part of his plan.

***

Tony scrolled through his cell phone numbers after hanging up with Gino, still upset that his man botched their plan. He punched in a number. The first thing he heard was loud music. "Lorenzo, you there?" He was mad. "Lorenzo!" he yelled.

Lorenzo finally answered. Turning down the car radio, he asked, "You okay?"

The answer was short, "Yeah, I need you, how long until you can get to the market?" Lorenzo could tell that something must have gone wrong. "I'll be there. I'm leaving now but it will take me about forty-five minutes; I'm with friends at Belle Isle."

It seemed to him that Tony didn't hear or even care what he said. "Meet me at the market; I need you to do something for me." The phone went silent.

Lorenzo shook his head as he yelled to his friend. "We gotta go." Leaving the island, they drove along Lake Shore Drive, through Grosse Pointe, past the Yacht Club and into St. Clair Shores. Dropping off his buddy, he followed the road past the Ford mansion, continuing north on Jefferson. He enjoyed the ride in his Mustang convertible as the radio blared out, *"Ain't no mountain high enough, ain't no valley low enough."* Marvin Gaye and Tammi Terrell's voices boomed out from the speakers. Lorenzo liked the music his mom always played; she'd sing the oldies whenever she rode with him. Turning left onto Nine Mile Road, he sped past the local McDonald's, a favorite high school hangout. Virgilio's meat market was east of Nine Mile on Greater Mack, just past Elizabeth. Lorenzo always chuckled when he passed the car dealership on the corner. He remembered hearing Tony sing the dealership's jingle, *"You're on the right track, Nine Mile and Mack..."* It always made him laugh. He wondered how such a tough guy like Tony would sing a car dealer's jingle. He never heard the old man sing anything else.

The market in St. Clair Shores was just down the street. The place was always busy with parking in front and an extra lot in the back. Lorenzo knew it must be pretty important for Tony to call him. He pulled into a spot along the front of the store and smiled at the two girls that walked by. "Hi, ladies." Lorenzo was known as a real ladies man, well known in the area for fast cars and faster women. He left the top down on the car, knowing no one would screw with his car, not Lorenzo's car, people knew better. It was close to six when he arrived, the sign on the building welcomed customers to the popular meat market. The young man strutted into the store and greeted the butcher at the counter, "Hello, Sal."

Lorenzo knew Sal since he was a young boy, calling him Uncle most of the time. Sal was waiting on customers. "How you doing, kid?" Most customers knew Lorenzo; he had worked in the store since the ninth grade. The lady at the meat counter smiled at him and he gave her a wave.

He answered Sal first, "Can't complain," then reaching over, he touched the lady's hand, "Mrs. Johnson, how's the family?"

She was pleased that he remembered her name. "Everything's good. Junior is in his second year at Wayne State. You going there?"

"No, I'm taking a couple years off, thinking about doing some traveling, then maybe college. Tell Junior, I said hi." He turned back toward Sal, "Is Tony in the back?"

"Yeah, he said you were stopping by." Pointing to the door that was along the right side of the wall, "I'm sure he's expecting you."

The young man smiled back and grabbed a smoked sausage stick from the case on the top of the counter. "Put this on my tab, Sal." The butcher just waved back as Lorenzo disappeared through the double doors. Lorenzo hadn't seen Sal for a while. Although he worked in the store all through high school, he'd only stop in once in a while now.

Tony Virgilio ran much of his underworld business out of the back room of the market. It had been located in St. Clair Shores since opening thirty years ago. Things had changed for Tony the past year since Vinnie La Russo was arrested and their drug business was shut down by the cops. Tony was determined to turn the tables on the people who stopped their lucrative business.

Virgilio's market was popular with locals and well known especially for their fresh meats and prepared sausages. Customers would have been shocked if they suspected the ties to drug trafficking along the Detroit River. When Lorenzo made his way into the back room he saw Tony sitting with two of his henchmen drinking coffee. Tony quickly got up, "Buongiorno." Standing, he hugged the young man. Tony had placed great trust in Lorenzo and made sure everyone showed him respect.

"Buonasera," Lorenzo said as he hugged the only father he'd ever known. He was always ready to perform any task assigned to him. Lorenzo was totally dedicated to the older man. Although adopted, Lorenzo resembled Tony, and had grown to be a handsome, six-foot-tall, olive-skinned young man. Tony walked with his arm around Lorenzo, moving to the rear door of the storage room. "We've got a problem," he said looking back toward the men sitting at the table. "Gino didn't finish the job I needed done and the cops are holding Franklin at the Second Precinct. That could be a problem." Shaking his head, Lorenzo knew that Tony was desperate. The older man patted Lorenzo's cheek, "Figlio," calling him son in Italian, "Figlio, I need you to handle this." He handed Lorenzo an envelope. "This is what I need you to do," as he went over the instructions in detail. "We've checked the location out and I can't trust Gino now. You know I'd never ask you to do this but it has to be done." Tony's original plans were clear but now John Franklin was in police custody because Gino failed; he couldn't trust the rest of it to him. Tony had to get Lorenzo to handle this, something he didn't want to do, especially because his wife, Rosa, wouldn't be happy if she found out. "You're familiar with the casino hotel. You and I have been on the roof a few times before. Make sure you build a good cover. We planned this for one day but I read in the paper there would be a presentation downtown. This will be perfect for us." Lorenzo was always Tony's back-up.

"I'll handle it," said Lorenzo, taking the envelope from him. He hugged Tony. "Consideralo fatto 'consider it done.'" He understood the assignment. "I'll call you when it's over." Lorenzo decided to cover for his sudden departure. "I'll see you all a little later, I've got a date." He smiled back at his father. Once Lorenzo left, the two men sitting at the able, laughed, "Hey, Tony, the kid must have a hundred girlfriends. Think he can spare a few for us?"

FOUR

Detective Sampson sat at the Second Precinct along with Harper. They were going over the details of the morning arrest of the deputy mayor. Harper leafed through the report and looked up at Sampson. "You've done a nice job, Jim. Last year you helped one of my colleagues, Detective Baker. He was assigned to a murder case and said you worked with him on a homicide at a party store on Jefferson."

"Yeah, I remember Baker, nice guy. We worked on a potential drug case that ended up with an undercover officer's body found in a vacant lot. Unfortunately we've had a few of those on the lower east side."

"Baker said that you were great to work with."

He nodded, "How's he doing, heard he got shot in a raid."

"He's good, back to work, but on desk duty for now." Harper hoped bringing up Baker's name would help Sampson be more willing to help her. "Do you mind if I sit in on the interview with your suspect?"

"No, not a problem, okay with you Captain?" The man nodded. Both Sampson and Harper got up and headed down the hallway to the interview room. Just before they entered, her phone chimed. "This is important, do you mind if I take it first?"

"Sure, this guy's not going anywhere."

She listened to what Spano had to say from his trip to the scene. Holding the phone in her left hand, she held a finger up to Sampson, "Wait Joe, let me ask Sampson." She turned, "Detective Spano is at the scene. He's wondering if you thought anything seemed odd or out of place at the condo scene."

"Funny you asked. It all looked pretty straight forward until they started to lift the vehicle off the woman who was hit. A lot of blood was on the Ford, especially the frame, but not much on the pavement. At first we thought she was hit and dragged but there wasn't any indication on the driveway. We know the suspect was blind drunk, he registered .08 this morning and that was after he claimed to have been in bed for five hours."

"Joe, Detective Sampson agrees with what you're saying. We're going in now to talk to Franklin. I'll call you once we're done." She looked at Sampson, "I'm not sure how you're planning to proceed, but maybe leave off the issue of blood at the scene."

He was thinking about what she suggested. "I'll see how this goes first."

They walked into the room where John Franklin sat looking terrified. "It's about time someone came in here; I need to know what in the hell is going on." The man had been left alone for a long time, maybe a ploy that Sampson planned to use. "I asked for my phone call that I haven't gotten and I want to talk to my lawyer." Sampson sat across from the suspect and Harper sat next to him. Taking his time before answering and leafing through a folder that he brought with him, he seemed to ignore the man.

"I want my lawyer, now!" Franklin yelled out."

Sampson looked up at him, "Okay, Mr. Franklin, give me the name and phone number of your attorney."

"It's about time." He rattled off a name for Sampson, but didn't have the phone number. "He's the only Peterson in that office. I'm not talking until I get to see him."

Sampson smiled, "Sure, we'll do what we can to find him for you." He rose from the chair and turned to Detective Harper. "Guess we'll wait until he gets to talk to his attorney."

They both got up. When Harper looked over at Detective

Sampson, she turned toward Franklin. "We've informed the mayor of the situation. He knows you're here, and asked Chief Mathews to get involved."

Franklin breathed a sigh of relief, "Finally."

"When we talked to the mayor, we told him you might be charged with vehicular homicide." It was quiet for a second, "Sorry but he can't help you." Sampson looked back at him; he could see the panic in the man's face, "Well it could take a while for your attorney to show up but first we've got to find him. You should talk to us now, maybe we can help."

Franklin felt he didn't have a choice. "Okay, okay, I'll talk to you, but really, I don't know much." Sampson sat back down but Detective Harper stayed standing. "I'm sure I didn't run someone over; I'm telling you the truth."

Sampson held his hands up, "Mr. Franklin, settle down and let's start from the beginning. Where were you last night?" Tears welled up in Franklin's eyes. He was breathing hard, and they could see his hands shaking. "Mr. Franklin, you've got to try to help yourself. If you can answer our questions it might help you with the trouble you're in."

"Okay, but you've got to believe me, I didn't run anyone over."

"It's hard to believe you when your Ford Explorer was found on top of a woman in the parking lot of your home. Franklin, you've already admitted to driving drunk. I'm sure you have no idea what happened. " Sampson waited for the man to gather himself.

Detective Harper had been standing at the back of the room and decided to move closer to the table. "Mr. Franklin, my name is Detective Harper. I'm here because the mayor called us. He's worried about you, but unless you talk to us, he can't help you. We know you're the deputy mayor, but if you've run someone over, you're going to be booked for vehicular homicide."

Franklin looked up at her. "The mayor sent you?"

"Yes, he called our chief and asked us to get involved. Mr. Franklin, you need to know, if you're guilty, there's nothing any of us can do to help, including the mayor."

Franklin seemed to understand what she meant and nodded. "Last night I was at the Gentlemen's Club on Eight Mile Road, just past Hoover."

"What time did you leave?"

He took a deep breath, shaking his head, trying to think. "It had to be after two in the morning. I tried to catch a few winks in my car but the bouncer made me pull out of the lot."

"Where did you go after that?"

"Nowhere, I drove home. I probably shouldn't have, but I drove slowly and I'm positive I made it home without hitting anyone."

"Did you see anyone who might be able to confirm your story, either at the club or on your way home?"

Franklin had a somber look on his face. "The bouncer can verify that I was there. After I pulled out of the lot, I drove straight home. When I turned down St. Aubin there was a car in my normal parking spot so I pulled into an open spot near the lake. After that I went into my condo. That's it, I didn't hit anyone, honest!"

Detective Sampson looked at Harper; he knew she had Franklin's trust by claiming that she was sent from the mayor. Franklin had given her many details that they could start checking. Sampson stood, "Mr. Franklin, I'll have an officer call your attorney. Detective Harper and I will check on your story and see if we can verify if someone may have seen you last night. We'll bring you another cup of coffee." They both walked out and for the first time Franklin felt a little ray of hope.

As they entered the squad room, one of the officers approached. "Sampson, there was a guy here earlier when you were in with the suspect, he asked about Franklin. Seemed kind of weird; he knew that we were holding him but not sure where."

"Who was he?'

"I asked but he didn't give a full name. He was writing in a note pad, probably a reporter."

"Did you get anything else?"

"No, just his first name; he said it was Gino. I told him that the captain couldn't talk to him and we weren't holding anyone here by the name of Franklin."

"Is he still around?"

"No, he seemed to look around, but because everyone was going about normal business I think he bought the answer."

"You're probably right. I'm sure someone from the press got a tip; it would be front page news. I'll make sure the front desk keeps everything on the down low."

Amy Harper had been watching Sampson and when he came back to her, she asked, "Everything okay, Detective?"

"Yeah, just a reporter looking for a story."

"I'm actually surprised we haven't had more of them hanging around."

"We tried to put it all to rest at the condo complex, but with so many neighbors around I'm surprised too." The two detectives called to update the captain on their investigation.

***

Chief Mathews listened to the report from Harper as she and Sampson headed down Eight Mile Road toward the Gentlemen's Club. "Detective, I'll let the mayor know what your team is doing; keep me informed."

"Detective Frederickson wanted me to update you while I was still working with Detective Sampson at the Second Precinct."

"I appreciate that, let the detectives in the Second know that it's important that we get it right."

"Yes, sir." Once she hung up, she saw Sampson looking back at her. "Something wrong, Detective?"

"No, nothing wrong, just not used to handling a case with someone important." He paused for a second, realizing that she seemed to be giving him a weird look. "So Detective Harper, tell me about this job you have that reports directly to the chief and mayor."

She was a little embarrassed by the question. "I don't report to the mayor, actually I've never talked to him." She stopped talking, hoping that she didn't have to explain more.

"I've been thinking all morning where I've seen you, and then it hit me: Front page of the Free Press, last year, you were involved in busting a crime syndicate operating out of the Eastern Market."

"I was only one of the detectives on the case."

"That's not what the Free Press said. You helped with the capture of the guys that caused the crash on the freeway, and it was your photo on the front page."

It was quiet in the car for a few minutes and Harper was searching for something to say. Sampson looked over at her, "I'm proud to work on a case with you Detective Harper." She smiled and could feel her face flush.

"Same here, Detective Sampson." They headed along Eight Mile and spotted the Gentlemen's Club on the south side of the street. "Okay Sampson, how do you want to handle this?"

"I'm thinking we need to see if anyone recognized Franklin, probably the bouncer from last night won't be there at lunch time. We'll need to confirm his story and the time he left there. Most likely they have surveillance video that will show the parking lot. If it's okay with you, I'd like to ask the questions."

"Your case, I'm just here to help," she said. They pulled into the lot that already had seven cars parked in it. It was close to noon. "Guess the lunch crowd hasn't arrived yet," she said laughing.

"You're not too far off," pointing to the flashing billboard that announced a lunch buffet special. Sampson asked, "Hungry, Detective Harper?" They both had a good laugh at that.

"I don't think I want to eat here." They agreed. Getting out of the car she looked up at the roof. "There's a video camera pointed directly at the lot. I hope we can get a look at the tape without a warrant."

Sampson nodded. "Let's go see what this place is all about." The two of them headed to the front door and were greeted by a tall burly man who pulled open the huge oak door. Sampson showed him his badge. "We need to talk to the owner."

"He ain't here."

"Okay, then the manager will do." The man must have been six foot five and three-hundred pounds. He nodded, leading them inside. He pointed to a mirrored glass door along the right side of the place. It was near what appeared to be a large stage. They followed the big man who opened the door and they entered.

"Boss, these two cops wanna to talk to you."

Sampson pushed his way forward, holding his badge in his right hand. "I'm Detective Sampson and this is Detective Harper from downtown. We need some information about one of your customers from last night."

The man behind the desk smiled, then standing he quietly said, "Thanks, Butch, I'll handle it." Turning toward Sampson he extended his hand, "I'm CK Johnson, the manager, "Can I get you both something to eat or drink?"

"No thanks. Last night one of your customers tells us he was here until two in the morning. We're hoping you will let us review your parking lot video to confirm his alibi."

"Sure, Detective, but I'm going to have to clear this with the owner and our attorneys first."

"I understand, but until we can review this, we'll have to put an officer in the lot and at the door to make sure no one tampers with the tape."

CK was a little uneasy. "Detective, that isn't necessary; we don't need a cop car in the parking lot. No one will tamper with the tapes, but the privacy of our customers is important to us."

Sampson was quick to answer, "Shit, I don't care if the governor was here, I just need to confirm that our suspect was here and what time he left. He said your evening bouncer made him leave the parking lot."

"That would be Sonny. He works the door and lot at night. How about I call him for you?"

"That's a good start, but we still need to see those tapes."

The man moved back to his desk and leafed through a folder. He grabbed his phone and dialed. After a few seconds they heard him saying, "Sonny, I need you to talk to a couple of detectives. They want some information about a guy from last night. Yeah, I know you can't remember everyone but they say this guy will stand out." CK handed Detective Sampson the phone.

"Sonny, this is Detective Sampson from the Second Precinct. The guy in question said you told him that he had to leave the lot around two." Sampson waited for the answer.

"I get a lot of problem people parked in the lot, but yeah, one guy was slumped over, sleeping in his car. I had to knock on his window and tell him this wasn't a hotel."

"Can you describe the guy?"

"Yeah, he was a white guy, driving a Ford Explorer. Only other thing I remember is he puked all over himself and the driver's side window."

Sampson took a deep breath, "We might need to show you a photo array if necessary. We'll get back with you." Sampson handed the phone back to the club's manager.

"Does that take care of what you needed, Detective?"

He looked at the manager, "Okay, we still need to confirm the identification from your video tapes." Sampson stood his ground. "If necessary, I'll call downtown and have a warrant issued. We'll have to close this place until it gets here." CK shrugged. "Detective, how about we compromise. I'll let you and your partner look at the tapes but if you want a copy you'll need that warrant."

Sampson looked back at Harper. "What do you think, Detective?"

It was the first time she entered into the discussion. "This is a good start but I'm sure we're going to need a copy for the court case."

The manager chimed back in. "How about we look at it together. If your guy is on it, I'll agree to make you a copy of the part of the tape that he's in."

"That would be perfect," Harper said. They followed the manager into a back room behind his office. The room was filthy, boxes on the floor, dirt everywhere, and a grimy guy sitting behind a console of television screens. Harper looked at the four screens surrounding the desk that the guy was watching. She had a puzzled look on her face, "What is going on there?" pointing to one of the screens. No one answered as they all watched a lap dance taking place on the video screen. The guy behind the desk didn't know what to do when cops showed up.

"I'm sure that isn't legal," she said.

Sampson jumped in, "We need to see the video from last night in the parking lot. Can you pull it up on one of these screens?"

The guy was happy to divert the conversation from the lap dancer to the parking lot. "Yeah, I can put it on the monitor right here." He started fumbling with some of the buttons and gadgets and the screen started a search from the parking lot. He slowed it down and they could see the lot and that it was dark. "What time did you say you were looking for?"

Harper said, "Pull up the time from one in the morning. We can fast forward from there." The guy nodded and did as she asked.

"Stop it there," Harper said. "Now go at normal speed; we need to watch from there. I want a copy of this too."

The guy looked up at his manager. CK was quick to say, "Do what they need." He pressed some buttons and slid a blank disk into the console. Then he started the tape. They all watched as people came and went from the front door. The view included the row of cars alongside the building. There was the white Ford Explorer parked around the corner. After a few minutes, John Franklin came stumbling out of the club. At first he appeared to be followed by a guy but the man strolled past Franklin.

Sampson and Harper both took note of the time stamp along the right bottom of the screen; it clearly showed 2:15 a.m. They continued to watch as Franklin fumbled with his keys and entered the Ford. It was maybe a few minutes later when they spotted a person, most likely Sonny the bouncer, walking up to the car. He appeared to be knocking on Franklin's window. This is what they needed. It confirmed that Franklin was indeed at the club and what time he was there. Although it didn't resolve the issue of him running someone over at the condo complex, but at least that part of his story was verified. They watched until Franklin's Ford pulled out of the lot. It was followed by another vehicle.

"That guy's right behind Franklin's car. Can we get an image of the driver, or plate number?"

The person running the video reversed the tape, "I'll try to freeze it when the car appears on the screen." He ran through the sequence again to where the second vehicle appeared. It was a dark SUV, maybe an import. "Here's the best view, Detective." Stopping the tape with the vehicle on the screen he added, "Do you want me to print this?"

Harper quickly answered, "Yes."

He stopped the footage three more times, printing a still each time for the detectives.

"Thanks, we need these and the copy of the whole tape." Again the guy looked back at his boss who nodded that it was okay. He pulled the disk out and handed it to Harper. As they started to leave the room, Harper turned to the manager. "You or your bouncer need to stop that lap dancer, she's gotten out of control." Both men looked at each other as the detectives walked out.

Once they were outside, Detective Sampson asked Harper, "Now that we know that our suspect was here as he stated, that still doesn't answer anything about the body under his car at the condo complex."

She knew he was right, but they had a starting point on John Franklin's activities that night. "At least we know he was telling us the truth earlier. Let's see what Detective Spano found out." She grabbed her cell phone and waited for her partner to update her.

FIVE

Lorenzo headed downtown on I-94 thinking back to the first time he learned that his father was more than just an owner of a meat market. His older step-brother, Anthony, and he were hiding in the back room of the market. Tony came in with two men, talking loudly. Tony was giving one of them a hit order on someone who was suspected of stealing drugs. The two boys never told their dad what they heard, but kept it a secret. Lorenzo and Anthony always remained close and guarded their secret.

Tony Virgilio and his wife Rosa adopted Lorenzo when he was only three years old. Lorenzo didn't remember his mom who was killed in a terrible car accident. Tony and his wife always showed Lorenzo old family photos hoping that he'd somehow have good memories of her. Lorenzo loved to hear Rosa tell him how happy she was to have a second child in the home. Rosa had hoped to have a bigger family but she had problems after Anthony was born; the doctors told her that she'd never have another baby. Rosa lovingly raised the two boys as brothers. In school, Anthony became a sports star, leading Notre Dame High School to a state championship in both baseball and football. Lorenzo on the other hand wasn't interested in sports but was the guy all the girls wanted to be with. He was outgoing and very good looking, but never seemed to have the same girlfriend for very long. Lorenzo was always proud of his brother, Anthony, who was a gifted student and helped Lorenzo with subjects that he struggled with. Although both boys were very different, they always got along. Anthony knew what his father's business entailed. He'd often tell Lorenzo, "Be careful, brother, you need to keep someone around you that you can trust. Dad's business isn't safe."

Lorenzo told him, "I'm not worried, brother; I've always got you at my back if I need you." He would put the back-up plan into action that he and Tony had discussed for weeks. After all, the announced event downtown was just what they needed. This was personal and he'd carry out his dad's wishes. Getting downtown was pretty easy since it was still early and Lorenzo was to park at the Greektown Casino Hotel. He planned to make a big splash, making sure he would be a memorable guest. Driving down Monroe and turning on Lafayette, he pulled into the hotel valet drive. A young man approached. "Checking in?" Lorenzo just nodded, tossed him the keys to the Mustang. "Put the top up. I want you to park it in the VIP area." He handed the attendant a fifty dollar bill and headed into the lobby. Looking back, he saw the kid, smiling, just standing there. *One witness set*, he thought. At the front desk he flashed his platinum players' card, "Reservation, Virgilio."

The lady punched in his name. "Welcome Mr. Virgilio, it's nice to have you back. Hope your stay will be enjoyable." She scrolled through the computer, turned and grabbed a key card and ran it into the machine to authorize it. "Is there anything I can add for you, maybe a dinner reservation?"

"No, thanks, I'm going to go to the ball game." Once he was checked in, he called Tony. "I'm in the hotel and will handle everything tomorrow morning, just as we planned."

"Good. I talked to Gino. He's down at the Twelfth Precinct hoping to get to Franklin. It might be our last chance."

"I thought he said he had a contact to get him in."

"Yeah, he said that, but lately things haven't quite worked out like he promised." Tony had lost all confidence in Gino who failed to kill Franklin after killing the stripper and planting the body. Somehow it didn't happen. He never explained why but that really didn't matter. "Lorenzo, if things don't work out down there, we will have other chances."

"I know, Dad, but I won't fail."

"Lorenzo, I'm always proud of you."

***

Spano was downtown at headquarters. He planned on going over the details with Detective Frederickson that he learned from the Stroh River Place condos. "Don, this isn't a clear cut case like we were led to believe. The photos I took make me think that the body wasn't run over in the parking lot." They studied the photos that he had taken of the undercarriage of Franklin's vehicle and the lack of blood on the pavement. While doing this, Joe's phone rang. When he saw that it was Detective Harper, he grabbed it. "Amy, how's it going there?"

Harper had been working the case with Detective Sampson from the Second Precinct, "Joe, Sampson and I are checking on Franklin's alibi. We're leaving the strip club that he said he was at before driving to his home. They confirmed he was here until after two. Although this really doesn't tell us much regarding the accident, it gives us a starting place. Did you get any other details that will help us from the scene?"

"Nothing for sure, but Don and I are looking at the photos I took. They just don't make any sense, Amy. There isn't a bloody trail on the pavement, just a body and a puddle of blood under the vehicle." I'm planning to go to the morgue to get the medical examiner's details from the autopsy. Maybe he's been lucky enough to figure out who she is and it might give us a better idea of what happened." Harper appreciated the update. Joe hung up, turning to Frederickson. "Boss, I'm going to head to the morgue." After he said that he remembered that Don told all of them not to call him that. "Sorry, Don, it's a habit."

"Yeah, I understand, but I'm not the boss, just another detective on the team." Saying that, Don got up. "I'm going with you, Joe. I have a bad feeling about this case."

The two men headed downstairs to the garage and Joe pointed to where his car was. He got in and Frederickson slid into the passenger side. The Wayne County Morgue was located on East Warren, not far from headquarters. Spano drove down Michigan Avenue and wanted to apologize for his previous remarks regarding a cover-up. "Don, I just needed to say sorry for doubting what our mission was earlier."

Frederickson turned, "Joe, I knew where you were coming from. Too many times in the past that's exactly what would have been the case. I hope you know that the chief wants us to always handle our cases aboveboard. No bullshit, we do it the right way every time."

The two men nodded, each one knowing that it would not be mentioned again.

The drive along Michigan Avenue took them past Campus Martius Park. They watched as a family of four crossed the street heading into the Lafayette Coney Island. "Joe, after we get the details from the M.E., let's come back here for lunch, my treat."

Spano was glad they cleared that up. "Sounds great." They followed the road around the park and continued to East Warren, a ten-minute ride. The morgue always had officers and suits coming and going, gathering evidence for their cases. Don Frederickson didn't know how many times in his twenty-five-plus- year's career he'd been there. "Although the work they do here is important, it's never good news for families, Joe." Spano silently agreed.

Walking downstairs to the lab, they passed two men from the district attorney's office. Frederickson stopped when one of them held his right hand up. "Don, you here on the mayor's case?" He was surprised about the comment, not sure how they knew about the case or where they got their information.

Frederickson tilted his head, "What case are you talking about?"

They looked puzzled. The first man said, "Thought for sure the mayor would get your team involved."

"I'm not sure what you're talking about. We're here to pick up evidence from the M.E." Don looked back at Spano. "You know anything about the mayor calling for help?" Spano played along, shrugged his shoulders and shook his head. Frederickson looked back at the assistant D.A. "So, you going to give us some details?"

"No, we don't really know much. Just heard the mayor's office is in a panic about someone in his administration involved in an accident. If it's true I'm sure the chief will want your help."

"Oh no, you're not leaving it like that, come on, details."

The two guys looked at each other. "Okay, but we only heard about it since arriving here. Looks like someone high up on the mayor's staff was involved in a hit and run. He may have been in a car crash. Heard he hit a pedestrian, ran her over this morning."

"Christ, don't want to be in his shoes," Spano answered.

They all agreed. "Bet you guys will be right in the middle of this sooner rather than later." They walked away chuckling.

Frederickson waited for the coast to clear, "Wonder how the story is already out there." Walking down the last few steps, Don pulled the door open and saw the M.E. sitting at her desk. He wanted to ask her about the rumors but decided to hold off.

She looked up and greeted them, "Figured you'd be here pretty soon; just completed the preliminary investigation." She stood up, holding a folder. "You want to follow me?"

They walked behind her, entering a cold room, flanked by three metal tables and a wall of large drawers. Spano felt a cold chill crawl down his back. "I can't come in here and not feel a sense of panic. Just knowing that you've got bodies stored along the wall in those drawers is enough to make me want to run."

Frederickson tilted his head, "Yeah, guess you don't want to spend too much time in here." Although they knew that an act of violence must be investigated by the medical examiner's office, they hated trips to the morgue. Everyone in the police department and district attorney's office knew the importance of this part of the investigation.

The M.E. moved closer to a metal table in the center of the room, pulling back a white sheet. The body was lying on the table that had a gutter that ran around it. She pointed, "Your victim is a white female, approximately twenty-six years old. She has broken ribs and a crushed right shoulder, all a result of possibly being run over. Pointing to the right side, "You can see the deep dark marks along this side of her body. It shows a heavy object, most likely a car tire, drove over her." She slid her hand under the victim's body, lifting it and turning it slightly. "What you don't see is the depression on the back of her skull." The body was badly mangled and both men looked pale as she continued, pointing to the damaged skull. Frederickson moved closer, but Spano took a step back. "Don, this didn't happen in a car accident. Someone hit her with a heavy metal object, most likely a hammer. This young lady was dead before she was run over."

Frederickson asked, "Do you know how long she had been dead before being run over?"

"No, not yet, but I can say with some certainty that the blow to the back of her head happened at least two hours before she was run over. I've taken her finger prints and run them through AFIS. It could take a couple of hours for results. We also hope to get something from facial recognition but so far no luck. I'm hoping that we'll have an answer for you soon. I plan to do a thorough autopsy to get you the other details you asked for."

Frederickson appreciated the quick results, knowing that she only had the body for a short time. "I know coming down here was premature, but due to the nature of the case we needed to know everything as soon as possible."

"Detective, there were a couple of other odd things, I found a large amount of Alprazolam in her blood, better known as Xanax. It's a potent drug that is normally used for panic disorders. It would also make your victim disorientated or in a sedative state. She would display the same results as someone who had been drunk."

"Thanks, if you find any other information or hopefully her identification, call me."

"Sure, I'll call your office when I have something more."

He turned, as they were about to walk out, Frederickson asked, "I've got one question, could anyone in your office leak the details of the case?"

She smiled, "No, but I heard one of responding officers has been spreading details to anyone who would listen. Surprised it isn't on the news."

He understood. Someone with half the information would make it seem like they knew the whole story. "We'll get to the bottom of this, thanks." As they left the office and headed upstairs, Frederickson grabbed his phone. "Lieutenant Jackson, I have some critical information for the chief."

She knew it was important. "Don, he will be with you in a minute, he's on the phone with the mayor."

Chief Mathews was pleased that Frederickson was calling already with an update. "Don, hope you have something to help."

"We're leaving the medical center right now. The M.E. is confident that the lady was dead before being run over. She didn't have an identification yet, but will call as soon as she does."

"How was the victim killed?"

"Fatal blow to the back of the skull, could be from a hammer. She appears to have been dead close to two hours before being run over. We've got to figure out if she was killed at the scene and pushed under the car to hide the body or if there is more to this."

"Okay, I'll update the mayor but we don't want to clear his guy just yet."

"I agree. Detective Harper is working with the Second Precinct and Spano and I plan to investigate further." After hanging up, he turned to Spano, "Joe, there's a lot of shit that doesn't add up." Joe Spano nodded, knowing that they had a lot of work ahead of them.

SIX

Lorenzo thought about what his dad had told him, understanding the importance of the assignment. This was personal, revenge often is, and it was the first step in his dad's plans. Although he was the back-up, Lorenzo was always prepared in case he was needed. When checking in, Lorenzo only carried a small duffle bag. He wanted to make sure that the hotel staff took notice of what he brought in. The optics were important. He knew that if he needed alibis, he'd have a lot of them. After checking into his room at the Greektown Casino Hotel, he called his friend. "Bobby, it's Lorenzo, I've checked in. Bring the items I want to the hotel. I'm in room 2950."

"Do you need anything else?"

"No, just the bag I told you to hide." Hanging up, Lorenzo knew Bobby would get there soon since he lived close in the downtown area off of Lafayette near I-375. Lorenzo moved to the bank of windows overlooking the shops and restaurants on Monroe. The streets were crowded with baseball fans wearing Tigers uniform hats and shirts. He stared at the casino sign flashing its call to fans, knowing it would be a busy night. The Tigers were in town playing a big series with the Indians. Although he wasn't a big baseball fan, many of his friends were; that gave him the perfect cover for his plan. Tomorrow there would be a day game, just what he needed. As he watched the activity on Monroe, he turned, grabbed the phone and dialed room service. "Can I get a burger, medium rare, with fries and six Bud Lights?" The lady repeated his order and said it would be forty-five minute to an hour, "Better make that two burgers and fries." After placing his room service order he plopped down on the bed. The rooms on the top floor had a wall of glass that looked across Monroe to the west. It was the best location for his plans. Lying on the bed, he could see trucks crossing the Ambassador Bridge, reminding him of small toys because they were so far away, then he turned his attention back to the fans on Monroe. It was close to six-thirty and the baseball game was scheduled to start in an hour. Monroe Street was lit up with small Christmas-type lights all the way from the hotel to Campus Martius. Lorenzo checked his watch for the third time, it was close to thirty minutes since he had talked to Bobby.

Just then there was a knock on the door. He moved toward it, hearing Bobby's voice. "Hey Zo, it's me, open up." Opening the door, he saw his friend, Bobby, holding a long black duffle bag. "What took you so long?"

"Tigers are in town, traffic sucks." Looking around, "Hey, nice room, check out that view." Bobby placed the bag in the far corner of the room and moved to the bank of windows.

Lorenzo moved next to Bobby, we got a break, the Free Press said there will be a presentation at Campus Martius tomorrow. Our target will surely be there."

"Okay, Zo, tell me what I need to do."

"Sure." They both moved to the table. "When I go up to the roof, you're going to stay in my room. If someone calls, you'll answer it and pretend to be me. I left a message at the front desk that I was expecting a call or a guy stopping by with my baseball tickets."

Bobby nodded, "Good move."

"I called my friend in housekeeping that handles this floor. We're clear until after noon. Once I've done the job, I'll bring you the rifle. You're going to get it back to the storage spot and hurry to the ballpark." As they talked, there was another knock at the door and the voice announced, "Room service." Lorenzo opened the door, and a pretty young blond wheeled in a metal table with two trays and an ice bucket with bottles of Bud sticking out. "Just put it over there," he said, pointing to the small table by the windows. She put the trays and bucket down and as she turned to leave, he handed her a twenty. She looked at it and gave him a huge smile as she said, "Thanks."

Bobby watched her every move and once she walked out, he turned to Lorenzo. "She's hot; did you get her name?"

He shook his head. "Not what I'm here for; grab me a beer." They both held a bottle of Bud and Lorenzo lifted the metal cover off a plate and grabbed a fry and looking back at his friend, said, "Bobby, this is critical, no screw ups."

"I know Zo, I'll do whatever you say."

"Okay. I ordered you a burger. Now give me the bag off the floor, let's see what we've got." Lorenzo started to empty the bag. Bobby watched him pull out a long rectangular box. The printing on the box said it was a Nightforce 34mm scope.

"Wow, new?"

"Yeah, can't afford to miss. Got it a few weeks ago, made sure the sight was set, took it to the range a couple of times." Lorenzo continued unpacking the bag. He pulled a black plastic case out and snapped it open. Bobby watched with envy as his friend assembled the high-precision, M40 sniper model and scope. "Bobby, grab me another Bud." With the telescope now mounted on the sniper rifle, Lorenzo stood and pointed the gun out the window, near where his friend stood.

"Hey, what the hell!" Bobby dove onto the floor, spilling the beer all over. "You asshole."

"I'm not going to shoot you." Then Lorenzo let out a big laugh, "Just making sure I have the feel of the new scope." Lorenzo laid the gun on the bed and moved toward his friend, still lying spread eagle on the carpet. "Come on, get up you jerk." Bobby let out a nervous chuckle He felt pretty dumb after diving to the floor. "Let's get a beer, mine is half empty." Lorenzo handed Bobby a new bottle of beer. "You okay?" Bobby nodded, as Lorenzo moved to the table, looking at the people still walking on Monroe. "Come on, let's eat then we can hit the casino."

Bobby shrugged his shoulders. "I smell like a brewery, I can't go out like this."

"We'll get you a new shirt across the street."

"Thanks, Zo."

"Sorry, Bobby, didn't mean to scare you, I know it was a natural reaction. Don't worry about it. Let's eat these burgers then we'll go out." Bobby grabbed the other plate with the burger and fries. He sat on the end of the bed, eating silently, keeping one eye on the rifle.

***

At close to nine-thirty, Lorenzo and Bobby strolled down Monroe. They could hear cheers from Tiger Stadium every once in a while.

It was only three blocks from Greektown to the ballpark and if the Tigers were scoring you'd hear the crowd. "Let's play some black jack," Lorenzo suggested to his buddy. "I want people to see me playing cards, fits perfect for our stay." Lorenzo looked back at the hotel, staring at the roof. He'd been up there twice, scouting out camera positions, distance to Campus Martius and wind patterns. He smiled at Bobby, "Let's go upstairs, they've added a lot of new gaming tables." Entering at the Monroe Street entrance, both of them were wearing Tigers shirts that they picked up at a gift shop across the street.

Bobby checked out every girl that they passed. "Hey Zo, there's a lot of hot chicks down here."

"I just want to play a little cards right now. Gotta be seen by as many people as possible." The aroma of smoke and noises from slot machines was overwhelming as they moved from the entrance past the guards.

"Yeah, that's a good plan." Bobby followed his friend and they smiled at a group that was watching the baseball game on the wall of televisions. "Zo, want a beer?" Bobby had been his friend since high school. He'd had it pretty rough. Parents went through a bad divorce, so he often spent time at Lorenzo's house. Because he was left alone so often, Bobby became a computer nerd, something that Lorenzo hoped would come in handy if needed.

"Yeah, a beer sounds good."

They were at the bar, standing with the group that was cheering a home run by Miguel Carrera. Lorenzo tapped his friend, "Let's head over to the black jack tables." Once there, he handed Bobby a few hundred dollar bills. "Bobby, I'm going to play at the tables over there," pointing to the line of green covered tables with people crowded around. "Why don't you float around, make yourself visible." Lorenzo moved into the crowded group and pulled up an empty chair, lying out a small stack of bills on the table.

"New player," the dealer announced to the pit boss standing at the end. She counted out the bills, laying them out across the table as the pit boss watched. "Have a player's card, sir?" Lorenzo slid his platinum player's card to her. She raised her eyebrows, thinking he looked pretty young to be a top-level player. "Welcome Mr.

Virgilio." He just nodded as he studied the stack of black hundred dollar chips in front of him.

The man seated in the last seat scoffed, "Hope you know what you're doing, kid, we've got a good table going here." Lorenzo looked over and smiled. "Deal those cards," the guy said, "My money needs to make some new friends." Everyone standing around laughed. Lorenzo placed two hundred-dollar chips on his spot and looked straight ahead as the dealer spun out cards to the seven players. The man at the end was dealt an ace and he chuckled, "Come to Papa."

Lorenzo had a king showing as the dealer dealt the second card to everyone. Lorenzo got an ace. "I think that's the name of the game." He looked back to the guy at the last seat, "My money can make new friends, too." That brought out a big laugh from those around the table. The dealer slid three black chips toward Lorenzo.

It was now after midnight and the casino was crowded. The baseball game had ended and many fans filled the bars and tables. The Tigers had a ninth-inning, come-from-behind victory. There were many happy faces cheering and recalling the rally that ended with a huge home run from Miguel Cabrera, his second of the night. Bobby was drinking a Bud and saw that Lorenzo was still playing black jack. Bobby talked to a couple of girls but most of them had dates. He knew his buddy attracted women; maybe with Zo here he'd get lucky. Bobby made his way to the black jack table and saw Zo had stacks of black chips and two young girls hanging on him. He whispered, "Zo, what's up?"

Lorenzo turned. "Just having fun; here's some money," handing Bobby a stack of chips. "Have a good time."

One of the girls standing behind Lorenzo looked over at Bobby. "Hi," she smiled. He thought she was cute, maybe five-foot-six, blond hair and short skirt. "Hi, I'm Bobby." He held out his hand and she took it in hers and followed him out of the throng. "Come on, we'll cash some of these in and get a drink." She gladly followed him to a cashier's window. Watching him cash out over a thousand dollars, she gripped Bobby's arm tighter. The two of them made their way to the bar, Bobby with that dumb smile and the girl with her arm tucked under his. He was thinking maybe he'd hit a homer, just like Cabrera.

It was a little after two in the morning as Lorenzo looked around but didn't see Bobby. There was still a couple of girls hanging around. He'd been buying them drinks all night. Leaving the table, he said, "Sorry ladies, I've got to go, maybe next time." One of them leaned in and gave him a lingering kiss and whispered in his ear, "Yeah, sounds great, maybe another time." She was disappointed but handed him her phone number, scrawled on a napkin. Making his way to one of the cashier's windows, he looked around, thinking, *Can't be too safe*. Lorenzo handed the cashier two handfuls of black chips and she gave him a large wad of bills. Moving along the wall past the cage, he dialed Bobby's cell. It rang a few times before Bobby answered.

"Hey, Zo, how'd you do?"

"Good, real good buddy, where'd you go?"

"Met a girl and we decided to get a room. Do you want me to head your way?"

"No buddy, have fun, big day tomorrow." Leaving the casino he headed across the bridge to the hotel, stopping at the front desk just as he had planned. "Hello, I'm Mr. Virgilio," sliding his players card across the desk. "I'm in room 2950. Can I keep the room until Monday instead of Sunday?"

She checked the computer while smiling at the high roller. "Yes, Mr. Virgilio, no problem. I'll change your checkout date to Monday. Is there anything else I can do?"

"No, that's great. I got tickets for the Tigers games; glad you could do this for me." Once he left, the clerk next to her smiled. "Of course he has a room, he's a platinum player."

"Yeah, not bad looking either." They laughed.

Lorenzo took the elevator upstairs. He entered his room, spotting two bottles of Bud still in the bucket of melted ice on the table. He grabbed one, opened it and sat on the edge of the bed. He pushed the duffle bag next to the bed. Laying back, Lorenzo was happy, knowing tomorrow would be an important day.

SEVEN

The SIU team was huddled together at police headquarters, going over the events of the past day. Frederickson recapped their investigation. Holding a folder, "Guys, at first blush, obviously Franklin was drunk, maybe super drunk given that his blood alcohol was well over the limit." He continued, "Once Amy and Spano did their checking, I'm not sure he ran anyone over. We've got to handle this carefully." Looking at Detective Harper, "Amy, we have that special presentation at Campus Martius today. Once we've finished, I want you to continue working with Detective Sampson at the Twelfth Precinct. Joe, you've got solid photos from the screen and we've got the M.E.'s report." He continued covering the details with the team.

Harper wiggled in her chair, knowing that the mayor and chief planned to present her with a special commendation. She asked, "Can't we cancel that event, this case requires our full attention."

Frederickson knew she didn't want to be singled out for capturing the escaped drug suspects last year. "Just consider this, it's good P.R. for the department." She reluctantly nodded. He turned toward Spano, "Joe, from what the medical examiner told us, it's obvious that the woman didn't die from a car accident." Looking over copies of the M.E.'s report, everyone leafed through the pages, stopping at the highlighted cause of death—blunt force trauma. "Most likely she was struck by a heavy object. We've got to dig deeper; who wanted to frame Franklin, and why? He's not an elected official, so if not Franklin then what was the goal?"

The meeting broke up and the detectives knew this was their number one case now. Harper was walking with Spano when Frederickson stopped them. "Amy, trust me, I know you hate the attention, but it is an election year and this is as much a political event for the mayor as it is recognition of your work. We've all been there."

She knew he was right, "Don, the whole team was involved, not just me. Joe deserves the credit as much as anyone."

Spano laughed, "Your turn in the box."

Frederickson smiled, "Amy, it will only take about a half-hour. We can ride to Campus Martius together. Once we're done, I'll go with you to the Twelfth. Detective Sampson was a great help last year and I'd like to thank him again." Looking at his watch, "We've got a couple hours before we need to go. I'm going upstairs to talk to the chief."

***

It was early and Lorenzo checked the emergency door again that led to the roof. He had checked it out yesterday and made sure that the magnetic lock could be tripped. He was able to reverse the polarity in both access doors with a special tool he brought in the duffle bag. It was six-thirty in the morning and still dark outside. The hallway was empty. Sliding the end of his magnetic bar into the slot above the locking mechanism, he heard the lock click open. Turning, checking the hallway to make sure he was still alone, he pushed the door. It opened. Now to get Bobby and set it up. He walked back to his room; 2950 was the second room from the access to the roof. He knew it would be easy to make his way to the doorway with the rifle and escape up the stairway.

Back in his room he assembled the rifle and scope. Looking out the window he surveyed the landscape toward Campus Martius. Lorenzo's research showed it was six-hundred-fifty meters to the downtown park. The M40 had a range of eight-hundred meters, over a half-mile, so it should be no problem. He was an excellent marksman, having spent the last two years in special training. Their cover, staying downtown, playing cards in the casino and going to the baseball game, was perfect.

His cell phone rang, "Zo, it's me; I'll head upstairs to your room in a few minutes."

"No, meet me downstairs in the lobby."

Once they met, Lorenzo said "Let's go across the street, I want to get us different Tigers shirts. So, guess you hooked up."

"Yeah, hope that was okay."

"Actually it's good. Did you get her name just in case we need it?"

"When she was taking a shower, I went through her purse and wrote down all her information."

Lorenzo smiled, "Nice going." They walked to the gift shop on Monroe. "We've got a few hours to get ready, I'd like to be seen by everyone that we pass in our Tigers shirts." They went back at the hotel and headed into the 555 Restaurant off the lobby. "We'll get breakfast then set it up."

***

The detectives were in their dress blues for the presentation. Amy smiled at Detective Spano. "Looking pretty sharp, Joe." The mayor and chief were talking near the presentation stand that was set up across from the Hard Rock Café on Campus Martius. Amy was watching them. She still felt funny being singled out. "Joe, you know this isn't right, the whole team should be recognized. I was just one of the people involved in the case."

He looked at her, knowing that he wasn't supposed to let her know what else was planned, "I wasn't supposed to tell you; Don and the chief wanted it to be a surprise." He looked around before telling her. "They're going to award Baker a special medal too."

That brought a big smile to her face. She punched him in the shoulder. "Why didn't you guys tell me?"

"Frederickson told me not to tell you but he knew you'd be happy. Tom doesn't know."

"I won't say anything, I promise." They walked toward Detective Frederickson. Chief Mathews and Lieutenant Jackson smiled at her. The chief said in his deep voice, "Harper, you deserve this recognition, it's a way for the city to know what your team accomplished last year."

She nodded, "Thank you, sir, but the whole team was involved."

"I know, but someone has to bite the bullet." That made everyone laugh. The group was getting their final directions, where to stand and that they'd be able to make only short remarks when receiving the medal. Amy was shifting from foot to foot as she listened to the mayor. She checked her watch. They'd been out there on the stand for ten minutes already. This wasn't the first time members of the team were honored, but it was a first to have the ceremony carried live on television with the whole city watching. Harper looked back at Baker, happy that he would also be recognized.

***

Lorenzo was perched on the roof of the hotel, the bipod positioned so the protruding barrel could not be seen over the lip. He was happy that there were people on the stage so he could check out the scope for accuracy one more time. He dialed the scope in, making sure he had everything handled. The setting was perfect. His target was standing in a group and soon they would be at the center of the stage and he'd have his shot then. Bobby was kneeling next to Lorenzo; his job was to keep a lookout. The rooftop of the casino hotel was the highest point in Greektown. The wind draft was minimal this morning, less than he had experienced the last time up there.

"Eleven-sixteen."

He looked through the scope. Lorenzo could see the mayor and police chief talking to Detective Harper. He focused on the mayor who was standing center stage. He was an even bigger target in the scope. The man was six-foot three and must have weighed two-hundred-fifty pounds. People seemed to be moving around on the stage and chairs were set up on both sides of the podium. One more adjustment to the scope. The mayor was now standing at the podium. Channel 4 along with Channel 7 moved their cameras closer. There were six microphones on the stand representing the local television and radio stations. The event was scheduled for live television with start time set so they could air it before the noon news shows.

The mayor smiled, standing tall at the podium in front of hundreds of people. He opened the ceremony, "The citizens of Detroit are safer today because of the efforts of our police department and we're very proud to be here to recognize their outstanding efforts." Turning he motioned toward the group of officers seated to his right. "Chief Mathews' Special Investigative Unit is to be congratulated." He introduced the chief and his commanders in attendance. "I'm pleased to acknowledge two of the SIU members today, Detectives

Amy Harper and Thomas Baker." There was applause as both detectives rose from their seats. The mayor held his hand out, motioning them to approach the podium. Tom Baker had a look of shock on his face, surprised that he would be singled out.

Amy Harper smiled at her partner, "Congrats, Tom."

He said, "This should be for you and Joe, not me."

They made their way to the side of the mayor who was now holding a blue velvet box in his right hand, "Detective Thomas Baker, your heroic efforts last year during the raid in Canada on the escaped drug suspects came at a great cost. You suffered severe injury and have been going through many hours and months of recovery. The citizens of Detroit and the State of Michigan offer you our deepest thanks with the city's Medal of Valor." Displaying the medal of valor to Baker, he then took it out of the box and pinned it on the detective's lapel. There was loud applause and photos were being snapped of the event. Tom looked out at the crowd, nodding in appreciation. Then he looked down with tears in his eyes, "Thank you." Baker stepped back, not able to say anything else.

The mayor smiled, "Detective Amy Harper, you have again performed outstandingly in the line of fire, heading the special team along with the Canadian authorities, arresting key suspects and bringing them to justice. I'm proud to award you the city's Medal of Valor." He held another blue velvet box like the one that held the medal he had given to Baker. Harper saw the two Royal Canadian Police in attendance. She especially appreciated their being in the audience.

Harper looked back to Joe Spano and Detective Frederickson. She smiled but had tears rolling down her cheeks. Shaking the mayor's hand, he motioned to the podium, offering her the opportunity to say a few words. She moved to the center of the podium and waited for the applause to stop. As she started to talk a shot rang out, sending an echo bouncing off the buildings surrounding Campus Martius. People ducked at the noise and many scrambled for cover. Harper stumbled, falling back, her blood splattered on those close to the stage. The mayor was rushed off, Spano and Baker along with the officers near drew their weapons looking for the shooter. People nearby were pointing in different directions, not sure where the shot came from. Baker and Frederickson rushed to Harper's side as Frederickson bent over her pressing on her chest trying to stop the flow of blood.

Baker knelt at her side and cried, "Amy, stay with me," while cradling her head. "Amy, Amy," he called out as Frederickson pulled open her uniform shirt where blood was bubbling out of her chest.

Spano was now at Amy's other side, "Captain, we've called the EMS." He saw where the bullet had entered her chest.

Baker was still holding her as he sputtered, "Why didn't she have a Kevlar on?"

Spano put his hands on Baker's shoulders, "Come on Tom, let the paramedics," who were making their way to the stricken detective, "do their job." Baker was crying, he knew it didn't look good.

The chief and mayor had been escorted to a safe spot as officers moved through the crowd looking for a suspect. A paramedic was treating the wound, putting pressure on it, trying to stop the bleeding, while the EMT was handing her a dressing. Baker was standing over them, still in shock. Spano was talking to an officer who pointed to a small group standing at the entrance to the Hard Rock Café. Joe waved Detective Frederickson over. "Don, these people think the shot came from down the street," pointing toward the east end of Monroe.

They got the names of the potential witnesses and Frederickson got on the radio. "We need to search all the offices and buildings on this street." There was now a mass of officers working the scene. The EMS team loaded Harper in the ambulance and Baker got in and rode to the hospital with them. Spano called out, "Tom, call us right away with any news."

***

Lorenzo grabbed the rifle off the stand and made sure he'd taken care of everything they had planned. He rested the bipod against the wall as he made his way downstairs. He disassembled the rifle before entering the hallway. Peeking out, making sure the coast was clear, he made his way to his room where Bobby was waiting for him. Placing the gun in the case, he handed the case to his friend. "Take this like we talked about and hide it in our special place. Once

65

you've accomplished that, take your baseball ticket and make your way to the game. Get a couple beers and bring them to our seats. I'll wait for you there."

Bobby left the room, Lorenzo headed to the elevators and down to the main lobby. He strolled outside and walked down Monroe toward the Old Shillelagh pub, planning to blend into the crowd of Tigers fans going to the baseball game. The pub's shuttle bus was parked in front with fans climbing aboard. Lorenzo bought a beer from the young lady peddling drinks to fans and jumped on the bus, cheering with the fans that packed the green shuttle, famous for taking patrons to and from the venue. He made sure that he talked to those around him so that he was obvious to others in case an alibi was needed. The people on the shuttle were not aware of what had just happened blocks away. The vehicle rocked back and forth as it crossed Grand Circus Park, in view of the stadium, with fans waving banners out of the open windows. Sounds of sirens filled the air but they went unnoticed to those waiting to enter Comerica Park. When the shuttle stopped on the corner near where the giant statue of the tiger stood, Lorenzo followed the fans that piled out and headed to Gates 3 and 4.

Security personal were checking tickets and scanning bags and backpacks of fans as they entered the stadium. Lorenzo smiled, pleased that he'd accomplished his goal. Once he entered the gate, he headed to the first vendor station and purchased a beer and hot dog and headed to Section 134. The usher looked at his ticket and escorted him to his seat. Plopping into Seat 3, he looked up at the giant scoreboard that told the current stats of the players starting the game. Now he sat back waiting for Bobby to make his way to the ballpark. Players were still on the field tossing baseballs about as fans were milling around. Section 134 was right behind the Tigers dugout and a premium spot. The tickets belonged to his uncle and Lorenzo had sat there many times in the past. Because they were season ticket holders, many of the fans in that area knew one another. This again played into his alibi for the day.

Two guys piled into the seats next to him and one of them said, "Great view." They were both carrying beers. Looking at Lorenzo, the first guy smiled, "Hi, I forgot your name."

"It's Lorenzo, but my friends call me Zo."

"Zo, this is my buddy, Greg." The young man reached over and shook Lorenzo's hand then stood, looking at the buildings that towered over the outfield. It must have been his first time in the stadium.

"Greg, ever been to a Tigers game before?"

"No, first time. Glad that I got to come. I'm really looking forward to it." Then he asked, "You here alone?"

Lorenzo was quick to answer, "No, I'm here with my buddy, he's getting us a couple of beers."

"He'll be awhile, the line sucks, took us fifteen minutes just for beer. Didn't even want to wait for a hot dog."

"Yeah, I was lucky and got the first round."

They were surprised, wondering when he arrived, "Man, what time did you get here?"

"I'm not sure, maybe twelve or a little earlier. I love watching batting practice." He turned, looking up the aisle, "Where in the hell is Bobby?" Lorenzo was pleased how it had gone, everything had followed the plan. He was actually feeling a little buzzed. Two beers on the shuttle, two more beers entering the ballpark, and Bobby would be bringing another round when he got there. What the hell, it just made the day that much sweeter.

EIGHT

The EMS unit pulled up to the emergency entrance at the Detroit Medical Center. Three nurses and a doctor came rushing out followed by a team pushing a gurney. Tom Baker and the paramedic piled out of the ambulance as the medic called out the condition of Detective Harper. "Gunshot right side of chest, looks like a through and through. She's stabilized, blood pressure holding at 95 over 60." Harper was loaded on the gurney as the trauma team went to work. Pushing the patient into Trauma Room One, Baker followed. "Sorry officer, you're going to have to wait out here." Tom sighed deeply as he nodded. He could see through the opening in the curtain; there must have been five or six people working on Harper. A portable X-ray machine was wheeled into the room and he saw the doctor hovering over her. He had blood all over his gloves and shirt. "We've got a squirter; I need two units of A Negative.

Another doctor came hurrying toward the room. Baker asked the nurse, "Who's that?"

"That's Doctor Guzzardo; he's the top thoracic surgeon in the city."

"Can you tell me what's going on?"

"They've got to stop the bleeding and check for pulmonary contusions. She's got the best team in the city." The nurse thought that Baker looked pale, "Officer, can I get you something, maybe a coffee or water?"

"No thanks, just worried about my partner."

"Why don't you follow me, I'll find you a seat and tell the doctor where you can be reached." He followed her to a small room where there must have been twenty people all waiting for news on their family members. "Officer, I'll let the doctors and nurses know where you are." She disappeared back into the emergency area.

Another nurse approached, "Excuse me officer, are you okay?"

Baker was surprised that she asked. "Yes, thanks for asking."

"You better have someone look at you, I think you're bleeding." Baker looked down, noticing for the first time that his uniform was bloody. "No, it's not from me, must be from my partner, she was shot." He feared that he'd tear up again. Standing, he thanked the nurse and moved back to the emergency room doorway. He asked out loud, "Why don't they tell me what's going on?" He started to pace as Joe Spano came in followed by Frederickson.

"Baker, how is she?"

"I don't know, they've got a half-dozen doctors working on her. They haven't told me anything." Baker was wringing his hands. Detective Frederickson listened, then turned and walked through the doors leading to the emergency room. "I don't think they'll let him stay in there." Spano laughed. He knew they'd have a hard time removing Frederickson out of the room. Both of them stood staring at the doors waiting for some news. It must have been ten minutes before Frederickson emerged, Baker right away gasped, "So?"

"Good news guys, they've got her stabilized, took her upstairs for surgery to sew her up. Doctor said she had a great chance. They have her on a ventilator; her vital signs are good." Baker was so relieved that he hugged Frederickson. Spano watched and wasn't sure what Don would do. Frederickson smiled, "We all feel the same, Tom." Turning toward Spano, "Joe, they said it was a high-power rifle, that's why it went through and through. It had to be from a high perch; we're possibly looking at a sniper shot."

"Sniper! Why in the hell would a sniper be shooting at Detective Harper?"

"Not sure, maybe the mayor was the target; after all he was on the podium too." Frederickson stopped for a second, "Joe, I wonder if this could be related to the incident with the deputy mayor." They looked over at Detective Baker who didn't appear to hear what they said. "Tom, we're going to rejoin the search for the shooter, you okay?"

"Yeah, I'm better now." He stepped back, tears streaming down his cheeks. "Thanks, Don, I guess you all realize she's more than my partner," he hesitated before finishing the statement, "I love her."

Spano started to laugh, "Tom, we wouldn't be much of a detective team if we hadn't figured that one out." Now all three of them were smiling. "Tom, they said you could go upstairs to the waiting room on the surgical floor. Why don't you go up; we need to see how the search for the shooter is progressing." The detective agreed and Baker thanked Frederickson again. Don smiled, "Let me know when she's out of surgery."

As they were leaving, Frederickson phoned Chief Mathews. While he was on the phone, close to fifteen officers arrived in the emergency room. Frederickson gave them the thumbs up sign and said, "She's stable." When they heard the good news, they cheered. "Chief," Frederickson continued, "Harper is in surgery, the doctor said it looked real good. Is there any update on the shooter?"

"We've got officers searching every building along Monroe and throughout the square. Based on the trajectory, the shooter must have been in a building along the route. There are three abandoned buildings that we're searching floor by floor."

"That fits with what the doctors here told me, including that it had to be a high-power rifle. Chief, they're saying it could have been a sniper. I'll be headed back with the other detectives on my team. Where do you want us to start?"

"Don, I'd like you to check with the guys at the stage area and see if your team, along with the investigators, can narrow down where the shot came from."

"Okay, we'll report back to you once we're on the scene."

***

The Special Investigation squad back at headquarters was still working on the identification of the body found under the Ford Explorer with the new details the M.E. supplied. The medical examiner called the SIU office, but after being told Frederickson was in the field, she gave the details to Detective Johnson. "Detective, I've got a hit back from AEFS. Your murdered subject is a local woman, Judy Bennet. I'll forward the details to your office."

Johnson walked over to Mindy, the team's secretary. "The medical examiner is sending an email that we need right away."

Mindy started checking her computer. "Here it is," printing the email and handing it to Johnson. Once she did that, she asked, "Do we have any more details on Amy?"

Johnson was quick to answer, "Last I heard she's still in surgery. I'm glad Baker's there, I'm sure he'll call as soon as he knows more." He walked toward his desk reading the report. When he got to his desk he punched in the name Judy Bennet; a photo and details scrolled across the screen: *Bennet, Judy; thirty-five years old; aliases: Judy Hitchcock, Judy Warren; last known address: 1565 East Warren, Detroit.* Johnson immediately called Detective Frederickson. "Lieutenant, we received the identification of our victim found under Franklin's car. Her name is Judy Bennet, local woman. Don, she has at least two aliases and a criminal record, all petty stuff. Bennet was a known hooker. I've got her last known address and was going to head there, unless you want to do it."

"No. That's a good lead. We needed somewhere to start. The rest of the team is working the shooting, so call downstairs and get a squad car to meet you there. Let me know as soon as possible if you have more."

"How's everything going?"

"We're now searching buildings in the Campus Martius corridor. The evidence now points to the shot coming from high up, maybe an empty building."

"If you need me to join the search let me know."

"Thanks but we've got a hundred officers out here. Let me know what you find at Bennet's address."

Frederickson saw Spano and three officers ahead. "Hey Joe, wait up." They were getting ready to enter a vacant building. "Did they complete searching the Compuware Building?"

"Yeah, we're now moving down Congress and east toward Greektown."

"Greektown? There isn't anything high enough except the casino hotel."

"Just doing what command has ordered." Spano turned toward the officers in his group. "Let's search every floor in two-man teams. Check any broken windows facing the park."

Frederickson said, "Joe, I'll call into the Chief and see where he wants me." Watching Spano and the three officers head into the building, he called Chief Mathews. "Chief, I'm here on the square and ready to help, what would you like me to do?"

The Chief asked, "Don, how's Harper doing?"

"No change so far. Once Detective Baker gets any news I'll call you. We've got the area covered. Right now every building from Campus Martius east has a team searching it."

Mathews asked, "How about Greektown? Spano said that you've got coverage all the way up to there."

Frederickson suggested, "I could take an officer with me and cover the casino hotel. I know it's pretty far from the park but it should be easy to check."

Mathews agreed, "Makes sense, at least we can mark it off."

Frederickson headed back to his vehicle and decided that he didn't need to take another officer with him. He was sure that this was an exercise in futility, but at least he'd be doing something to help. The casino hotel was less than a mile and it would take about fifteen minutes to park and get upstairs. Parking in front he flashed his badge, "Here's the keys, I'll be back out in a little bit." Walking inside he approached the front desk. Showing his badge, he said, "I'm Detective Frederickson, I need to get someone to take me upstairs to the roof."

The young lady at the desk was surprised at the request, "Let me get my manager." A few seconds later another woman came out. "Detective, my name is Ms. Samuels, I understand you need to gain access to the roof. Can you tell me why?"

"It's probably just routine, but I've got to confirm everything is okay up there."

She wanted more, but didn't ask. "I'll get one of our attendants to head upstairs with you." She waved a young man over. "Take the detective upstairs, he needs to get on the roof." Handing the young man a square, metal-looking box that was maybe two inches long, she asked, "Do you know how to use this?" He shook his head. Pointing to the slot on one end, "Place this spot on the same spot next to the door handle, slide it downward and the magnetic lock will click then the door will be unlocked. Reverse that when you're done." When he turned to walk away, she reminded him, "Make sure it's locked before you leave." He nodded.

Frederickson looked back, "I'll check it. Thanks for your help."

As they headed to the bank of elevators, the young man asked, "So what's this about?"

"Just routine. Once we get the door open, I want you to wait down here for me."

Entering the elevator, the young man slid a key card in the slot and pressed the button for twenty-six. The ride was quick. When they exited, he pointed to the right. "The access door to the roof is at the end of the hallway.

They headed down to the end. Frederickson was surprised to see so many trays outside of rooms. "Why so many trays out here?"

"Housekeeping should have already picked these up." He also seemed surprised. They continued toward the end access door. The young man took the metallic box the manager had given him, and looking at the slot on the end, lined it up to the one on the door. Sliding it down, the door clicked. "Hey, it worked."

"Step back now and unless I call you, under any circumstances do not come upstairs. Do you understand?"

"Yeah, don't worry, I'm afraid of heights."

Pulling the door open, Don climbed the stairs leading to the roof. There was a second door at the top. Pulling his weapon, Don pushed it open and peered out, nothing or no one was in sight. Don stepped out onto the roof where he could see the front edge of the roof that looked directly toward the west and Campus Martius. Moving slowly to the edge, he stopped. Foot prints, and they looked fresh. The detective moved back, reaching for his cell phone. "Chief, I'm on the roof of the Greektown Hotel. There's a two-legged bipod leaning against the wall. I've seen these before, it's something a sniper would use. I didn't get too close, it could be booby trapped. We've got a lot of foot prints up here; they look pretty fresh. All of them are concentrated near the edge of the wall facing Campus Martius."

"Don't go any further, I'm ordering a forensic team right now."

"I'll keep the area clear. Tell them I already have access to the roof, it's off the twenty-sixth floor." Hanging up he headed back down the stairway. The young man who brought the key was standing in the hallway, "Thanks, I'll take that key and lock up. You can go back to work."

The guy looked back, "I don't think I can leave without approval from the manager."

"I'll call the manager, do you know her extension?" He shook his head. "What's the number to the desk?"

"Thirty-six-twenty-one."

Detective Frederickson dialed the switchboard and asked for the managers extension. "We've got an issue on the roof and I'll be sending the attendant back down without the key." Before she could answer he added, "There will be a team of officers arriving, have them sent upstairs. Once we know more, I'll be able to fill you, and only you, in." Don hung up before she could say anything else. Turning to the young man, "Your boss said to go back down; I'll bring the key down when we're done." The young man walked away, looking back twice, not sure what was going on, but he knew it couldn't be good.

***

Joe Spano was on the eleventh floor of the empty building down the street and was heading back out when his cell rang. He saw it was Detective Frederickson, "Yeah, what's up?"

"Did your team find anything?"

"No, I'm headed back down, how about you?"

"Joe, this is where the shooter was. I'm at the Greektown Hotel. I went on the roof and there is a bipod stationed against the outer wall, also a lot of foot prints up here. They're leading to the western edge. This is the place."

Spano was stunned, "Hell, the roof at the Greektown Hotel is too far away!"

"I guess most of us would have agreed with that, but Joe, now that we've found out that it was a high-power rifle that shot Amy, it had to be on a stationary object and the bipod fits that scenario."

Joe Spano was silent for a minute, "I'm coming there right now."

"Joe, I've informed the chief. He's sending a forensic team. I didn't touch anything, just keeping everyone away. When you get here take the elevator to the twenty-sixth floor. The exit to the rooftop is all the way to the right end of the hallway. Don't say anything to the people downstairs. Let your team join another search group."

"I'm on my way."

Detective Frederickson sat on the bottom step of the roof doorway.

He wondered, *Was this a potential hit on the mayor that missed? It couldn't have been aimed at Detective Harper, could it?* It didn't add up. He wanted to investigate the roof more but thought it was better to wait for the team the chief was sending. Why would they leave the bipod? He heard voices coming down the hall. Stepping out into the hall he saw four officers walking with Detective Spano. "Joe, who're your friends?"

"We met downstairs, said they were coming to find you."

Frederickson extended his hand, "Glad you got here so quick. When I went on the roof, I spotted a bipod up against the wall and foot prints in some of the gravel near the western edge." The group followed him back up the staircase and headed out on the roof. Frederickson stood near the door opening with Spano and pointed in the direction he had described. Watching the officers from the forensic team mark the area, Frederickson asked Joe. "Tell me, what do you make of this? Why leave the bipod? That's too easy for us." Looking over at Spano, "Joe, do you think Harper was the target, or did the sniper miss?"

"Same thing I've been wondering; it had to have been meant for either the mayor or possibly the chief." Both men nodded as the team was placing markers at several places near the short wall facing west and placed the bipod in a forensic plastic bag. The detectives hoped that they'd identify fingerprints from the item left behind. It could be the thing they needed to break the case. They knew the bipod would be taken back to headquarters and put into evidence.

NINE

Detective Baker was seated in the surgical waiting room when Dr. Guzzardo and a nurse came walking in. Baker jumped to his feet and the nurse introduced him, "This is Doctor Guzzardo." Guzzardo smiled, shaking Baker's hand. "Officer, will you follow me?" Baker's face bore a concerned look. "Officer, your chief wanted me to give you this information privately. I'm pleased to inform you that your partner is out of surgery and that the surgery was a success." Baker teared up. "She's lost of a lot of blood and it will be some time before she's up and around. We were able to clear out any fragments of the bullet and repair the wounds. I've sent her blood work downstairs to the lab. Dr. Nagappala will check everything to make sure there isn't any further complications. It has the highest priority."

Baker was relieved as Doctor Guzzardo covered the surgical progress. "Thank you, thank you." He hugged the doctor "When can I see her?"

Guzzardo continued, "She'll be headed into recovery in a few minutes. Once they have her situated, one of the nurses will come out and take you in. Officer, she had a shattered rib that I repaired. It was damaged by the bullet. Actually that turned out to be a blessing—the rib deflected the bullet so it missed her vital organs. She's going to be pretty sore for quite a while but she will recover without lasting effects except for two scars."

Tom Baker was so happy, he again shook the doctor's hand. "I can't thank you enough."

"No officer, it is us that thank you and your fellow officers for everything you do. I'd like to see her at my office in ten days. The stitches will dissolve but I need to see how everything is coming along."

"Thank you again, Doctor." Tom was so happy that he walked around in circles before remembering that he needed to call

Frederickson to let him know how Harper was doing. Grabbing his cell phone, he punched in the lieutenant's number. "Don, it's Baker, Amy's fine, surgery went great."

"That's super, I'll let everyone know. What can we do for you?"

"Nothing Don, just let the team know. The doctor said she had a shattered rib from the bullet, but the rib may have saved her from more damage. She's going to be off for a long time."

"She can have all the time she needs for a full recovery."

Baker asked, "Any news on the shooter?"

Frederickson didn't want to have Baker worrying about that. "Tom, we've got a few leads. Don't concern yourself with that, just take care of Amy."

"Thanks." Tom was pleased that he was able to give Frederickson the good news. He'd only been part of the SIU team for a little over a year, but felt like part of a family. A nurse walked into the waiting room.

"Officer Baker, will you follow me please. We've moved your partner into a recovery room. She's coming out of the anesthesia." Baker clenched both fists and thrust them into the air, so happy to see Harper. "Right this way, Officer."

***

Detective Frederickson called back to the SIU office. Mindy answered and he gave her the good news. "We heard from Baker, Harper is out of surgery and in recovery. The doctors are glad that they got to her so quickly because it gave her a better chance for a full recovery. I'd like you to let the rest of the team know."

Mindy was pleased to get the call. "Thanks for letting me know, Detective. I'll call the team. Do you want me to call the chief?"

"No, I'll do that. He will want to update the news teams that were covering the event." After talking to Mindy, he called the chief and informed him about Harper's progress. "Chief, I'm still on the hotel roof and the forensics team has found more evidence, most likely where the shooter was positioned. No shells were found, but they've got the bipod. It was set up at the edge of the wall. They're looking for any fingerprints and making a cast of the foot prints they found."

"At least we've got the location of the shooter. Don, do you think Harper was the target?"

"I don't think so. It seems to me that someone would have been aiming at the mayor. I'm wondering if this has anything to do with framing his deputy."

"Not sure, but I agree. Harper couldn't have been the target. Glad you discovered the shooting location. I'm sending you a team of officers to help search the hotel for possible suspects."

"First let Spano and I do some recon work. The staff might have someone who looked suspicious staying here or hanging around."

"Okay, I'll hold off. Keep me informed. Don, I'm glad Harper is doing okay, she's a heck of a cop."

"I agree." Once he hung up, Frederickson grabbed Spano. "Joe, someone here had to see something, they might not know what but we've got to start with the staff. I want to know everyone who had a room on the top floor." The two of them headed down to the lobby. "Let's start with the manager. I've already talked to her to get access to the roof." As they approached the bank of elevators at the end of the hallway, Frederickson was surprised to see trays still in the hallway. "Joe, you ever stay here?"

The doors opened and they got in. "Do I look like a high roller?"

"No, but I'm wondering about the housekeeping staff, did you notice all the trays of half-eaten food and dishes in the hall?"

Spano put his hand on the elevator doors before they closed. Looking down the row of rooms he saw what Frederickson was referring to. "Don, even at the Holiday Inn they'd have picked up trays by now, hell it's close to three." They let the doors close and headed to the lobby.

They exited and approached the front desk, Frederickson nodded toward Joe. Undercover officers were stationed at the front and side doors. "The chief has it all covered." Walking to the desk, Frederickson asked for Ms. Samuels, the hotel manager.

She came out right away, "Detective Frederickson, how's everything going upstairs?"

"Can we talk someplace private?"

She seemed stunned. "Sure, my office okay?"

"That would be perfect." They followed her to a hinged door off the right side of the long mahogany desk. She lifted it to allow them to enter and they walked to her office. Frederickson called her by name. "Ms. Samuels, this is Detective Spano. We've got a few questions for you."

She was really puzzled. "Did you find a problem on the roof?"

"Possibly, but we need to cover some other issues. What time does your housekeeping staff clean the trays and dishes from the hallway on the twenty-sixth floor?"

This she didn't expect. "Why are you asking that?"

"We need an answer first."

Picking up a folder off her desk, she leafed through the pages. "Our staff starts cleaning rooms after nine when the front desk sends them the list of guests who have checked out. They also take a cart upstairs to pick up any empty dishes and trays in the hall. At times it isn't done until ten but not later than ten-thirty."

"It's after three and there are trays and dishes in the hallway from the elevators all the way to the doors leading to the roof."

"That's not right." Now she wondered why the detectives were concerned about housekeeping.

"I thought the same thing. Is the individual or individuals responsible working now?"

"I need to make a call. That isn't my area of responsibility; our housekeeping manager handles it."

She picked up her phone and Frederickson stopped her. "Please ask them to come to your office. I'd like this to be confidential for now."

Nodding, she waited for someone to answer. "Maria, this is Angie. I have a problem. Could you meet me in my office, oh, and bring the list of staff on duty this weekend." Hanging up she turned back to the detectives, "Now are you going to tell me what's going on?"

"Not yet but I promise I'll fill you in later." They waited for the housekeeping manager to arrive. Spano was feeling a bit suspect, just standing there. Frederickson broke the silence, "Ms. Samuels, how long have you been the manager here?"

She looked at Don first then at Joe. "Detective, I've worked here since we opened. I started as a desk clerk and was made the front desk manager three years ago." She looked at Frederickson. "So, how long have you been a detective?"

He chuckled, "Fair enough. By looking at me, you'd guess a

hundred years. I joined the force twenty-six years ago and was promoted to detective in 2013. Joe and I are both in the Special Investigative Unit, we report to the chief of police."

"Thanks, Detective, I didn't mean to sound like a smart-ass but I wish I knew what was going on."

"That's understandable."

There was a knock on her door and she called out, "Maria, come on in." An Hispanic female came into the office. She looked surprised to see two police officers standing there with Angie.

"What's going on?"

Before the desk manager could answer, Frederickson stated, "We're heading an investigation that has brought us to the hotel and we have some questions. Is it okay to ask you a few things?"

"Sure, I've got nothing to hide."

"This isn't about you; we've got questions about a guest on the twenty-sixth floor and maybe some members of your staff."

Happy that it wasn't about her personally, "Okay, ask away."

"Why don't we all have a seat, we might be here a while." After they sat down, Frederickson said, "First thing we'll need is a list of all the guests who were on the twenty-sixth floor last night and those with reservations for the past week."

Angie Samuels nodded. "I'll print that out for you right now."

"The second question is regarding the staff that works on that floor. We'll need their names and addresses. Did anyone call in sick today?"

Maria took out her listing, "I had one girl call in sick. She usually works that floor. I assigned it to another person who fills in for us."

"What's her name?"

"Sophia Valentine. Is this related to immigration? I know she's a citizen; we check for that during the interview."

"No, we're not immigration agents. We were wondering why there are still trays and dishes in the hallway at this time of day."

She didn't expect that question. "You're here about trays in the hallway?"

"Please, just answer the question."

"Sophia works both the twenty-fifth and -sixth floors. She's been with us for a long time, at least six or seven years. I think she has a sick child, that's why she called in. We usually pick up the trays between nine and ten."

He said, "We were surprised to see them this late in the day. That's all for now. I want you to go back upstairs but please don't say anything about our questions."

"I won't. Is there anything else?"

"Not right now. We'll go over everything with Ms. Samuels. She'll fill you in later. Thank you for your help." Frederickson stood as Maria got up. She left the room wondering what this was all about. Once she left, Don asked Angie, "We'll need the address for Ms. Valentine and the rest of the staff that work those top floors."

"I'll print that out too." Angie handed Frederickson the list of everyone who made reservations and stayed on the top two floors. "Detective, I listed everyone who stayed for the past week. Only two names appeared twice." She pointed out the names on the second page: Lorenzo Virgilio and Bob Booker. "Mr. Virgilio requested the same room last week, 2650. Detective, both of them are platinum players. It isn't odd that he stayed here two weeks in a row and requested the same room. Most people on that player level like a certain view or amenities the room may offer." As she scrolled through the list, she stopped, "Detective, Mr. Virgilio is still checked in. Mr. Booker was in room 2610. They've both been here in the last week, guests of the management."

"Guests, what do you mean 'guests.'"

"Both guys are high rollers, platinum players. They will gamble thousands on every visit."

"Okay, I appreciate your help." He marked the two rooms on his list. "Joe, let's check both rooms."

"Detective, you promised that you'd fill me in."

"Yeah, I did, didn't I?" Frederickson looked over at Spano. "Joe, we need to let her know," looking back at Angie. "Did you hear about a shooting at Campus Martius today?"

"Yes, not any of the details but the bell staff was talking about it. Someone was shot during a presentation or gathering; we're not sure about the facts."

"Well, that someone shot who was one of my detectives. We've had to check every building from the park to Greektown. When I inspected your roof, it appeared that people had been up there recently, maybe our shooter. A forensic team is up there gathering evidence. It's imperative that none of this gets out."

"Do you think the shooter was here?"

"Not sure, but we've got people checking every possible location. Have you had any workmen on your roof in the past two days?"

"No, no one; there are only three keys. I gave you mine, the building manager has one and the third one belongs to the superintendent. It's a special key designed for added protection. He's only here if we have a building issue."

"I'll return your key once the team is done upstairs."

"Thanks, I promise I won't say anything."

Don stood up, followed by Spano. "That's greatly appreciated. We won't be upstairs much longer. Thanks for the two lists. If I need anything else, I'll let you know." Both detectives went back upstairs, surprised to see all of the trays gone in the hallway. "Guess we scared Maria; someone cleaned up these trays and dishes pretty fast."

Detective Spano asked, "Do you think they had anything to do with the guy on the roof?"

"I don't know, Joe, but we've got to get a squad out to check on Ms. Valentine. Maybe someone paid her to take the morning off. We need to see if either person that has been here the past two weeks is in their rooms." Heading down the hallway they stopped at 2610 first. No one answered their knock. The same thing happened at the second room. "We'll get the staff to get us room keys."

Joe dialed the manager's extension, "Angie, this is Detective Spano, can we get someone to let us into rooms 2650 and 2610?" It took less than five minutes for her to send Maria from housekeeping. She let them into 2650 first. Joe said, "Wait in the hallway while we check the room out." The room was empty, the bed unmade and an empty beer bottle in a bucket sitting on a small table. Joe turned to Detective Frederickson, "I never realized it but you have a clear view of Campus Martius from here."

"The shot could have been taken from any of these rooms. Whoever did this must have had a contact or been here many times, how else could they get on the roof?"

Joe replied, "With that special key. Either someone gave it to the shooter or let them up."

"Guess we should check room 2610 now, and then check every room that faces west." They headed down the hall to the second room. They saw a maid's cart in the hallway and once they entered 2610, they found that the room had been cleaned. There were clothes in the closet, just like the previous room, but nothing else in clear view. Nothing unusual in either room. "I'll ask Maria to let us into the other rooms on this side of the hallway. Joe, why don't you go upstairs on the roof and see how the team is doing."

Once he was on the roof, Spano found the forensic team wrapping up their inspection. They had taken photos of the disturbed area confirming that someone obviously had positioned themselves at the edge facing west. They also had taken casts of the foot prints. These might be their best key to solving the case. Unfortunately, there wasn't any other tangible evidence to take back except the bipod. Whoever was up there did a pretty good job: they didn't leave anything else up there, no cigarette butts, no handprints, the only other thing that confirmed a shooter was up there was a trace of gunpowder on the roof's edge. It was swabbed and would be taken back to the lab. A second team was completing the inspection at the stage in Campus Martius. Their main search priority was finding any fragments from the bullet that struck Detective Harper. They were gathering everything that would help solve the shooting and then would be heading back to headquarters.

Frederickson got a call from the officer that went to check on Ms. Valentine. "Sir, I talked to the lady you wanted me to check on. She said her son was sick, had to take him to the hospital during the night. Guess she forgot to call into work."

"Thanks officer." Don wasn't sure, but this was to suspicious, especially given the events of the day.

TEN

The captain at the Twelfth Precinct arrived downtown at headquarters and brought John Franklin as the chief requested. He headed upstairs to the chief's office. Mathews' orders were clear, "As soon as they arrive, bring them to my office." They were sure now that Franklin had been set up. The feeling was that the mayor might have been the potential target at Campus Martius.

"Welcome, Captain." Mathews was happy to see both of them. "Mr. Franklin, I'm sorry about all of this, you probably heard about the events today."

Franklin was still shocked over being arrested, but happy that people were starting to believe him. "Thank you, Chief. I heard the news from the captain. How's your detective."

"Still touch and go. We're not sure if she was the target." He turned toward the captain, "We need to keep Franklin out of sight. My team is thinking about letting people think we're still holding him for the incident at Stroh River Place.

The chief planned to only give the captain from the Twelfth Precinct some details. "John, I'm going to have Lieutenant Jackson take you upstairs for now. You'll be our guest until we figure this out." Once Franklin was gone, the chief turned to the captain, "We've got too many possibilities in this case. We're planning to announce that Detective Harper died today of complications after surgery. If we can let this shooter think he succeeded, they might slip up. I'm going to cover the details with Harper and the SIU team first." The captain asked, "Did Franklin have any idea who may have had it out for him?"

"No, Chief, so he's a perfect suspect. Our officers said he was still drunk this morning and doesn't have an alibi."

"I'm going to go talk to him. We'll keep your office in the loop once we've got more details." When the captain left, the chief went upstairs to talk to Franklin to question him. "John, do you have any idea what's this is about?"

"Not really. All I know is that I'm being arrested for killing someone with my car. This whole thing has me puzzled. I didn't do it."

"We're starting to believe you, but you haven't helped yourself with your behavior."

"I'll admit that I've been off my game a little lately."

Mathews didn't like the way Franklin brushed it off. "Hell man, off your game! You're a damn liability. The Free Press barbequed your ass in last Sunday's edition. They pegged you as a drunk and an embarrassment to the mayor and his team. Three council members called for your resignation!" Franklin couldn't say much, he knew the chief was right. Mathews thought maybe he'd gone too far, but knew the mayor was entrenched in an election battle and Franklin's actions hadn't made it any easier. "We've got to figure this out and I'm going to need you to go through recent events with my team. Someone went to a lot of trouble to set you up."

Franklin hung his head, knowing that his actions had been a problem. "You're right, Chief. I'm willing to do anything to help. Maybe I can go through letters we've received. Maybe it has to do with some people upset about neighborhood issues."

"I think it's deeper than that. We're going to find a spot here to keep you under cover. I'll get Lieutenant Jackson to get you a place to stay. It should only be for a few days." Mathews called Jackson and she said she'd handle it. As Franklin was being shown to a secluded area on the fifth floor, Mathews contacted Detective Frederickson, "Don, I want to run a few things past you."

"Okay Chief, what do you have?"

"I'm putting Franklin up here at headquarters; best to keep him out of the public's eye. I'm thinking that we've got the same people involved in both the Franklin issue and Harper's shooting. I still think the shot was meant for the mayor."

Frederickson understood. "We're on the same wavelength, but why did they try to set the deputy mayor up, and then shoot at the mayor? That's a bit of overkill." After saying that, Frederickson shook his head, "Sorry, I didn't mean to be funny."

"Yeah, I understand. I plan to announce to the press that Harper died after surgery."

"Oh no, I don't like that..."

"Now wait, before you finish, Don, listen to my idea. Someone obviously wanted to frame Franklin, and kill someone at the podium, most likely the mayor. So we hide Franklin and they still think he's been arrested. We tell them they succeeded in killing an officer today. Maybe we can flush them out. I'll put a twenty-four-hour guard on the mayor."

The detective took a breath. "I'm not sure; how do we get the staff at the hospital to keep quiet?"

"You're a pretty smart guy, Don, I'm sure you'll come up with something." Once he finished saying that, the chief started laughing. "Sorry, Don."

"Okay, but you owe me big time," Don Frederickson chuckled as he hung up. He knew he should handle it in person with Harper. Should be easy to get the staff on board. He first called the SIU office. "Mindy, I need you to call everyone and fill them in for me. The chief plans to let people think Harper was killed so we might be able to flush these guys out."

"She's okay, isn't she?"

"Yeah, I'm going to go over there right now. Want to fill her and Baker in so they don't freak out."

"Okay, I'll handle it." She started by calling Johnson who was searching Bennet's last known address. Once he answered she covered the situation.

"Thanks for the heads up, Mindy. I haven't made any progress here. Bennet hasn't been seen at her apartment for the past week. I did find out that she danced at a strip club on Eight Mile."

Mindy stopped him, "Johnson, you might want to relay that information to Harper." She realized what she just said. "On second thought, call Detective Spano; he's handling the case with Detective Harper. They were working on what tied the Franklin case to events at the strip club on Eight Mile."

"Good lead, thanks, Mindy. I'll do that right away." Johnson called Detective Spano, "Joe, I've got a lead on the woman that was found under Franklin's vehicle. I understand that you might have some information about a strip club on Eight Mile?"

"Actually Harper handled that with Detective Sampson from the

Twelfth Precinct. I've got his number if you want it."

"Thanks, I'll do that. You hear anything else about Harper?"

"Baker is with her. Last we heard she's come out of the anesthesia. Of course she's in a lot of pain but everything's looking good. You know that the chief is going to keep her under wraps and announce that she died from the gunshot wounds."

"Yeah, guess they're not taking any chances. What if she had been the target? That's good that they'll protect her."

"Why do you want to know about the strip club on Eight Mile? Planning a big night out?" Spano laughed, thinking he'd really gotten Johnson with that one.

"You're really funny. How long did it take you to think that one up?" Spano didn't answer. "Looks like the woman who was found under Franklin's car was a known stripper at a club. There's not many clubs left on Eight Mile since they closed a bunch of the strip joints down."

"You're right, Johnson, good job. Let me know if you need some help."

"Just let Lieutenant Frederickson know that I'm headed out there to see if this Bennet chick was on their payroll. Who knows, maybe the owners of the club are involved in our case."

Once Johnson hung up, Spano thought about what he'd said. *Wow, that makes sense. I'm going to run this by Don. Maybe we should stop him before he gets to the club.* Joe strolled over to Frederickson. "Don, Johnson had a good idea about the body that was found under Franklin's car. She may have been a stripper at the place that Harper and Sampson investigated yesterday. He's going to head out there."

"Yeah, I agree that could be a great lead. It might be what we're missing. He should check out the connection."

"Should we let him walk into that alone?"

Frederickson looked back at him, "The club owner would know if one of his girls had any family and if she's been missed. Call Johnson, tell him we'll meet him there right after we leave the hospital. I want to go in together." Spano passed the information on to Johnson as Frederickson made their way to the Medical Center. He pulled up to the side entrance and he and Spano went up to Harper's room. When they walked past the officer guarding her room, they saw Tom Baker sitting next to the bed, holding Harper's hand and looking pitiful. "Baker, is she okay?"

He hadn't noticed them coming in, "Oh, yeah, Don, it's just hard seeing her like this."

"I understand. We just wanted to come by and see her ourselves. Spano and I need to head out to Eight Mile, but I wanted to let her know something." He shuffled his feet, "Tom, I've been where she is, so have you, but she's a strong person, she's going to be okay."

"I know, sir, I've just got to make her believe it."

"I'm going to tell you something that you'll have to relay to her. I wanted to tell her in person, but Johnson has a lead that we need to follow up on." Frederickson thought back to his surgery last year, hoping Amy's came out as well as his did. "Tom, Chief Mathews is going to tell the press that Harper died after surgery."

"What?" Baker was now standing.

"I know what you're thinking, but first, sit down. We don't know if Harper was the target but the chief thinks we can keep her safer by announcing that she died. Whoever shot her, will think they succeeded and that way maybe we can flush these guys out."

Baker was nodding, "I guess that makes sense. When is he going to do that?"

"Today. Tom, are you okay telling this to Amy?"

"Yeah. Now that I think about it, that's a good idea. How will we handle the hospital staff?"

"I'll handle that. I've already talked to Dr. Guzzardo and he will cover it with everyone who's been involved with her care. We're going to keep an officer guarding her room when she's moved to another floor. He'll be here all the time."

Baker smiled for the first time since they walked in. He reached out and shook Frederickson's hand, "Thanks, Don, I know she'll understand."

"Tom, we've got to go. I'll call once we know more." Harper was still sleeping as they walked out of her room. Frederickson turned to Spano, "I wanted to tell her myself but we've got to see what's going on at that club. Johnson could walk into a mess."

***

An hour had passed since Frederickson and Spano left the

hospital. As Detective Baker was holding Amy's right hand, he saw her eyes open and he slowly started talking to her. "Amy, can I get you anything?"

She looked over at him and in a hushed tone, "Yeah."

"What? I'll do anything for you, honey."

"I want a new body, one that hasn't been shot."

He smiled, "It might take a while."

She was still groggy, but asked for a drink. Harper had tubes and gages all around, "What?" She tried sitting up but was too weak.

He handed her a cup of water with a straw. "Go slowly." He thought that maybe he'd tell her a few things about the investigation. "Amy, Don and Spano were here; they hoped to talk to you but didn't want to wake you." She turned toward him, seemingly understanding. "They needed to meet Johnson at that strip club on Eight Mile that you've been to. The woman that started this whole investigation, well, she's a stripper. They want to know if she might have worked there."

"They're going where?"

Baker stood. "You can't sit up, Amy, lay back down. You don't need to get excited."

"Then why tell me about this?" She gave him a stern look.

"Sorry, I thought you'd want to know."

"You're damn right I want to know." Coughing, "Ow, that hurt."

Baker wasn't quite sure of what to do next, "Can I get something for you?"

A nurse came in, checked her blood pressure and heart rate and asked Amy, "Ms. Harper, are you feeling okay?"

"Yeah, like I just got hit by a train."

The nurse looked back at Baker. "You need to keep her laying flat until the anesthetic wears off. I'm going to come back in a little while and get you up and moving Ms. Harper. I brought you some pain pills; you can take them every four hours. Dr. Nagappala in the lab sent up a report showing all your blood work came back great." She handed Harper a sheet with notes detailing the blood work. "It's going to be rough the first few days but by tomorrow you'll start feeling better, I promise. Can I bring you a ginger ale?"

"How about a glass of wine?" Harper laughed. "Oh, shit, that really hurts," she said, holding her chest. Baker was still standing, hoping he could help, but there wasn't anything he could do. She looked up at Baker, "Sit down, Tom, I'm okay. Sorry about being a pain, I appreciate everything you're doing. Now tell me again about the strip club."

The nurse chuckled, "I'll leave on that note."

"Amy, sure you're up to this?"

"Yeah, tell me what's going on."

"Frederickson and Spano have a possible break in the Franklin case. They're wondering," he stopped for a few seconds, "Amy if the woman found under Franklin's vehicle is a stripper, maybe she worked at the club that Franklin claimed he was in."

Harper was now fully alert and into the discussion, "That makes sense. Maybe the owners of the club were in on the frame-up. Tom, they need to know that the manager is kind of a flake, he's not anything more than a babysitter. Sampson and I were able to bully him into doing what we wanted."

"I'll call Frederickson and let him know. You need to rest now."

Harper laid back down, flat on her back. She started to close her eyes, then looked back at him. "There's something else you wanted to tell me, Tom, what is it?"

Baker was hoping that the pain pills were starting to work by now. "It's not important, you need to rest." It had been a tough day. Tom Baker was just glad that she was alive.

"I'm not sleeping until you tell me the other thing you're hiding from me. What did the doctors say, am I going to be okay?"

He had to tell her now, "You're doing great, the doctor said everything is fine, better than expected."

"Than what is it?"

"The boss said that Chief Mathews is worried about you, so to keep you safe, he's going to announce that you were killed in action." He was afraid of her reaction.

She looked over at him, nodding and quiet at first. "That makes sense, maybe they can flush out the shooter if they think they were successful."

Baker laughed, "Christ, you're so great." He leaned in and hugged her, kissing her forehead. He watched her close her eyes and drift off. She'd been sleeping for a couple of hours when the nurse walked in. She motioned to Baker and he smiled, "She's good."

"Glad everything seems to be okay." She checked Amy's vitals again and pressed lightly on Harper's side. Amy opened her eyes and took a deep breath. "This is going to be numb for a day or so. Trust me, you'll want it that way. I'd like to get you sitting at the side of the bed first, then later maybe we can get you standing."

"Guess there's no time like the present." Amy looked back at Tom, smiling, "You better leave, I'd hate to have you see me cry."

He had tears in his eyes. "I know you're just happy to be alive." Touching her hand, he left the room.

***

The Tigers game was in the bottom of the first inning and Bobby walked down the aisle, carrying two beers, "What took you so long?" Lorenzo asked.

"Line at the beer vendor. Did I miss anything?"

"Yeah, Verlander struck out two for a quick first half." He introduced Bobby to the two guys sitting next to them. They exchanged handshakes. It was going just as Lorenzo hoped; they'd sit back and enjoy the game. "Can we buy you guys a beer?" That was met with smiles. Their seats were right behind home plate, and they'd surely be caught on one of the television cameras. Bobby, Lorenzo and the two guys cheered a solid performance by the Tigers ace and watched Miguel Cabrera hit a couple of homers. The home team took another win versus Cleveland, and moved the two teams into a tie for first place. People poured out of the ballpark and many of them headed to Greektown to celebrate. Lorenzo grabbed Bobby. "I got one of those guys' names in case we need it."

Bobby knew the plan and was pleased that Zo was happy it was working out. "What're we gonna do now, Zo?"

"Let's head to my room first, then I want to play some cards."

After riding the shuttle bus back to Monroe Street, they walked to the Greektown Hotel and headed upstairs. When they exited the elevators, the first thing they saw was a police officer standing in the hallway, right past their room. "No problem, Bobby, we're in the clear. Let's go." As they walked to 2650 the officer approached.

"Excuse me gentlemen, are either of you Lorenzo Virgilio?"

"Yes, that's me," Lorenzo said. "Can I help you, Officer?"

"There was a problem here on the twenty-sixth floor. The hotel let us into all the rooms. We're checking with everyone on this floor. If that's okay with you, I'd like to ask you some questions."

"Sure, we were going to clean up after the ball game first. Do you want to come into our room?"

"Yes, that'll work, I just have a few questions."

Lorenzo opened his door. "Come on in." The officer followed him and Bobby into the suite.

Looking around the room, the officer noted that it was neat, bed made, nothing out of place. "Where were both of you this afternoon?"

Lorenzo calmly looked directly into the officer's eyes. "Ball game, why?"

"I need you both to give me a rundown of your afternoon, specifically between eleven and noon."

"I'd like to know why before we tell you. We're just a couple of Tigers fans."

"We're checking on a crime that took place near here, now where were you both?"

"We rode on the shuttle from the Old Shillelagh bar to the ballpark. Not sure what time it was but it had to be about that time. We had a couple beers there before grabbing the ride to the stadium."

"Both of you?"

"Yeah, we got to the ballpark about noon. Had great seats. I enjoy watching batting practice."

The officer nodded, writing it all down. "Is there anyone who can confirm that they saw you there?"

"Hell, I'm not sure. There were a lot of people on the shuttle, I'm sure people saw us. We did sit with two other guys at the ballpark. They were there early too." Lorenzo pulled his ticket stub out of his pocket. "Not sure if you need this, but these were our seats."

"Thank you." He wrote down the seat numbers in his note pad. "Can I get a contact number if we need anything else from you?"

"Sure, Officer, now can you tell me what this is all about?"

The officer looked back at the two men, "What do you know about a shooting at Campus Martius?"

They looked at each other. "Shooting, what shooting?"

Looking at Bobby first, who hadn't said much, "What about you, where were you today?"

"We've been together all day. Just like he told you."

The officer made sure he had everything written down. He confirmed their contact information and told them, "Thank you, we'll be in touch if we need anything else."

The officer walked out. Lorenzo looked at Bobby pressing his finger to his lips. He motioned to Bobby to come closer. He whispered, "They may have the room bugged so don't say anything, just listen to me." Looking toward the bank of windows, he loudly said, "I wonder what that was all about," smiling at Bobby and quickly changing the subject. "Man that was some game. How about going to the casino, we can play some cards and get a beer."

Motioning for Bobby to answer, "Sounds great Zo, I'm in." They walked out of the room and headed back to the elevators. Once they got in, Bobby said, "We okay, Zo?"

"Great, Bobby, we're good."

***

Joe Spano entered Detective Johnson's number on his cell phone. "Johnson, where are you right now?"

"Pulled up in front of the club; I'm parking on the east side of the building."

"We're about five minutes away, wait for us." Spano turned to Frederickson, "Johnson's there, he'll wait for us." Pulling down Eight Mile, they saw the flashing lights on the club ahead. It was now six-thirty. "How do you want to handle this?"

"We'll ask for the manager. I'm going to tell them we need their employee information for the past year. I'm not leaving until we get it. If necessary, I'll threaten to get a warrant and shut the club down until I get that list." Spano chuckled, knowing that Frederickson would kick ass and take names. They entered the parking lot and parked next to where Johnson was staking out the place. Getting out of the vehicle, Frederickson said, "Let's go." Detectives Spano and Johnson hurried to catch up with Frederickson who was striding ahead of them at a fast pace. When they walked past the bouncer, the glittering lights flashed on dancers gyrating on stages around the bar and lit up the place. Frederickson looked at the bartender as he walked up to the tall man. Showing him his badge, "We need to see the owner, now."

The guy sneered, "He's not here."

"Then I want to see the manager, or do I need to have the dozen officers outside come in and close this place down?" Spano had a puzzled look on his face, wondering if Frederickson had called in a team.

The bartender picked up a phone from under the bar. "Boss, I've got two officers out here, they want to see you."

The manager, CK Johnson, wondered why the cops were back. He was cooperative yesterday with the two detectives who wanted tapes so he asked, "What do you mean two officers?"

"I've got two of them standing here and they've got squad cars outside."

"I'm coming, tell them to hold on." Walking out from the back room, he saw the men standing there. These weren't the same detectives from yesterday. "Officer," extending his hand, "I'm the manager, Chris Johnson, but everyone calls me CK. What can we do for you?"

Frederickson didn't move to shake his hand. "You've got a problem, maybe more than one, but one of your employees may have been killed yesterday. I've got a squad of officers parked down the street. We want all your employee records or we're prepared to close this place down." Not only did that statement make the manager step back, but Johnson and Spano wondered who was in custody. When the manager didn't answer right away, Frederickson grabbed his radio, "Officer, bring your team in here!"

"Wait, wait, I'll help you, what exactly do you want?"

"First, we want all your employee records for the past year."

"Can we go to my office? I don't know what I have here, but I'm willing to work with you."

Frederickson turned to his two detectives, "Detective Spano, call the officer, tell him to hold off for a few minutes. Joe, follow us." They walked with the manager. Turning, Frederickson called out, "Detective, five minutes. If I don't come out or call you, call in the outside team."

The manager immediately turned and stopped, "Hey, I'm going to help you!"

Frederickson said, "We'll see, let's just get that information." They entered the back office. "Joe, stand watch at the door."

The manager was now holding his hands up in front of his face. "I'm doing what you wanted, how about cooling it."

"Maybe we need to take you downtown and just search the place after we board it up." It wouldn't be the first time a strip club on Eight Mile had been closed by the police in the past year. There were three other clubs sitting empty. The manager didn't want his to be the next one.

"Okay, Detective, here's everything we've got." He entered the requested information into the desktop computer, handing Frederickson a printout. "This is the list of employees that we've had for this year."

Frederickson didn't even look at it. "Not so quick, there can't be more than ten names on that. I want all your strippers' information too."

"They aren't employees, they're independent contractors. We don't keep those records."

Frederickson wasn't having any of that. "Bullshit!" Turning toward Joe, "Call the team in."

"Hey, I'm doing everything you asked, don't do this."

"You can stop all of this by pulling the list of *all* your employees, including dancers, and do it now!"

CK was in a panic. "I'll need to call the lawyer for the club first."

"You can tell him that the place has just been closed until further notice."

CK knew he didn't have a choice. "Hey, I helped your officers yesterday. I'll do what I can." He reentered data in his computer, handing Frederickson a second list. This time it printed two pages.

"I hope you've got it all, because this is your last chance." He took the list and scrolled down. There was the name he hoped to find, Judy Bennet. "Your information has names and phone numbers for these people but no addresses, why?"

"Many of these girls never have a permanent place. Often they room together. As long as we can reach them, that is all we need."

"Guess the IRS will be interested. You'd have to send them a 1099 for tax purposes so somewhere you must have addresses." Frederickson thought for a second, "Do you pay them hourly?"

"Yeah, but it's just minimum, their real money is from tips. All the pay details would be at our central location; the owners are responsible for handling all of that."

Taking the list he said, "You can tell the owner we'll be back." He turned toward Spano, "Joe, call this in to the squad. They'll need to stay in place until the district attorney decides our next move." Walking out without addressing the manager, he kept talking to Spano. The club manager, CK, called the club's attorney as soon as the detectives left his office. He didn't know exactly what would happen next but knew his boss needed to know.

ELEVEN

Tony Virgilio anxiously watched television with anticipation when the breaking news banner flashed across the screen. The reporter had a somber look on her face as she announced the grim story. Rhonda Walker, from Channel 4, was speaking while a film of the events at Campus Martius was being shown. "For our viewers who are just tuning in, Detective Amy Harper was shot earlier today around eleven-thirty. Harper, along with fellow police officer Detective Thomas Baker, were being presented with special medals from the mayor for their actions last year. Although Harper was rushed to the DMC and doctors removed the bullet, she lost a lot of blood and sadly died in surgery." The local NBC station was showing their filming of the presentation and ran footage of the events as Walker continued, "According to Chief Mathews, his team discovered where the shooter was positioned but no arrest has been made. When we get more details, we'll report it as soon as it comes in."

Virgilio knew that six hours had passed and the cops didn't have an identification on the shooter.

Lorenzo carried off the perfect plan, he covered all the evidence and went to the baseball game. They all went on as if nothing happened, Tony operated the meat market and Lorenzo and Bobby were enjoying their time at Greektown. The instruction he gave Lorenzo was: Just do as you would normally do, play cards, have some drinks and enjoy yourself. Tony worked behind the butcher counter and conversed with customers, just like he would do most weekends.

Two customers stood waiting for their order. "Tony, did you hear the awful news?"

He didn't want her to think he'd been keeping up with the events in downtown Detroit. "No, Mrs. Bradford, what happened?"

"Someone killed a police officer. She was shot downtown at Campus Martius." He stopped, giving her a puzzled look. "What a shame, when did all this happen?"

Mrs. Bradford went into a long explanation. "Tony, there was a special celebration downtown and right in the middle of it, a female police officer was shot and killed. It's just so terrible. Too many guns out there." The lady standing next to her, nodded in agreement.

Virgilio agreed, "Did they catch the guy?"

"No, there's a manhunt going on downtown, they've got all the streets and buildings blocked off around Greektown. Must have a hundred officers searching for the shooter."

Tony shook his head. "At least we know this wouldn't happen here in St. Clair Shores." Both customers agreed as he wrapped their orders. "Here's your steaks Mrs. Bradford. Tell Jim I cut them the way he likes them for your barbecue tomorrow. Is there anything else?"

"No, thanks, Tony. Your meat is always the best." She waved goodbye to her friend who was waiting for Sal to finish her order.

Virgilio Market was always crowded, especially with such nice weather the past few weeks. It was only a few miles to the marinas off of Nine Mile and many people would be boating or having a barbecue. Tony kept hoping that the events downtown continued to be a search for the shooter, without any arrest. Every chance he had he'd check the television in the back room, not wanting to call Lorenzo. They had decided that was the best way to proceed. Tony also hoped, although it was slim, that Gino would have some good news and that he had found John Franklin. Last thing he heard from Gino was that Franklin wasn't being held at the Twelfth Precinct. He wanted Gino to complete the original mission of killing the deputy mayor. That was looking slim, but he held out hope that Gino would have something positive to report.

***

John Franklin looked around the stark interior of the room on the fifth floor of police headquarters. *Not exactly the Ritz*, he thought. The chief had Lieutenant Jackson show him around. "There's a small kitchen with some things in the fridge. We use this during emergencies. The chief and other officials stay here overnight when they can't leave." He looked bored. She turned on the television, "Detective Frederickson put the new television in last month." Standing in front of the thirty-two inch screen, she stopped talking. When she saw he was staring off at a blank wall, she yelled, "Hey, jackass!" Franklin jumped, "You're pretty lucky that they're taking care of you; you could be stuck in a cell. Maybe that's where you'd rather be."

That got his attention, but before he answered he noticed the stripes on her uniform. "Sorry, I just can't believe that someone put a body under my car."

"Chief Mathews must be on your side otherwise you'd be in that jail cell, like I said."

"Where is the chief?"

She turned on the television. "Right here," pointing to the news conference playing on the screen. "He's handling a press conference, no thanks to you."

Franklin realized, it had to be right outside of the building. He carefully listened, hearing him say that one of his detectives had been killed today. *"What?"* he stuttered. *"Killed?"* Who and how did that happen? He watched the press conference. No wonder Mathews was pissed at him earlier. Franklin knew the police chief's job was tough, but the events today had to be the worst. Franklin sat alone, because Jackson left him staring at the set. He watched the reporter as she continued her coverage after the chief made the announcement. Franklin thought, *That could have been me dead instead of the woman under my car. What's going on? Maybe someone who planned to kill her is the same person who now killed a detective.* It had been close to forty-eight hours since he was rousted out of bed and arrested for supposedly killing someone with his vehicle. Now he was under police protection and hidden on the fifth floor of police headquarters. "I want to call Misty." She was his estranged wife, but he knew he couldn't call her, not now. *How long will this last and what if they never found these guys?* Franklin still hadn't talked to the mayor. Was his boss the target of the shooter the chief described? So many questions and no answers right now. Franklin was surprised that his name didn't come up in the report, wondering how that stayed out the news. He thought back to the nights he spent at the strip club on Eight Mile. *How dumb could I have been, leaving my beautiful wife alone at home while I drank and ran around with strippers.* Gambling and drinking had taken its toll on many men before, John Franklin was just another one to fall.

***

Frederickson was now armed with two lists, the first one naming club employees and the second one all the dancers who worked at the club. When he and Spano looked it over, it was just what Detective Johnson had thought, Judy Bennet was listed as a dancer. This could be the clue they needed that would connect the club to the events with John Franklin's vehicle at the condo at St. Aubin Place. He said, "Why else would a dancer, who worked at the club that Franklin frequently visited, be found dead under his vehicle? We need to talk to the deputy mayor one more time," Frederickson suggested as they studied the list. "I want to make sure what he knows about her. Maybe there's another connection that we're missing."

It was agreed, they'd go back downtown to talk to Franklin. Don turned to Spano, "I'm going to put a car outside the club. Can't have the manager leaving without a tail. He's probably going to report to someone; they'll need to know that we've been there." The SIU team was getting some answers in the case, at least the name of the dead woman and that she worked as a stripper. How this fit into the framing of the deputy mayor was a mystery, and now Harper being shot, how did that fit into the case? The team was still thinking that Harper wasn't the primary target. They had to be shooting at the mayor.

Spano looked at Frederickson, "You know this is only becoming more tangled. Looks like someone's trying to frame the deputy mayor and now we've got a person taking a shot, presumably at the mayor. We need to know who owns that club."

"You're right, Joe. I'll have Johnson continue to watch the club and get him some back-up in case it's needed." As they headed back downtown Frederickson called Mathews, "Chief, we've uncovered important details on the case. We've found out that the body of the woman found under Franklin's car was a stripper. She worked at the same club where he spent his last night before being arrested. Chief, we need to get the records to see who owns this club."

Mathews knew this was becoming a quagmire of events loosely tied together. "I'll get our people working on it right away. Do we need to close the place down?"

"No, I'm sure they're circling the wagons, but I've got a car stationed outside keeping an eye on the manager. If he leaves, he might lead us to the owner or whoever is running the place."

"Good move. Don, on another front, the investigative team from the Greektown Hotel rooftop found very little to help us. Whoever was up there cleaned up without any fingerprints or material left that could lead us to a suspect. Where are you headed to now?"

"I've found recent photos of the stripper who was killed from the internet. We need to run them by Franklin, maybe he had more interaction with her than he's told us. At least we've got a lead in this part of the case, but until we get more, we don't know if Harper or the mayor was the target today."

Johnson was stationed outside the strip club keeping an eye on everything, with a second car dispatched in case he had to follow the manager. The team planned to record everyone entering or leaving.

While headed back downtown, Frederickson decided to talk to Amy Harper. "Joe, I'm going to call Baker. I haven't talked to Amy since she was shot, I'd like to hear her voice." Spano agreed, "Me too. Use my phone. We can both talk to her with the Bluetooth option."

Frederickson looked back at Joe. "Another new gadget, I hate them." He dialed Detective Baker's number. They knew he hadn't left Amy's side. When Tom answered, Frederickson was the first to talk, "Baker, I'm with Joe and using his phone, how's Harper doing?"

"She just got back from a short walk down the hallway. They've had her sitting on the side of the bed and moving a little. Spano, how did you get Don to use the Bluetooth?" They both laughed. Baker said, "I'll give Amy the phone."

Frederickson was happy to hear that she was up and walking. "Amy, Joe and I want to know how you're doing."

She sounded weak, "Fine, how's the case going?"

He wasn't surprised at her answer. "I'm so sorry we couldn't stay with you. I wanted to tell you the chief's plans in person."

"I understand the reason he had for the announcement. It's just a little chilling hearing that you're dead. Baker said some of the guys have been calling offering support and condolences. Wish we could tell them the truth."

He heard her cough and felt that they needed to stop at the hospital first. "Joe and I are headed your way right now, we'll be there soon…"

She stopped him, "Boss, you've got more important things to do. Go get those guys, don't worry about me, I'll be fine. Baker is here taking good care of me."

Spano jumped into the conversation, "Baker taking care of someone?" He laughed, "Then who's going to take care of him?" They all chuckled at making fun of Baker. Laughter was a good relief. Spano continued, "Amy, don't eat anything if Tom makes it, remember that pie he brought in?" That got a big laugh out of her.

Frederickson wanted to get serious. "Amy, we're all rooting for you, the chief and our team will do everything to protect you. I know you've got the best doctors working for you."

"I know. I'm going to be okay. Go get those bastards."

"Will do, you get better." Once they hung up it was quiet in the car for a few minutes. Frederickson took a deep breath, "Joe, head back to headquarters, we've got to talk to Franklin one more time. The chief has him upstairs in the crash pad. He'll be out of sight there. Maybe Franklin was involved with this Judy Bennet." The ride to headquarters was pretty quick. They parked and headed upstairs. "Joe, let's check in with Mindy first, then we'll go and talk to Franklin." Mindy was happy to get a firsthand update on Amy Harper's condition. Mindy told them that the chief left them a message. Frederickson read the note. "The chief has a team working on ownership of the strip club, Joe. Still no further developments on possible suspects in Harper's shooting." Both Joe and Don wondered how someone could have pulled off that difficult of a shot and disappeared into thin air. Frederickson crumpled the note and tossed it into the trash can next to the desk. "Mindy, we're going upstairs to talk to Franklin." The two of them walked out of the squad room hoping that Franklin could help unravel the puzzle.

When they entered the upstairs room, Franklin jumped up. "Man, I'm glad to see someone, I've got a thousand questions."

Frederickson didn't want any of Franklin's crap, "Sit down! We've got some questions for you. Understand, you're still a suspect in the murder of a woman in your condo parking lot." Franklin was shocked, but sat back down. Frederickson pulled the photo out of his pocket that they got off the internet. "Okay, how do you know this lady?"

Franklin took the photo and looked up at the detectives. "Her name is Diamond. I'm sure it is her stage name. She is beautiful, tall, slim and very well put together." Franklin looked back at them, "That's one of the dancers from the club on Eight Mile. What's she got to do with anything?"

"What's she got to do with this? You idiot. She's the woman you ran over. Unless we can prove otherwise you'll be charged with killing her in your parking lot!"

"No, I couldn't have!" His voice cracked, stumbling through his words, "Your chief said that he's sure that I've been framed, Detective. I only know her as a dancer, like I said, her name is Diamond." He looked up to the ceiling before finishing. "I promise, I don't know anything else."

"Did you ever tell her where you lived?"

Franklin was still holding the photo in his right hand. "I was never with her outside the club."

The detective wasn't happy that Franklin didn't have any information to help them, "Listen, I need to know what you may have told her personally about yourself."

Franklin kept looking at the photo. "Maybe I did tell some of the girls that my wife and I were having problems. I'm sure I never told them where I lived, never."

Frederickson knew he needed to lighten up on the deputy mayor. He moved to the seat next to him. "John, you think I'm being too tough on you, but this is turning into a major case that not only has the mayor involved but one of my detectives was shot, a bullet maybe intended for the mayor. It's important for you to answer me honestly. Did you ever take one of the girls home with you, and this isn't the time to lie to me. It's vital to both your case and the recent shooting."

He looked back at Joe who stood in the middle of the room, "Look guys, things have been pretty rough with my wife, Misty, and me for a while. When she moved out I really was in the dumps. Yeah, I took a girl home a few times."

Frederickson asked him again, "John, was this the lady you took home?" He pointed at the photo that Franklin was still holding.

"No, although she was really friendly and offered me her cell phone number, I took home another dancer, a blonde, her name is Jasmine. She came to my place a few times."

Frederickson looked at Franklin. "Okay, that club was your last stop, and now one of the dancers is found under your car, dead." He knew that the guy was set up and maybe aided in it, although unwittingly. He continued, "Listen John, we're getting closer to connecting the strip club with the dead girl. The chief and your boss figure you've been set up. But if we can't prove it, you'll go down for this. We're working to clear it up, but you've got to help us any way possible. Look, you're not in jail, we're protecting you, and unless you're truthful we're never going to solve this."

Franklin realized that he had to do everything to help them. Unless this was solved, he'd still be on the hook for the dead body under his vehicle. "Thanks Detective, you don't know how sorry I am for all of this. I appreciate what your team is doing." He extended his hand and Frederickson shook it. The detectives had more information now, hoping that it could help break the case open.

Once they left Franklin, they called Detective Johnson who was still watching the club. "Any action at the club?"

"No, the manager hasn't left and I've got a second car down the street making sure that no one leaves out of the back."

"Good, we're going to get a warrant for another of the dancers. Her name is Jasmine, most likely her stage name. I'm sending you her photo. I want you to make sure none of the dancers or bouncers leave. Once we have it, we'll have to move fast so they don't hide her, or worse."

***

The forensic team at headquarters had gone over everything multiple times, especially analyzing the bipod that was found on the Greektown Hotel rooftop. It was a standard Caldwell Pivot bipod, two legs versus three, that was available at many gun shops and outdoor stores across the country. One of the team explained, "It's actually called a bipod because it only has two legs and is designed for snipers and hunters to lean against something to get a stable shot." When Frederickson looked at the item closer, he understood, "The shooter must have had it pressed against the wall for stability. That's why there was gun power on the wall." He was hoping that they'd find prints on the wall. The investigators checked everything including the wall on the rooftop without any luck. They were also running the foot prints cast they made at the scene. At headquarters they worked tirelessly looking for any fingerprints on the bipod. After checking the two legs and concentrating on the connecting brackets that were used to adjust the legs, it brought nothing. They checked each piece for any prints. The chief inspector was stunned, he asked, "How did the shooter not leave any prints on this, especially on the joints that were used to adjust the height?" He knew the bipod was normally light weight and easily adjusted. The tubular legs, although these were heavier than you'd expect, were still collapsible and adjustable for height. One of the inspectors asked, "Is this supposed to be this heavy?" Another tech suggested, "Maybe it's heavier so it would be stable." They agreed. Nothing odd about the bipod. It was the Cadillac of units. Once they completed their inspection and it offered nothing to help the case, the chief wanted the item put in the evidence room upstairs across from the SIU office at headquarters.

This lack of fingerprints at the scene or on the bipod was a major disappointment. The question existed, how did the shooter get the bipod into place and adjust it without leaving so much as a smudge; that was almost impossible. "You can't do all that with gloves on," one of the men stated, "you'd have to at some point do it with your bare hands." The news was passed onto Frederickson who was pissed that it didn't offer them a lead.

Chief Mathews tried to comfort Frederickson, "We'll keep the bipod upstairs in the evidence room downtown. I know you'll want to check it out yourself when you get back." He knew his officers very well. They put it in the locker across from the SIU office.

TWELVE

The events at Campus Martius filled the front page of the Free Press. The lead story was about the attempt on the life of the mayor and the death of a Detroit detective. Under the story's details, the reporter stated that the police thought the shooter missed his apparent target, the mayor, and killed Detective Harper instead. The article had photos of her lying on the stage, blood splattered on the podium and emergency personnel tending to her. This was exactly what Chief Mathews wanted, hoping that if Harper was the target, the shooter would figure he was successful. If the mayor was the target, he would try a second time. Mathews had ordered special protection details for both Harper at the hospital and the mayor. Tom Baker didn't want Amy reading the newspaper, but when she demanded to see what it said, he relented. He watched as she turned the pages. Tears welled in her eyes when page three had pictures of her and her mom at the police academy graduation ceremony. Turning to Baker, she asked, "How did they get these photos?"

"Guess they got them from the police department; they must keep graduation photos in the archives." He knew how hard it was when she saw the pictures of her mom. Knowing that Amy's mom died the year after she graduated from the academy of stage four colon cancer.

"Tom, my mom looks great in these pictures, who would have ever known that she had cancer."

Baker didn't know how to answer. Trying to comfort her, he held her hand. "Your mom was beautiful, just like you. Looking back at this must be tough, but at least you have such great memories. You and I were in that same graduating class. My dad made it and I'll never forget his words, 'Life is filled with many events, some will make you smile but others will bring tears.' Amy, photos like this one of you and your mom will always bring smiles."

She looked over at him, "How did you get so smart?" She kissed him on the cheek as he leaned toward her. The two were perfect, supporting each other during hard times. After a few seconds, Harper tried to sit up, Tom helped her by putting a second pillow under her back. "Tom, did you hear anything more from the team?"

"Last news I got was that they followed up on the interview you and Detective Sampson handled at the strip club and it appears that the club owners may be involved in the body found under John Franklin's vehicle. Sampson helped Spano and gave him the details you both got on that visit. The woman found under the car was a stripper at the club. They figure that Franklin was some kind of a target, but why? They still didn't have anything on the shooter at Campus Martius." He didn't want to say the person that shot you, but that was all he could think of.

"Tom, maybe you're needed more on the two cases; I'm going to be fine. I want you helping catch those assholes."

"I asked Don about that. He's got the team covering both cases. He's more concerned about you and your safety right now. I promise, as soon as possible, I'll be out there too."

Smiling at him, she said, "Okay. I'm glad you've been here with me, but number one, I want to get that son-of-a-bitch that shot me!"

He looked at her, pursed his lips, then said, "I'll leave you a loaded gun baby; maybe you can get your own revenge soon."

Harper quickly turned when he said loaded gun, then she felt her hip. "Where *is* my gun?"

"It was kinda hard to strap it to the hospital gown." Baker said laughing. "That would be a great photo for the next police gazette."

A nurse knocked then entered. She saw them smiling. *A good sign,* she thought, "Ms. Harper, how are you doing today, ready for a walk?"

"Absolutely! Is there a possibility that I can get out of this gown? The breeze from the back isn't any fun. I'd hate to scare everyone in the hallway."

"Let me see if I can get you one of the full-wrap-around types before we take that walk." She grabbed the chart and noted the readings off the machine that monitored Harper's vital signs. "Ms. Harper, your blood pressure and other indicators are looking good. Let me go find you that other type gown."

Once she left, Baker stood. Harper asked, "Hey, where do you think you're going buddy?"

"Christ, I need to hit the head." He smiled, "Plus you need to let the nurse help you with that gown. I'm going to check on the team."

"Promise you'll fill me in?"

"You bet."

***

Tony Virgilio held the morning Free Press, reading the headlines, speaking Italian, "Figlio mio, Sapevo che potrei contare su di te. My son, I knew I could count on you." His pride showing by a big smile on his face, as he re-read the story of the detective who was shot and later died. This was sweet revenge from events last year when Harper and her team foiled his drug connection out of the Eastern Market. He swore he'd get even. Killing Harper was the first step in his plan. The second was to ruin the life, both professionally and personally, of the mayor. He hoped that Gino would still find the deputy mayor and finish the job but that prospect was looking slim. The last time Gino called he was at the Second Precinct looking for his target. Tony had the second step already in the works. Documents would be mailed to a local television station reporter showing that Mayor Sanborn had taken big money from a known syndicate, a group that had a contract to clear abandoned buildings in the city. He knew the reporter would check it out. When it hit the news, it would lead to further investigations. Tony's idea was to plant the story with underworld friends making sure that when investigators checked, it would show that Sanborn had an account in the Cayman Islands with thousands of dollars. The underworld group was entangled in a collage of international companies, some that would take years to unravel. He also figured to plant photos of Sanborn with a couple of the dancers from a club on Eight Mile. Tony knew that the press would soon figure out that they were photo shopped but the initial shock would take a toll on the mayor's family. He'd have to answer all of the allegations one way or another. He wanted to call Lorenzo, but better to keep a low profile. It was quarter to ten and the market would soon open for business. Sunday was always a busy morning: picnickers, boaters and families would come in for that special cut of meat for their events. Tony heard the front door open. He looked out from the back room and saw Sal unlocking the doors and greeting two guys waiting to get in. "Good morning, Sal," the first guy said. "Hope you can make up a special order for us."

Sal was walking back toward the meat counter. "Anything that you need Mr. Roker. What can I do for you?"

He handed Sal a list. "My wife has her friends in from Florida; it was a surprise visit. We're going to take them out on the boat. We're hoping that you can fill a quick special order." Sal nodded, looking over the list. The customer continued, "I'd like to have eight to ten filets and a dozen burgers."

Sal smiled and made a note. "Not a problem, Mr. Roker, how big do you want the steaks?"

"Maybe six to eight ounces."

"I'll get this going right away. I'll put the burgers in a separate package for you."

"Thanks Sal. We're going next door and grab a cup of coffee. How long do you think it will take?"

"Give me a half-hour, I'll have them wrapped and ready." They appreciated the personal attention. Sal waved as they walked out.

As the men left, Tony came out of the backroom. "Sal, I'll cut that order for you; I know you're just opening up." Sal nodded and handed him the list. Tony opened the large refrigerator door and disappeared inside. He knew that staying busy was the best medicine to keep his mind from going over the events of the past few days. He had re-read the newspaper article detailing the shooting at Campus Martius and the account of Detective Harper's death. Killing her was personal; she had engineered the events that captured his partners in their highly successful drug business. Next would be to wipe out the rest of the SIU team. Once he accomplished that he'd concentrate on the mayor. Killing him would be too easy. Better Tony thought, to destroy the man's reputation and eliminate his political career. Tony figured that setting up Franklin, then killing him with a dead hooker under his car would crush the man. But that didn't quite work out. He hoped to hear from Lorenzo soon, knowing that they agreed not to communicate unless absolutely necessary for three or four days. Keeping busy was helpful for Tony.

Virgilio's Market would be busy this Sunday, especially with the great weather. Tony decided to open up on Sundays during the summer a few years ago and although they were open shorter hours, it was always busy. He was cutting the special order when his cell phone went off. Wiping his right hand, Tony looked at the screen, it was Lorenzo. He quickly answered.

"Hi Dad, just wanted to see how you're doing?"

This was the coded message that they agreed on, signaling that Lorenzo had handled the part of their plan by leaving the bipod on the rooftop. Tony smiled, knowing his son had completed the first step and the next one was in place. "Good to hear from you. How was the ball game?"

"Good, the Tigers won. Dad, I'm thinking about heading out of town, is that okay with you?"

"Yeah, we can handle things here, you have a good time. Where are you going?"

"My girlfriend and I are planning a trip to the Bahamas. Might as well use that condo you and mom bought years ago."

"Yeah, we need to get down there some time too." Once the call was over, Tony hummed that silly car dealership jingle that Lorenzo always laughed at, *"You're on the right track, Nine Mile and Mack..."* If Lorenzo could hear him, he'd laugh out loud, maybe even finally ask his dad, "Why that song?"

Tony hadn't heard anything from Gino in the last day and a half. Gino lost control of knowing where John Franklin was and the deputy mayor could be a problem. He had been to the strip club many times and might be able to name some of the dancers. Hopefully he wouldn't remember the key dancers, Diamond and Jasmine, who helped Gino execute the frame up.

***

The SIU team was getting closer to gathering all the individuals and film footage from the strip joint on Eight Mile. This part of their investigation was critical to confirm who or what involvement the club had in framing John Franklin and how that might fit into the recent shooting downtown. Judy Bennet was dead, found under Franklin's truck; Jasmine, the stripper Franklin admitted taking home, was someone they needed to talk to. Frederickson hoped to interrogate her once they had her in custody. Detectives Spano and

Johnson were headed back to the club. Their team back at headquarters was trying to find out who owned the place. Like so many of these places, it registered under a multi-nation corporation listing with layers of ownership. Frederickson talked to Spano, "Joe, we've got the warrant. I've sent a squad with a panel van to bring everyone in. Askew has the warrant and is headed your way."

"Are we going to close the place down?"

"Yeah. We've got everything we need to close it legally, Joe, this should get someone's attention."

"They'll just send a lawyer in to get all these people out."

"That's what the district attorney said, but Joe, maybe we'll see who is paying for the attorney. We've got to do *something*."

Spano knew that his boss was grasping at straws. They hadn't made any headway into the shooting at Campus Martius. Harper was still recovering in seclusion at the hospital and Franklin hadn't been able to give them information enough to help much in the case. Frustration in both cases was evident. "Don, maybe we can get one of these people to talk and give us something to go on."

"That's what we're hoping for, Joe." Once he concluded the conversation, Frederickson headed to the area where they were holding Franklin. He wanted to go over the situation again with him. The man had to have more to add to their investigation.

Spano and Johnson sat in front of the strip club, going over their plan one more time while waiting for Detective Askew to arrive with the warrant. "Johnson, looks like we've been spotted," pointing to the huge bouncer who was on his cell phone, looking right at their vehicle.

"This is a pool car, how in the hell can he know we're cops?"

"Not sure, but we better move now or our suspects will be gone." The two men piled out of the car and headed to the entrance. As they reached the front door, Askew pulled up. He saw them going in and quickly followed. The bouncer followed Spano inside, and Askew headed right in behind them. Joe turned and saw Askew. "I've got a warrant and want everyone out of here except employees."

The bouncer held his hand up. "I don't think so. None of our customers are leaving!"

To Joe's surprise, Johnson spun the big guy around ramming him into the wall and cuffing him. "You're the first one to the paddy wagon, asshole." The man was stunned. People turned, watching the action at the doorway.

Spano moved forward, holding his badge up high as he said, "Okay, this place is closing. Everyone except employees needs to leave, now!" He watched as people moved, grabbing their jackets and looking puzzled, but the group, mostly men, headed for the front door.

While Spano oversaw that, Askew headed toward the bar. The bartender, along with a few dancers, was escorted to the stage area by Askew. "You're all to remain here until the other detectives have completed getting customers out of here." One of the girls started to move away from the stage area. "Where you going?" She pointed to the back. "I said, where do you think you're going?"

"I need to change."

"Come back right now or you'll be cuffed and taken in too." She lowered her head and sat at the edge of the stage alongside the other dancers. The bartender was a lanky guy, maybe in his mid-forties. He kept looking toward a door near the front side of the bar. The man knew that the manager would be watching everything on the closed-circuit cameras set up throughout the place. He was sure that he'd appear soon, trying to stop this.

Detective Johnson had been in the place before and knew where the manager's office was. Once he and Spano had the bouncer under control, he headed to the office. Before he got to the door, the manager came walking out. "What in the hell is going on?"

Johnson announced, "We've got a warrant and we're enforcing it. The details are listed." He handed the warrant to the manager who looked at the document. The man slowly read the warrant as Johnson walked through the doors into the backroom. There was a man still in the office who was now going through the manager's desk. "You, move away from the desk!"

The guy looked up at Johnson. "Who in the hell are you?"

Johnson held up his badge with one hand, and took out his gun with the other one. "Either move away from the desk or I'll put a new hole in your head."

The guy backed away from the desk, with both hands up. "Okay, okay, I'm just doing my job."

Johnson moved closer, "Turn around." He cuffed the man and

took him out of the room. Once in the main club, he pushed him toward the stage. "Sit down!" Now the team had everyone from the club sitting on the stage except the manager who was standing with Spano, still going over the warrant. Two more officers entered and stood at the doorway. The people who were positioned by the stage were all starting to ask questions when Johnson stepped forward. "We need everyone to stop talking. I'll go over the details with you." They looked at each other, puzzled, but followed his orders. "We're all going downtown, I've got a van outside. One by one, you're going to head to the front door and follow the directions of the officers outside."

One of the dancers stood, "I'm not going anywhere until you tell us why."

"Here's your choice: Go quietly or we'll cuff you and take you out gagged and bound!"

She stood as tears welled up in her eyes. "I just want to know, what did we do?"

"I promise we'll tell you once we get downtown."

Another dancer asked, "Can we change?" Johnson shook his head and pointed to the door. They filed past, one by one, toward the two officers standing at the front door and into the two vans that were parked in front. There was still a low buzzing of conversation, but they did exactly what they were being told to.

Spano stood with the manager who was still holding the warrant. "We're locking this place up."

"What're the charges?"

"Racketeering is one of the charges listed in the warrant. You can read, can't you?"

The manager, CK, looked back at them, "I'm not sure what that means."

"I'm sure the district attorney will go over all of it with you." The guy took a step back. Spano said, "Turn around, I'll need to cuff you for the ride downtown."

"Hey, I didn't do anything, I'm just an employee, like everyone else here."

"Take it up with the D.A." He cuffed him and Askew led the man to a waiting squad car. Once everyone was removed from the building, Spano, Johnson and Askew headed back to the manager's office. "Okay," Joe said, "we've got to box everything from the desk and take it in with us." As they searched the office, Johnson looked up at Spano.

"Joe, there's a secret panel in this desk." He pulled a lever and it slid open. Lifting a five by eight inch booklet, he held it up. "Joe, this must be pretty important."

"We'll give that to Frederickson; I'm sure he's going to want to go through it first."

Joe took it from Johnson. "You two did a great job today." The men smiled at each other.

Johnson nodded, "Hope I didn't overstep my bounds, Joe. I know you're the one in charge Sorry if I went too far."

Spano laughed, "Hell, Johnson, you even scared me, especially when you spun that bouncer around. You've got to show me that move sometime." All three detectives chuckled. Spano decided, "I better call Frederickson and let him know what we've accomplished." Askew and Johnson were happy that they were involved and that Joe let them handle what they did. The group had grown closer the past two years what with Frederickson out after his car crash and now with Amy Harper in the hospital, they were working even closer together. "Okay guys, let's head back; the boss is questioning Franklin one more time and we've got to find out what the people from this place can help us with." Turning to Johnson. "Was that dancer, Jasmine, among those we put in the van?"

"Yeah, as soon as we had them standing at the stage area, I recognized her from the photos that Mindy sent us. She wasn't hard to miss, a real looker." Askew nodded.

"Good, let's start with her when we get back."

Johnson smiled, "Joe, I'd be happy to question her."

Both Spano and Askew answered at the same time, "Bet you would." Askew punched Johnson in the right arm as they walked out. While Joe was on route to the office, Mindy called letting him know that Baker had arrived from the hospital. He was glad to hear that, hoping it was good news about Harper's recovery.

The staff at the hospital who were attending to Harper had all been sworn to secrecy as to her location and condition. Those who worked in the ER were told that she died of complications after surgery. Detective Baker had been at her side for two days and now that she was moving around, Harper convinced him to get back to work. He didn't want to leave her but knew that she was right, plus he wanted to get the bastard who did this to her.

Baker was in the SIU office when a parade of dancers and staff from the strip joint were ushered into the briefing room. The bouncer was booked downstairs for resisting arrest and the club's manager, CK, was put into an interrogation room. When Johnson and Askew entered the SIU office, they were surprised and happy to see Baker. "Baker, how's Harper doing?"

They were all delighted to get a firsthand report on their partner's condition. "She said she felt like she went through a wood chipper. What's with all the strippers?"

"Pretty nice, huh?" Johnson had a big smile on his face that caused both of them to look at each other. "The brunette, Jasmine, is the best looking stripper I've ever seen."

Spano moved into the group, "Johnson, I think you need a cold shower." Now they were all laughing at the tall, single, detective, who stood with a frown on his face. Spano then brought them to loud applause when he said, "Johnson, you don't have enough singles in your bank account to even talk to that lady."

Mindy called out, "Joe, Detective Frederickson wants you to join him in the interrogation room with the club's manager."

"Thanks, Mindy. Okay, Askew, I want you to get everyone from the club's name and I mean real name, address and background. They're all in the briefing room. Take Baker with you." When Spano walked away, Johnson just stood in the middle of the room, pouting that he hadn't been given the assignment.

THIRTEEN

The investigation now centered on the staff from the strip joint. Everyone taken in had been taken in and questioned, hoping that anything they said would help the case. The SIU team knew that the strip club had to be involved somehow in framing Deputy Mayor, John Franklin. Frederickson wasn't about to spend too much time talking to the manager without getting information. He'd already informed the district attorney's office that he might arrest all of them. They read everyone their rights, hoping to scare the hell out of them and after hours of questioning, most had been released. The two key suspects, CK the manager and the stripper Jasmine, were still being held. They could be held for twenty-four hours without charging them.

Frederickson entered the interrogation room and stood in front of the manager holding his driver's license in his right hand. "Okay, Chris, or as you prefer, CK, let's make this simple, who owns the club?"

The manager hadn't been very helpful, maybe he didn't know who the owners were. He gave the same answer that he'd given the other detectives. "I don't know who owns it, I just work there."

"You're the damn manager, you have to report to someone!"

CK had been cross-examined by the detectives for over an hour. He looked up at Frederickson, "Every night a messenger comes in and I give him the sales receipts. They send a copy back the next day. I don't report to anyone."

Frederickson figured that this would be a dead end but he hoped that the manager had something to help them. "Okay, so how about the cash, you've got to take in a lot of cash. What do you do with all the daily receipts?"

CK cleared his throat, he was stalling. "I want to talk to my attorney."

Spano looked over at Johnson then back to Don. Frederickson was still standing and moved closer to the manager, "Okay, we'll contact you're attorney, again. We tried once and no one has responded. We might be your only help. Why not tell us who owns the place."

Chris looked up. "If I talk, they'll kill me."

Spano decided to jump in, hoping this was the opening they needed. "CK, you've got only one real choice, talk to us and let us protect you. We called the number you gave us and no one has responded, so maybe your owners are looking to erase you too." He stood patiently waiting for an answer. "Once this is over Chris, you could end up in witness protection. Who knows, maybe you'll get a sweet deal and end up in a sunny location." Frederickson gave Joe a stern look. Although Spano saw it, he continued, "CK, even if you don't talk, I'll put the word out on the street that you gave us a lot of details you're screwed." Spano continued with the interrogation. "It's us or you're back on the street, and they'll be looking for you right away."

"How can you protect me?"

Detective Frederickson let Spano keep going, "We can talk to the D.A. for you, but your information has to lead us to the club owner."

The man had been under their questioning for close to two hours now, and although they had advised him of his rights and tried calling his attorney, he never refused to talk to them. Frederickson saw an opening. "Listen, CK, if we talk to the district attorney for you, and you're willing to be a witness, I'll make sure you're protected."

CK was breathing at a rapid pace, they hoped he'd break soon. "Will you put it in writing that I'd get protection?"

Frederickson had enough, "This is bullshit." He pounded on the wall above CK. "Spano, take him downstairs to the drunk tank. We'll let him rot down there."

"Wait, I'll try to help you. I have a ledger, it's in a hidden compartment in my desk. Go back to the club, get me that book; I'll need it to give you what you want."

Frederickson smiled, "Well you're in luck, CK. We emptied your desk. My detectives found the secret compartment and the book hiding in there, we have everything downstairs, I'll ask one of our guys to bring it up." They saw that CK had a look of panic when he heard they had the ledger. He knew this was it, he'd have to show them where the details were hidden in the book.

Spano made the call to the squad room, "Mindy, I need one of the guys to bring me the box marked 'Manager's desk'." CK squirmed in his chair. Frederickson stayed right in front of the man, keeping up the bad cop routine. It didn't take much time before Askew walked in with a box with the ledger and two other small booklets. Spano nodded as he took them. "Okay CK, you've got two minutes to give us what we want." He handed him the book, "This is a onetime shot, don't screw it up."

The man thumbed through a few pages near the back of the ledger and stopped. "Here's what you want," pointing to a page. Holding the book in his hands, he said, "Remember, I'm doing this but I want that protection order, I'm going to need it."

Frederickson took the ledger. "If this tells us what we need to know, you'll get your protection order. He looked at the information. It was a list of words or names they couldn't make out. Maybe the letters and symbols were scrambled. The last column listed dollar amounts. "Exactly what are we looking at?"

"You said you wanted to know who owns the club; these are the four men who own the place. I wasn't supposed to know it but one night when it was slow, I was staring at the page. I figured it out." CK pointed to the four lines of letters, "These names are scrambled, they're in code." He then rearranged the letters as they were out of order, a little like pig Latin but much more confusing. "When I get the money totals from that period, a guy comes in and I have a packet for each one of them. Detective, they've never come into the club themselves. No one knows that I figured this out. I put the packets in a larger envelope. I give it to the guy who handles it. He's kind of their go-between. I'm the only one who has this information."

Spano looked surprised. "Who is this go-between?"

"His name is Rossi, Gino Rossi. The guy hangs out in the club almost every night. I'm sure they thought I'd think he was one of the owners but the guy's a thug. I knew he didn't own the place."

Now they had a name to go along with the list that CK gave them after rearranging the coded letters. Frederickson told Spano, "Get an APB out for this Rossi. Now we're getting somewhere." After handling the new information they sat together, reviewing the list of owners. Frederickson and Spano studied the list that CK rearranged for them, "Shit! Joe, look who's on this!" They couldn't believe it.

***

Detectives Frederickson and Spano stood across from Chief Mathews who sat back reviewing the list of names in front of him. They waited for his reaction. *"What?"* Mathews jumped out of his seat. Frederickson looked at Spano, "I told you he'd do that. Chief, we had the same reaction."

Mathews was livid, "How could this be true and none of us had any idea?"

"I'm not sure, but if this list is as accurate as the manager stated, we've got a big problem."

Mathews sat back down. He was still looking at the list, shaking his head. "Don, you know we've got to make sure this is true before moving forward."

Spano wanted to make a suggestion, but waited for Frederickson to give him the okay. "Chief, Joe is really responsible for getting the manager to give us the details. We owe him credit for getting this list." Turning toward Spano, "Joe, tell the chief your idea."

Joe was pleased at the opening. "Yeah, sure, okay with you Don?"

"That's why I asked. What have you got?"

"In order to make sure this list is accurate, after checking out the information, we've got to find this Gino Rossi. Once we do, maybe he can give us the way he normally delivers each person their money. We get someone, maybe an undercover detective, to take the envelope to our guys and see what happens. If they accept them without question, we've got them."

The Chief stood, "I like that. Of course it could be considered entrapment, so let's run it by the D.A. first."

Frederickson smiled, "Good idea. Mathews picked up the phone. Once the D.A. answered, he said, "Brandon, we've got an unusual situation here, can you come to my office?" Brandon must have asked when he was needed, because the chief said, "Right away." This wasn't the first time Mathews requested help from the district attorney, but this time was different. Mathews hung up, "He'll be here in about an hour. When he gets here, I'm going to share the details and list with him. Understand, we've got to make sure we're okay on this." Both men left the office and would wait until they heard back from the chief's meeting with the D.A.

As they walked to the elevator, Joe asked, "Why would someone like Perone be involved in a strip club?"

"Joe, there's a bigger question: Did Council President Perone plan this to unseat the mayor? He's the one running against him in the coming election."

"Yeah, I thought about that. A few years ago Perone was under review for possible ties to underworld mobsters."

Frederickson said, "Let's look that up when we get upstairs." The two of them decided to do some research. Frederickson asked the team's secretary to help. "Mindy, can you pull up some details for us?"

"Sure, what do you need?"

He gave her Councilman Perone's name along with the other three men. "Mindy, I need everything you can find on all of these guys, especially Councilman Perone such as any accusations in the past about ties to underworld activities." She raised an eyebrow, knowing that the councilman was just featured in a front page article in the Free Press. He finished, "Mindy, keep this quiet, I don't want anyone to know what we're doing." Turning toward her desk, she started the search. Frederickson looked at his partner, "Joe, what if the councilman is behind more than just running against the mayor. What if he and his friends framed Franklin, hoping to discredit the mayor? More importantly, what if he and his friends were behind the shooting at Campus Martius? Joe, we may have uncovered the person behind many of the events this week that have gone unsolved."

***

District Attorney, Brandon Hanson, sat in Chief Mathews office, staring at the file that was handed to him. "Where did you get this list?"

"Our detectives were following the scope of the warrant that was signed earlier on the Eight Mile strip club. It allowed us to bring in all the people who worked at the club and any documents stored there. The manager, who we've got in custody along with the bouncer and the stripper, Jasmine, gave us his ledger. It detailed that Perone is one of the four men that owns the place. Through our investigation, we've tied members of this club to the possible killing of a stripper who worked there and even more importantly the framing of Deputy Mayor, Franklin."

Hanson looked up at the chief. "Okay, I agree, you came by this legally. What do you plan to do with it, and how do I fit into your plans?"

Mathews went over his teams' idea. "We want to make sure we're not going to be accused as using or entrapping the councilman."

You could see the D.A. studying the plan, touching a finger to his temple. "I think you're on solid ground. Your team got this when they were completing the investigation into the findings. I'll support what you're doing." Hanson stood, "Chief, have you thought about how this could explode if it's true, and what about the other three names on the list?"

"Yeah, that's a good question, but we need one more thing."

"What?"

"In order to get the manager talking and agreeing to be a witness, we've offered him possible immunity and relocation."

"You know that's something I'm supposed to handle, not your detectives, however, I'm sure he's going to need that if we get these guys. You're also going to have to treat everyone on the list with the same attention, even if you feel that Perone might be the ringleader and involved more than the others in ownership of the questionable club."

"Brandon, that's why you're here. Once we get more details on Perone's involvement, we'll bring all four in, charged with whatever you think will stand up in court. If we find more on any of them, we'll address it later." The two men stood and shook hands. Once the D.A. left, Chief Mathews called up to the SIU office. "Mindy, please ask Frederickson and Spano to come to my office."

"Yes, sir."

As Don and Joe Spano headed to the Chief's office, Joe asked, "What if the D.A. says we can't do this with the councilman?"

"Joe, we've got a good case. We just need to find more evidence."

Spano understood. "I'm just afraid they'll say it's all speculation. We'll need hard facts."

As they entered the chief's office, Lieutenant Jackson followed them inside. She often sat with the chief when he was going over details with members of his teams on pending investigations. Neither man said anything and followed the chief's direction to take a seat. Mathews started the conversation, "District Attorney Hanson understood our request, and I gave him all the details that we've gathered." Frederickson slid closer to the edge of his seat. "He agreed that there's a lot of smoke so there must be a fire. He warned us that we've got to treat all the parties listed in the ownership of the strip club the same. We can't just focus on Perone."

Spano raised his eyebrows, "What exactly is he okay with us doing?"

"I'm getting to that, Joe." Spano lowered his head. "Joe, don't worry, we got the okay to go ahead with your idea." That perked the detective's mood up. He pumped a fist and smiled. "What Hanson was worried about was if we only concentrate on Perone, he might say we were on a witch hunt and doing the mayor's dirty work."

Frederickson nodded. "That makes sense. I'll put a team on each one of the people on the list, but we're going to carry out the plan on Perone first. We've got to get all of them. Who knows how much any of them are involved. If we get Perone to take the envelope, and, according to CK, the men have to open it and sign off, we'll have him at least for ownership of the club. We'll use an undercover officer. We have to confirm Perone's involvement in any of this. Hopefully we'll have him by the nuts." Lieutenant Jackson smiled at the detective's reference.

Mathews made sure his team understood what this could mean to the political landscape. "I need to be in on every step of the investigation. We can't, at any point, go rogue on this." Frederickson and Spano understood the ramifications of this case, and that it could have lasting effects. "Detectives, none of this information leaves our team, that includes saying anything to the mayor's office. Until we know the depth of involvement by these four individuals, we cannot have it leaked." Everything was agreed on and the two detectives stood and left the chief's office, determined to make their plan work. As they headed back to their office, Spano asked, "Who do we want in on this?"

Frederickson didn't answer right away. "Let me think about that." They still needed to get the details from the detectives who questioned Jasmine, the other person still in custody. She might have key details to help in this case."

FOURTEEN

The meeting at the Special Investigation Unit office was set. Detective Frederickson sat with Spano and Johnson. "We need to keep the information regarding the list of four men found in the club's ledger within our team. Guys, I know you all realize the potential implications involved in handling a case like this; it could become a political football. For the time being I'm suggesting that we keep this between us. We can't have it leaked."

Spano asked, "How do you suggest we proceed?"

Detective Frederickson knew what concerned Spano. "Joe, first, if we find more details showing how or if Perone is really involved, we'll have to bring in the district attorney's office." Turning toward the wall that held their case board, he stood, "Let's go over what we've got so far." He pointed to the list of names, photos and details under each. "I want to make sure we aren't missing something." Frederickson stood, moving to the board. "I'll add all four men listed in that ledger on our board." He wrote down the names with Perone in the third spot. "I plan to tell the team that we will divide the names between us. Joe, you and Johnson will take Perone. We'll put Baker and Askew on Singleton and Swinton. I'll take Ramos. Swinton is a businessman out of Fort Wayne, Indiana. They'll need to do some internet research and maybe do a little traveling."

Spano looked at him, "I suggest you don't put Baker on them; he'll want to be closer to home with Harper still recovering."

"Joe, that's a good point but maybe Harper can use a break, and she'll have some therapy that might be better without Baker hanging over her." The two detectives realized that he was probably right, knowing that Frederickson had just gone through a similar situation last year. Frederickson continued, "Singleton seems like a mysterious person to be involved in this. I'm intrigued that an automobile executive is part owner of a strip joint. The potential ramifications of it getting out not only would affect him but his family.

The team had their assignments and Frederickson told them that they need to meet every evening at five to update the investigation. "I'm going to call Baker and Askew and have them meet us here in a few hours; we'll go over all of this together, one more time." As they broke up, Frederickson asked Mindy to call both Baker and Askew to come back to the office once they left the Detroit Medical Center. The two detectives wanted to visit with Amy Harper, so they had headed to the hospital.

Detectives Spano and Johnson moved to Joe's desk. They started to review the material Mindy had looked up for them. Joe was surprised that Perone's father owned a business at Eastern Market. Looking at Johnson, "We need to find out more about that business his dad owned." Searching through the articles, they found the address of the vegetable delivery service. "I think this is the same location that Vinnie La Russo operated in at the market."

Johnson quickly punched in the address and it popped up. "Joe, it's the same building." The two men stared at each other for a few seconds. "Can this be related to the drug business that we busted last year?" Spano shook his head, not sure, but he didn't believe in coincidence. The two of them kept leafing through the papers on the desk. Perone's father sold the business to Vinnie La Russo in 1995, the same year that Perone entered politics. He was the youngest member of the Detroit City Council. The man had a lot of positive press until an investigation linked him to a crime family. Although it was soon dropped, Perone lost his seat on the council in the next election. It took five years for Eddie Perone to regain his political footing and he soon won his seat and was voted as the council president. Eddie Perone had been a strong leader proposing many measures to help the poor in the city. His political star had risen and it was no surprise when he entered the mayoral race some months ago.

Spano kept talking to himself. Finally he jumped up. "I've got to get Frederickson, now!" Johnson watched as Joe rushed across the office heading into Don's office. Johnson could see Joe's arms waving through the office glass, and then both men headed his way.

"Johnson, Spano isn't making any sense; he wants me to see what you have on your computer." Don slid a chair next to the desk and scrolled through the documented history that detectives had been researching. "Johnson, print this for me." He continued reading the details about Eddie Perone, his father, and the business at the Eastern Market. The connection between Perone and La Russo shocked him. Although he wasn't asking anyone in particular, Don said aloud, "Could Perone be involved in the drug trade? Was he one of the silent partners that the team missed last year when we arrested La Russo and Castellanos?" Both Johnson and Spano just listened, knowing he was thinking out loud. This connection was too close to Frederickson personally. La Russo planned to kill him last year, now there's maybe another partner and he's a councilman! "Joe, we need to let the chief know about this." He kept reading and talking to himself, just as Spano had done. Johnson watched, somewhat amused, thinking both men mirrored each other in so many ways. The next step would be to question both La Russo and Castellanos who were in the custody of the Canadian government for international drug trafficking. The Canadians had stronger drug penalties than the U.S. Anyway, if they were released, the U.S. still had an order for extradition.

***

Tony Virgilio saw the name on his cell phone, it was Gino calling. He hadn't heard from his hit man in two days. "Tony, I found our guy." He waited for a reaction, but although Tony didn't answer, he could hear the man breathing.

Virgilio was stunned; he'd given up on Gino ever finding out where John Franklin had disappeared to. "Where is he?"

"The police are holding him at their headquarters. My contact at the Twelfth Precinct just called me. The information I'm getting is that the police are still going to charge him with murder."

Virgilio didn't think so. "Why would they charge him and keep him in hiding?"

Gino hesitated before answering. "Tony, my contact is good. He believes that they are closing in on the murder investigation. The cops raided the strip club."

Tony was stunned, "When did they raid the club?"

"Earlier, today. Questioned everyone. I understand that some have been released but the manager and one of the dancers are still being held."

That news was troubling. Virgilio knew that none of the dancers had any information that would cause them a problem but the manager could have important details. Tony wasn't sure if he knew how to read the information. "We've got to know where they're keeping them. I'll get our attorney involved. Get me a name that he can contact."

"I've got that, but you're not going to like it. It's Detective Don Frederickson. Word is he's the one holding our people." Gino took a breath. "Tony, I'm concerned that the manager, CK, can give them my name in connection with the club. I'm going to keep a low profile."

Virgilio knew Frederickson's name all too well. His organization had ordered a hit last year on Frederickson, unfortunately they failed. He swore they wouldn't fail again. They even attempted to get Frederickson's wife at her workplace. "Get me as much as you can. I know after he recovered, he and his wife moved. I want to know where he moved to. We've checked records and there isn't a listing. No one knows where they've relocated. Gino, I'm sending my son the address of where his wife works, it's off of Hall Road, east of Romeo Plank. I want you to finish the job on Frederickson and do it now. There's a big pay day in it for you." Tony didn't tell Gino about the plan that Lorenzo put in place, leaving the bipod at the scene of the Greektown shooting. He was concerned that Gino might be a liability since the police were holding the club's manager. He and Lorenzo planned to utilize the bipod soon.

"Mr. Virgilio, I promise, I'll get him for you." When Gino hung up he was happy that he had been able to give Tony some news even if it didn't get him exactly what he wanted. He had feared that the man would retaliate after he failed to get rid of John Franklin. Now he had a new assignment, one that he couldn't fail at. He headed downtown, hoping to get into the police headquarters garage.

After Virgilio had completed his conversation with Gino, he made an important call. Dialing the unlisted number, he started the conversation, "It's me. I just heard they arrested our people from the club." Waiting for the response, he listened to the man on the other end who obviously wasn't happy. Tony knew he had to add some information before the man totally blew up. "I've got my man Gino working on it. Bubba has an informant at the Twelfth Precinct and the guy said they're holding all of them downtown. Detective Frederickson is at it again. We've got to eliminate him and do it fast."

The man didn't say much; he wanted action, not promises. He had already placed a call into his attorney but feared that it might be too late. "You might have to use that bipod sooner than you planned."

Virgilio had to have an answer, "I've put Gino on it; maybe we can succeed where we failed last year. We've got a new plan." The man wasn't happy, but agreed. Virgilio thought about getting Lorenzo involved as a backup to Gino. They couldn't fail, not again.

***

The SIU team put their plan into action; linking Councilman Perone to the case was a major break. Frederickson made sure his team understood the ramifications. Everyone had a suspect and they needed everything they could get as soon as possible. Spano heard Detectives Askew and Baker planning to head to Fort Wayne, Indiana. "When are you leaving?"

Baker turned back, "Joe, I'm thinking, if we leave now, we'll get there tonight and can start early tomorrow." Spano nodded, thinking it was a good idea. Baker told Askew, "Let's head to the records department; we'll have to take your car, mine is in the shop."

Frederickson heard them. "Hey, you should take my car."

Askew looked back at him, "You sure it's okay, Lieutenant?"

"Yeah, makes sense, besides no one has used it for months. I haven't driven it since I've been back." He tossed the keys to Askew.

Baker smiled at his partner, "I'm going to grab the material we printed out, and I'll meet you downstairs."

Askew fingered the keys, "Boss, do you need anything from your car before we go?"

"No, I don't ever leave anything in it."

"Okay, in case I find something, I'll bring it up."

Frederickson nodded, "Okay. The car's downstairs in my usual spot."

Baker grabbed the folder as Askew headed down to the garage. Askew looked back, "Baker, I'll wait for you." Askew arrived in the garage and saw Frederickson's vehicle. It was parked on the outer rim of the basement parking garage, just as he was told. Askew popped the rear tailgate and walked back to his vehicle and transferred a small duffle bag. He always kept a change of clothes in his car in case he was on an overnight assignment and decided to grab it.

Tom Baker made his way into the garage and was waving to Askew who moved toward the SUV. "I'll be there in a second." Baker was close to a half-dozen cars away when Askew jumped into Frederickson's vehicle.

The noise was deafening. The explosion sent chunks of cement across the garage and knocked Baker to the ground. Flames shot out over a ten-foot area engulfing vehicles on both sides of the SUV. Baker was stunned and tried to get off the pavement.

"Help! Help!" A voice came from the stairwell.

Baker's eyes were filled with smoke as the vehicles in front of him disappeared as the inferno jumped across the pavement. A second explosion and Baker couldn't get off the pavement. On his knees, he saw Frederickson's vehicle eaten by the raging fire. Baker let out a cry for help before collapsing.

FIFTEEN

The building above rattled and the shaking sent people running for cover. Windows were blown out of the second floor as alarms overhead sounded; Tom Baker was stunned and found himself laying on the ground, surrounded by a wall of flames. He watched the vehicle in front of him being lifted off the pavement, flying into the air, blazing. All of this right in front of him. Covering his eyes, Baker ducked as shards of concrete came flying, covering him. He couldn't catch his breath, couldn't move, his mind was rattled. *"What happened?"* He looked right, then left, watching as the fire jumped across the line of vehicles parked close to one another, he knew it had to be from the initial explosion. Stunned, a third blast occurred as he yelled out, "Askew!" to no avail. As flames ravaged the garage, Baker began dragging his body, crawling for cover, not sure if he'd make it out but he had to get to the screams he heard from the stairwell. "I'm coming, where are you?" Black smoke filled the garage. He was disorientated and holding his ears, the only sound a loud, shrill buzzing, so strong he couldn't tell where it was coming from. Baker looked up. He was getting wet; the sprinkler system was triggered but it was too late. Sirens filled Michigan Avenue and fire trucks from the Third Street station headed to the building. Covering his face, Baker tried to clear his eyes from the smoke and dust that filled the air. Again he wondered, W*here's Askew, how did this happen*? Pushing chunks of cement off his feet, he got to his knees, only to have flames above him send him back down, flat on the ground. Starting to crawl again, he finally saw the stairway ahead. A body was at the base of the steps. Baker felt for a pulse, there wasn't one. The garage had become a giant tomb, one of burnt cars and trucks, and who knows how many people. Tears ran down his face; he couldn't go on.

Officers and city officials scrambled to safety as rescue squads surrounded the building trying to put the blaze out. Detective Spano yelled, "That explosion was downstairs." he ran down the stairway leading to the garage but once he made it to the first floor's garage entrance, he was held back by searing heat. A guard in front of him yelled, "You can't go down there, the whole area could collapse."

Spano shoved past, only to be overwhelmed and pushed back by secondary explosions, most likely from gas tanks blowing up. "We've got to do something!" Spano crouched down staring into the smoke that billowed up the stairwell. Firemen made it to the stairway. Others joined in trying to help save any survivors. The firemen poured water into the opening as Spano and the guard continued standing behind them. Spano yelled, "Wait, I see someone coming up the stairs!" Two firemen wearing masks moved out of the smoke-filled stairwell carrying Baker. They had an oxygen mask on him and took him outside. Spano helped carry his partner, as paramedics started to administer first aide. Baker opened his eyes, not sure he made it out of the burning abyss, his face bloody and his shirt torn and saw Spano.

Spano called out, "Tom, what happened, where's Askew?"

Baker was shaking not sure where he was. He held his ears; his head went side to side. The paramedic looked up at Spano after securing the mask back on Baker. "I'm sure he can't hear you now; if he was anywhere close to the explosion his hearing might be damaged."

They carried Detective Baker to a waiting ambulance and rushed him to the same hospital where Amy Harper was recovering. Spano watched, not sure what happened or how he could help. The firefighters were spraying the garage area with water and foam, from both the stairwell and through the garage openings. It would be a long time until the blaze would be under control. They had to get the cars inside covered in foam, hoping to stop the explosions. Buildings downtown had emptied. People describing it thought there was an attack; most didn't know what had happened. Others told news crews that they were sure a bomb went off. Every news channel was on site, sending pictures to thousands glued to their television sets. Bars were lined with patrons, many holding their hands to their faces in horror.

An investigative team arrived and was on site, unable to do

anything except take photos and samples for their investigation. It might take days or weeks to figure it all out.

***

The young man circled through the construction on Hall Road past Garfield and made his way past Romeo Plank. Turning right into the complex that housed the Macomb Daily, he parked and studied the buildings layout. His Mustang convertible was pulled up behind a large white cube van that was delivering furniture to one of the offices. He watched as one man pulled a long truck dolly down a small ramp, it held a tall grey cabinet. Lorenzo exited his car and headed toward the propped open door. "Can I help you?" he asked the man pulling the dolly.

"Thanks, I've got it."

Walking a few feet behind the delivery person, he watched him enter the office on the first floor. The writing on the frosted glass read, "Law Office of Smyth & Smyth." Peeking in, he saw the office was empty. The delivery man was placing the cabinet against the wall next to three other cabinets that were exactly the same. Lorenzo strolled in, "You're doing a great job. I really appreciate how careful you're handling my furniture."

The man was startled, "Oh, I didn't know you were Mr. Smyth when we came in, sorry about that."

"Don't worry, I wanted to stop by and see how this was coming along."

"I've got one more cabinet in the truck. We put all the other furniture in your two offices earlier."

"Yes, I saw that; very nicely done. I thought my partner was here."

"A tall guy was here when we finished the two offices but he left about an hour ago. He said you were out of town."

"Just got back, wanted to check it out before going home. Did he say if he would be back?"

"No, sir. Just waited until we done with the two offices. I hope everything's okay."

"Perfect, what do you still have on the truck?"

"Just a few more pieces—a secretarial desk and some chairs."

"Tell you what," looking at his watch, "how about taking a break and getting something to eat." Lorenzo handed the guy two twenties,

"You've got a lot done and it's close to two o'clock. Bet you could use a break. There's a good restaurant down the street in Partridge Creek, Max & Erma's. Maybe grab a burger and cold one."

"You sure it's okay?"

"I'm not going to tell, besides, order me a burger and I'll join you there."

"Thanks, I just need to close up the truck."

Lorenzo smiled, "By the time you do that and get to the restaurant I'll be right behind you. Get me a burger with cheese."

The guy was pretty happy, "I'll do that; see you there." As he sang a little tune while walking out of the office suite, the guy was pleased that even a lawyer could be a cool dude.

Lorenzo watched until the guy headed to his truck. He knew that he would have a little more than thirty minutes to check out if Nancy Frederickson still worked in the building. When he entered, he checked the listing of businesses and people who worked there but her name didn't appear. Maybe she was still employed but they removed her name to help shield her from anyone looking for her. Lorenzo moved into the open foyer that was banked on both sides by large indoor trees. There were three floors; the law office along with an advertising firm occupied the first floor. The third floor belonged to the Macomb Daily. He knew she didn't work there. That left just the second floor. Going back into the law office, Lorenzo grabbed the overalls that the workman had taken off to go to eat. He was glad that they were close to the same size. Pushing a tall empty cabinet onto the dolly, he headed toward the elevators, with the cabinet. Lorenzo exited on the second floor and saw just one business listed, Canfield Marketing.

When he entered, a lady approached, "Can I help you?"

"I hope so; I've got a delivery for Nancy Frederickson."

She had a puzzled look, searching to see if the man was with anyone else, "I'm sorry, we don't have anyone who works here by that name."

"I've got an order for her, you can call my boss, my truck is outside." Lorenzo pointed to the white cube vehicle outside.

"Mrs. Frederickson used to work her but she left, I think it was last year."

"Maybe I've got the right name but wrong location. Can you help me? I need to get her new address to deliver this furniture."

"Sorry, she didn't leave a forwarding address. I think she moved out of state." She watched the young man nod.

"Boy, my boss is going to pitch a fit. Can I use your phone to call in?"

"I wish I could help but I can't let anyone into our offices. Don't you have a cell phone?"

"Yeah, but I ran out of juice."

She said, "Sorry, I can't help you."

Once he was downstairs he pushed the dolly with the cabinet where the delivery person had left it. Slipping out of the overalls, he headed back to his car and sped off.

***

The Public Safety building was now a five-alarm fire because of the magnitude of the blaze. The fire chief directed trucks from both downtown fire stations, as well as those close by, spraying water and foam on the headquarters building for over five hours. The pure white façade was scarred with black streaks extending to the second and third floors. Hundreds of people were now standing outside as crews of fire fighters worked to put the last of the blaze out. Chief Mathews stood next to the fire chief, hoping they'd soon be able to evaluate the damage. He listened to the report, "Two bodies were found, a man's body in one of the burnt vehicles and what possibly was a woman in one of the stairwells. The man found at the base of the stairs has been identified as Detective Thomas Baker, but until the medical examiner checks it out we can't be sure who the deceased were."

Mathews knew one of the bodies was Detective Askew, but no one knew who the second person was.

The inspector standing at the base of the garage looked back. He came as a courtesy to the fire chief. "I'm surprised there wasn't more structural damage."

Mathews was surprised. One pillar was cracked and the ceiling structure seemed the worst part.

The chief heard the inspector say, "I think it can be shored up in a couple of days. I've placed a call to our engineers to head on down and do a final check. We've found ten or eleven vehicles that were burnt in the fire and many others with severe damage. Most had glass blown out and shards of concrete and glass over them."

Although it was late, many detectives and officials still stood outside waiting to hear about those lost. The SIU team was among them, standing silently.

Mathews looked at the rescue team. He asked, "Have you recovered anyone?"

"Yes, I understand that one of them is a detective of yours. Beside Officer Baker who was taken to the hospital with injuries, we've got two bodies found in the garage."

"My men will want to help. I know you don't know which one was our detective, but they're both officers of my force."

"Absolutely, Chief, follow me." Mathews waved to Frederickson as the rest of the team followed. They made their way to a waiting EMS vehicle. As the medics exited the gaping hole in the structure carrying two stretchers, one of them signaled that the two stretchers carried the two lost officers. Spano rushed over followed by Frederickson and Johnson. Mindy stood, tears flowing, not sure what she could do but knowing she had to do something, after all, this was her family. Spano grabbed the back handles of one stretcher and everyone around scrambled to help. Tears flowed from those watching, knowing what was taking place. Frederickson moved in and took one handle with Johnson, Mindy and Spano. Chief Mathews joined them as all four men and Mindy carried the remains of Detective Robby Askew, and the yet unidentified other officer to the waiting EMS vehicle. Mindy placed small American flags that the chief gave her over both bodies. There wasn't a dry eye anywhere, as they escorted the two officers to a resting place in the waiting vehicles. All the news shows were televising the event for the evening time slot.

Once they slid the remains into the EMS vehicle, Chief Mathews grabbed his cell phone, "Captain Harvey, I need you to form an escort for us." The two bodies followed, carried by a fire truck and EMS vehicle.

Harvey knew that the chief wanted a group of police vehicles in line with the order to lead the two units to the medical examiner's office on East Warren. Michigan Avenue had been closed all the way to Campus Martius which was blocked off, as well as Third Street past the MGM Casino & Hotel. Police cars had their flashers and sirens blaring and personnel from headquarters stood at attention, along with most people watching the event. The two emergency vehicles led by a parade of police cars passed by. All saluted along the path that the EMS vehicle passed, honoring their comrade.

***

Olivia, the office manager at Canfield Marketing, who dealt with the delivery driver made an emergency call. "Nancy, it's Olivia from the Hall Road office. Did you order cabinets for your place?"

Nancy was surprised to hear from her. "No, I haven't ordered anything, not after I moved, why?"

Fear gripped Olivia. "Nancy, there was a guy here just now, said he had an order for you. He called you specifically by name. Said you ordered a cabinet and wanted to know what office location you were working at."

Nancy had goose bumps as she listened. "What did you tell him?"

"Nothing. I said you left the company last year, thought you moved out of state. Nancy, he looked legit, had a cabinet on a dolly, said you ordered it."

"Can you identify him?"

"Yeah, I'm sure I can." She stopped for a second. "Nancy, we probably got him on camera."

"Oh great, I forgot we added the cameras in the lobby and on each floor. Get someone to pull the tapes. I'm going to call my husband; he'll send an officer to you. Thanks Olivia." Nancy dialed her husband's number, surprised that it went to his voice mail. She left him a message hoping that he'd return it soon. Nancy had been working on a special project all day. Walking into a conference room, she turned on the television, staring as Carolyn Clifford reported on an explosion downtown at Detroit Public Safety headquarters. The news bulletin flashed across the screen, two dead, serious damage and the entire administration building closed. "Oh God!" She cried out to no one. Clifford said, "We're going to join our reporter on the scene, Carole Newton."

Nancy slumped into a chair, glued to the action. She watched the reporter who stood in front of the building at 1301 Third Street. "This is the scene from earlier." She watched flames leaping from the garage area below, climbing up three floors. "My information now is that at least two bodies have been found in the garage and paramedics are searching the rest of the building. The report is that a vehicle exploded about seven-thirty this evening. We don't know the identities of either person thought to have been in the garage yet, but I'll stay here until we have that for you."

Carolyn Clifford, the ABC news anchor, asked the field reporter questions, "Did they know what caused the explosion?"

"No, we haven't been able to get confirmation on that, only that it happened in areas used by the police department."

The news switched back to Clifford and she told viewers, "We'll stay on this breaking story as more information comes in."

Nancy Frederickson who watched couldn't take it. "Not again!" she screamed at the television. Grabbing her cell phone she dialed her husband, wringing her hands waiting for an answer, one ring, two, three, it went to his voice mail. She knew she couldn't call the office, hell, it had been blown up, or at least something at headquarters had been. She paced the room, calling her husband's cell phone again.

One ring, second ring, then his voice, "I'm so sorry, I couldn't answer before. I planned to call you but forgot, I'm so sorry." He could hear her rapid breathing, "Nancy, you okay?"

"Oh my God!" She started crying, her hands trembling, hoping she wouldn't drop the phone. "Don," she said through her sobs, "are you okay?"

"Yeah, honey, I'm fine. Please take a breath." He waited a few seconds, "Nancy, we lost Barry Askew today." After saying that he became very quiet.

Nancy was rummaging through her mind, *Barry, Barry, yes, Askew, young good-looking detective.* She knew her husband usually never called any of the team by their first names. "Don, what happened? I'm watching television; the whole place looks like it went up in flames. Were you guys the target?"

He couldn't answer that, not yet, besides, he'd never tell her the truth. "We don't know for sure, it may have been meant for anyone. Many of the cars were damaged, burnt to ashes. You're going to be upset; my new jacket was in mine." He hoped by making light of it she'd stop crying and asking questions.

"Your jacket, you're worried about the jacket? I never liked the damn thing anyway." She let out a nervous laugh. "What can I do, would you like me to come down there?"

"No, you stay home. I don't need to worry about you too. We haven't released any names yet. Askew's family doesn't know. I am going to head there in a few minutes. Got to tell them myself. Spano will go with me."

"I can meet you."

"Thanks hon, you're the best. It will be better if just Spano and I go right now. I'm sure his parents are watching the news coverage just like you. It won't be pretty when they see us at the door." It was always a difficult sight for family members, whether it was military or police, when officials showed up at the door.

Every year Nancy and her husband hosted a small party, usually a barbecue, very informal. Nancy made sure she knew all the people on his team and their families. Askew was new to the team. He and Johnson joined them last year when Don was recovering from his accident, at least that's what they referred to it as. He was a young man, nice looking, dark hair and blue eyes. She heard the others kid him. They called him a real ladies' man. She took another deep breath, "Okay, okay, as long as you're fine. Will you be home tonight?"

"Not sure, if so it will be very late. Please don't wait up."

After everything he told her, she decided not to mention the delivery guy who was looking for her; it was probably nothing anyway.

SIXTEEN

Tony Virgilio had been waiting for the call from Gino, knowing that he'd want to gloat about the successful bombing downtown. Virgilio watched the coverage on every channel, but none of them gave the names of the people who died in the explosion. When his cell phone rang he didn't even look to see who was calling; it had to be Gino. Grabbing the phone, he gruffly answered, "Yeah?"

"Dad, it's me. I decided to search for the detective's wife one more time. I'm headed back from the advertising company on Hall Road where she used to work. She doesn't work there now, but I think the lady I talked to knows where she is."

The news excited Tony. "Lorenzo, I hope you were careful."

"Yes, I pretended to be a furniture delivery person, had a uniform and even a cabinet on a dolly."

Tony laughed, "You're a good son. Did you see the news?"

"Yeah, looks like Gino might have finally finished the job."

"I hope so. They're not releasing the names of the people killed yet." Lorenzo knew his dad had more than a few disappointments regarding the impending death of Detective Frederickson. And until the news confirmed that the detective was dead, Tony wouldn't be celebrating.

"Dad, after I left the advertising company, I headed to the main library on Romeo Plank."

Virgilio laughed, "Got an overdue book?"

"Probably a few. I decided to run some searches through the library's database. I didn't want to leave an email trail on my computer so I used someone else's password." Lorenzo took a minute while he scrambled through his notepad. "I hacked into the police department payroll database," he paused, "Dad, I found Frederickson's new address."

Tony was surprised. "When did you learn to do that?"

"That's not important, just thank Bobby the next time you see him. Guess him being a computer nerd paid off for us. Dad. If Frederickson isn't dead, we can get to him and his wife with this information."

"Where does he live?"

"Downtown. Shit, he bought one of those high-rise condos on the riverfront, the address is 1001 West Jefferson. There are three buildings there; he's in the third one on the river, number three-hundred, seventh floor, unit 7E."

"Lorenzo, I think we need to check that out now."

"I understand, but now that we've got his location, I can make the visit to his place anytime with this information."

Tony knew Lorenzo was correct; he just wanted confirmation that the blast got their target. Just then he was getting another call; looking at the number, he smiled. "Lorenzo, it's Gino. I'll call you back after I talk to him." He connected to the caller and waited for Gino to talk.

The man sounded pretty pleased with his work, "Hope you enjoyed television earlier."

"Yeah, I found the evening news very interesting."

"Oh, I'm sure I got him. Put it right under the fuel tank, triggered it with my cell phone when he got in the vehicle."

Tony felt a rush of excitement. "So you're sure it was him?"

"Yeah, I hid behind a pillar and watched him get in. Damn, I was a little too close for comfort. I was pinned down at first and when I crawled out, I had to avoid the firemen."

"You're okay, no one saw you?"

"Pretended to be with the rescue squad. Everyone was running around, it was crazy. Just got a few bumps. Going to lay low for a few days."

"Good job, Gino. There will be a nice package headed your way." Gino knew this would be a big payday. He finally pulled off what Tony wanted.

When Gino Rossi hung up he had a big smile on his face. He decided once he collected his reward, he'd head out of town. *Maybe Miami, that's a good place for a vacation,* he thought.

***

It was early the next morning when the inspector concluded his tour of the fire-charred building along with the mayor and the chiefs of police and fire departments. "Looks like we got pretty lucky, the only major building damage is in the corner of the lower level, above where the first vehicle blew up. Our team of forensic analysts was able to determine that this was the origin of the blast. We found pieces of a pretty sophisticated trigger that most likely set it off. We've concluded that it was a bomb, probably planted under a fuel tank." He stopped to answer a cell phone call. "Sorry about that, of course we'll have a couple dozen windows to replace on the floors above, but structurally everything appears sound. My men are placing covers over the busted windows and we've contacted the insurance company. They'll order glass when they get here. I've got a team that will do a clean-up of the smoke damage. That may take a week or so."

Chief Mathews was the first to ask, "When can we move back in?" The fire chief wondered the same thing.

"Gentlemen, I'd say Monday morning would be fine to move people back in from the second floors and higher once the glass is in place. This being Friday morning, it gives us the weekend to work on everything, but I'd rather keep everyone out of the first floor and the garage. A crew is inside sweeping up and taking inventory of the damage as they put boards over the openings. You'll have to keep people clear of those areas. We also plan to put supports under the first floor corner this evening. We'll have to block off the parking garage where it all happened until the ceiling is patched and new supports are added."

The mayor was surprised that the building didn't sustain a lot more serious damage. He turned to Chief Mathews, "Chief, the building repair is one thing, more importantly, how did this happen?"

As the fire inspector left, Chief Mathews turned, "That's the million dollar question. I've got security checking the cameras to see when and who might have been in the garage and possibly planted the bomb. Mayor, our investigation is just starting but I'll put everyone on it."

Mathews wasn't sure how he'd put people on the case; he had the

SIU working on the shooting of Detective Harper at Campus Martius and now the explosion at headquarters, not to mention the issue with the deputy mayor and potential conflict with Councilman Perone. He didn't know if the mayor would have anything else to say but he wanted to close the conversation, at least until he viewed the film footage from security. It was better not to say more about the case, after all they had the deputy mayor under guard upstairs and were investigating a sitting councilman. He knew the mayor and fire chief didn't need to hear about that, at least not now. Mathews told them, "Frederickson and Spano went to Askew's parents' home to inform them about what happened. They wanted to do it personally." Both men nodded, knowing at times like this it's important to remember the people who were lost. Once the meeting was over, not much was left to do except inform department heads that the building would be operational Monday morning with the exception of the first floor offices that would be closed until repairs were completed, hopefully by Wednesday.

As Chief Mathews and the mayor walked toward their vehicles, Carole Newton approached. She had a cameraman with her and held a microphone in her left hand. "Mayor, Carole Newton with Channel 7 news. Could we ask you and Chief Mathews a few questions for our viewers?" Before either man answered, she started, "Chief, we understand that one of the people killed was a detective of yours. Can you tell us who it was?"

"Carole, I appreciate your inquiry, however, until the family has been notified, we'll have to wait to release the name."

She tried another approach. "I understand. Mayor, any identification on the second person found in the fire?"

"No, Carole, the medical examiner will be working to determine the identity of both persons. We should know something soon. You know it's only been a day since the explosion."

She nodded, "Do you have any idea how this happened? I'm sure our citizens thought that such a high profile building would have been more secure."

Both Mathews and the mayor knew she was fishing for a story. "Carole, our concerns are first for our employees and the two lives that were lost. I promise there will be a thorough investigation of this incident." The two men thanked the reporter and walked away together. Mathews smiled at the mayor, "Nice job ditching her."

The mayor nodded as he walked to his vehicle then turned back toward Mathews, saying, "Tomorrow I won't be that lucky," guessing he'd be under fire for more answers from the news teams.

***

The events of the past several days were front and center on everyone's mind. Chief Mathews had many concerns, including those about his SIU team, especially now after losing another detective. The chief had the news from the medical examiner on the second body found in the garage. It was Angela Sowers, a detective from the Third Precinct. He contacted the commander and informed him about the loss. This was a tough part of the job, one that none of the people handled well. He planned to visit both Askew's and Sowers' parents along with Lieutenant Jackson and the commander.

Mathews asked Detective Spano to come down to his office. He wanted another set of eyes going over the footage from the security team. The team pointed out a man entering the garage, but none of them recognized him. The guy had hidden from the cameras. Mathews wanted Detective Spano to go over what they had from the security unit. It was the second time around for both of them viewing the film. They found the best angle of the dark figure slipping into the downstairs garage, along the side of a van. "He must have been waiting there until a large vehicle entered. Look at how he goes in using the van as cover. He appeared to know where the cameras were. This might have been an inside job."

Mathews looked over at him. "I agree, he definitely knew where the camera was. Like you said, he covers his face just as he comes out of the bushes and moved along with the van."

They kept looking at the footage. Once they finished, Spano looked up at the chief. "Chief, with the evidence the inspectors found, and the view the surveillance shows, we've got to secure the entrance."

"I'll make sure when the construction team repairs the wall, they take care of this problem. Joe, I'm concerned about what we've seen. If the guy knew where the cameras were, we might have an inside leak. I'll send the best photo we've got to administration.

They'll run it through the employee database. I'm also sending it to the FBI to see if they can get something from their systems."

Spano headed back upstairs. Mindy was at her desk signing a large card with an oversize envelope attached. He looked over at her, "Guess that's for Askew?"

"Yeah, the guys started a collection for his parents. Robby didn't have very much time on the job and won't get much of a death benefit."

Putting his arm around her, Spano tried comforting the secretary. "Mindy, the chief is also putting something together downstairs. Maybe you need to call Lieutenant Jackson; she can fill you in so that we don't duplicate efforts. I'm sure everyone will want to support this."

Spano looked up when he heard the door open. He saw Frederickson enter. "Don, the chief let me see the surveillance footage."

"Did it give us any clues?"

"Not really, but it did capture a guy slipping into the garage along the side of a van. Looks like he knew where the camera was because he turned his head. We just have a partial side view of him."

"Any hope of identifying the guy?"

"I don't think so, but the chief is sending it to everyone, looking for help. Did you tell Nancy what happened?"

Frederickson stared back at Joe for a second. "I just told her about Askew; I didn't say anything about my vehicle."

"What?" Spano suspected that she'd blow up if she heard it on the news. "She needs to know that we've still got some asshole possibly gunning for you."

"No, Joe, she doesn't need to know that. We've already had to move once. She can't work out of her office and the last thing she needs to know is that some nut is running around with me as his target."

"But…"

"Joe, you don't understand. I know Nancy and the worst thing I can do now is tell her that someone is trying to kill me." Both of them agreed that it might not be a good idea to give her something else to worry about. "Now, tell me what you and the chief talked about."

Spano grabbed for his note pad. "We decided to go over the footage again from the garage. Like I said, the surveillance caught the guy on the camera but he hid his face the whole time. The chief wanted me to check it out in case I could help with the identification."

Frederickson agreed. "He knew where the cameras were, Joe. Guess you both came up with the idea that we've got an inside job, maybe a mole."

"Yeah same thing I said. The Chief's running the best photo we've got through the FBI and our admin department."

"They won't find anything; this is never going to end." Frederickson took a deep breath, turned and walked to his office. Spano followed as he heard him still talking, "I want to find this asshole. He's put Harper and Barker in the hospital and killed Askew. I'm not taking this laying down. I'll turn over every stone to find him!"

Spano had never seen him like this, not even last year when he was in the hospital after that terrible crash on 1-94. "Boss, how about we put someone outside your new place, keeping an eye on Nancy for you?"

Frederickson stopped dead in his tracks, "No, not now, not ever." He pounded on the desk, "I'm not hiding from these people."

Joe stepped back, "I got it, but how about Nancy; if they are still coming after you, they might find out where you're living."

"The new place has a full-time guard in the lobby. You've got to have a key to operate the elevator. There is video surveillance in our unit covering the hallway and our front door. Short of an armed guard, we're good."

Spano knew he should quit asking about Nancy and protection. "Do you want to check out the video from the garage?"

"No, not now. I don't know if I could ever watch that again." He moved into his office and slammed the door and slumped behind the desk.

Spano forgot to tell him that Baker was in. The hospital released him that morning. He was on desk duty, but refused to go home. They still had a case and he decided to leave Frederickson alone for a while. Baker and Johnson were talking in the conference room. Johnson asked, "Baker, what did the doctor say about your injuries?"

"He was surprised I didn't have a concussion; it pays to have a hard head. They released me. I've only got a few cuts and bruises."

"How about the smoke inhalation, that has to have a lasting effect!"

"Believe it or not, they pump your system full of oxygen. I'm good."

As Spano walked into the conference room, Baker turned. "Johnson and I thought we needed to run everything on all four of the owners of the strip club on the Internet. Maybe we can find something on them that will help the investigation."

"Baker, that's a great idea; you start on that. I'm going to follow up on Councilman Perone. Johnson, how about you taking Buddy Swinton? He's the one who lives in Fort Wayne."

"Okay, I handle it."

"Let's first get the three local guys covered and then we'll see where that leads us." Johnson and Baker started working on data searches, and Spano walked back into Frederickson's office.

Frederickson looked up when Joe entered, "Don, did you know that Baker was released from the hospital?"

"Yeah, sorry, we've been so busy, I should have told you. They called me earlier. He's going to be on desk duty but I really think he should have spent another night in the hospital. Where is he?"

"In the conference room with Johnson."

"I need to see him." Frederickson jumped up and headed to the room. Spano followed. Frederickson continued telling Spano, "Baker is relegated to desk duty because of his injuries but he can help doing Internet searches on our suspects."

Spano said, "I tried to ask Baker about the bombing but he didn't want to say much except the details he first gave the investigators. Unfortunately not much of it helps; guess the blast took its toll on his memory. None of us have come to grips with what happened, not yet."

Frederickson walked in. Seeing Baker he put his hand out and pulled him into a tight hug. "Tom, I'm glad you're okay. I promise, if it's the last thing I do, we'll get these guys." The two men held onto each other for a few seconds. The team had been through a lot, but this week was the worst.

SEVENTEEN

Tony Virgilio was surprised that the news stations hadn't released the names of those killed at headquarters. He watched Carole Newton from Channel 7 do a recap of the events as she stood in front of the damaged building.. He hoped he'd have more details today. Tony turned the volume up higher. Newton opened the news briefing with, "You can see the spot where the blast burned the outer surface of the building. My sources said that one of the detectives was in a black Chevrolet SUV that blew up when it was started. The explosion caused the vehicles on both sides to catch fire and then spread to others that also blew up." Her cameraman panned across the opening in the garage, catching the repairs taking place. "The mayor's office said that the building sustained only cosmetic damage. You can see the windows being replaced behind me and workers are in the garage fixing the ceiling. I hope to have more details as they come in." Once the camera stopped, Carole shook her head. Looking at the cameraman, she said, "Let's head inside, I want to talk to Chief Mathews now."

Lieutenant Jackson got word that a news team was in the building. She buzzed the chief, "Chief, Channel 7 is here and headed our way. What do you want me to do?"

"Hold her for a few minutes. Let her know I'll talk to her, but not on camera." Mathews called upstairs to the SIU office. "Mindy, is Don in?"

"Yes sir, I'll put you through." She sent the call to the conference room where Don was talking to Baker.

When he looked out to her desk she motioned that it was the chief. Grabbing the phone he said "Morning sir, sorry I didn't stop in first."

"Glad you're in, Don. I've got Channel 7 and one of your favorite reporters, Carole Newton, coming in my office."

"Yeah, my favorite."

"Don, this is your choice, I can still tell her you're the one killed in the blast. We'll find a safe spot to hide you and Nancy. Maybe it will help bring out the guy who did this."

"I appreciate what you're offering, but I'm on my way down."

"I'll let her know."

"We can talk to her together."

Mathews knew that Frederickson wouldn't want to go into hiding, not with Askew killed in the blast meant for him. Once he had the answer, he told Lieutenant Jackson to show Carole in, but leave the cameraman in the outer office. Mathews stood, "Carole, glad you're here, the mayor and I told you the other day that we'd have details for you."

The reporter was surprised but not sure she'd get what she hoped for. "Thank you, Chief. We've had a good relationship. I plan to keep my part of the bargain and glad you're keeping yours."

As they talked, Frederickson walked in. Reaching out, he shook her hand, "Carole, thanks for waiting."

She was surprised to see him. "Detective, I'm glad to see you're okay. Sorry that it's under such sad circumstances." Carole Newton had known Detective Frederickson for a few years; they met when he was working a case of a missing teacher. They both sat down across from the chief.

Mathews looked over and asked, "Lieutenant Jackson, would you please bring in some coffee." He smiled at the two across from him. "Hope you understand Carole, I can't tell you this with a camera in my face or for a news team." She slid to the edge of the armed chair and waited for his comments, knowing that it wouldn't be the whole truth but what they wanted her to hear. Jackson came in and poured coffee for all three of them and left. Mathews looked over at Frederickson, "I'm going to let the Don fill you in."

Frederickson surprised both of them, first by sipping his coffee and then sitting back in the big chair. He looked over at Carole. "We've been friends for a few years now, so I'm not going to bullshit you. It was my car that blew up. Our investigative team discovered that someone, we're not sure who, planted a bomb in my vehicle. Detective Barry Askew was going to use it. We didn't know..." He stopped talking, looked up at the ceiling for a second and took a deep breath. "It was Detective Askew in my car." He looked over at the chief before continuing, "Carole, that information isn't for the news.

I'm telling you this because we need to catch the bastard who did this. I'll give you an interview, but some things will not be for public consumption, not yet."

Carole's eyes darted back and forth from the chief to Frederickson. She knew he was on the level. "Oh God, I'm so sorry." Carole laid her hand on Don's and both of them nodded. She turned back to Mathews. Any leads?"

"I wish I could say we have one, but we don't. We're working on a partial photo of someone entering the garage. We suspect he planted the bomb. I've got the FBI working on this along with our detectives. Until we have more, I'd like to keep most of this out of the news. Carole, we've agreed in the past to give you the exclusive. In this case, we'd like you to keep as much quiet as possible, at least until we've got a lead."

Frederickson turned to Mathews, "Chief, Detective Askew's family deserves to know that their son was a hero. I'd like to at least be able give his name as one of the people killed in the blast."

Mathews looked at Don, "I understand."

Frederickson told Carole, "Were going to have to leave out that it was my vehicle. We'll also get the medical examiner to get us the identification of the other person killed, so you'll have both names. You can tell your viewers that we're still working on the cause of the blast."

Carole put her head down, jotting down a few notes. "Okay, which one of you is going on the air with me?"

Frederickson right away answered, "Me, I'll do it, but only giving you what we agreed to."

"Deal, I need to call the station, it will be breaking news." Carole left the office as the chief gave a weak smile.

Don stood, "Boss, I don't want you in front of the camera spilling bullshit in case this backfires. I'll handle this."

"You don't have to."

"Yes, I do, we'll get to the bottom of this, I promise." Turning back to the chief, before he walked out, "I'm going to get these guys if it's the last thing I do." Frederickson moved into the atrium as Carole and her cameraman set everything up. This was the normal place where officials gave media updates. An American flag draped the wall along with symbols of the State of Michigan and City of Detroit. Frederickson was resolved, he'd get the people who did this to his team.

Tony Virgilio was wrapping up two special orders for customers when he saw the television in the corner of the meat market flash "Special Bulletin." He stood at the counter and turned to Sal, "Take care of the special orders for me, I want to see what's going on downtown," pointing up at the television. Sal nodded knowing that his boss had been following recent events with great interest. Tony hurried into the back room and turned the television set on. He stood, mouth open, as he saw Detective Frederickson in the middle of the screen. "Son-of-a-bitch!"

Carole Newton made sure the newsroom turned the segment to her as she opened the news conference. "I'm standing with special Detective Don Frederickson of the Special Investigation Unit."

With that initial announcement and the sight of the detective standing there, very much alive, Virgilio went nuts. He stormed out of the back door of the market, yelling once he was in the empty loading area. His rant was directed at everyone. "Damn you Frederickson, you must have nine lives. How in the hell could you escape this?" He turned his attention to the hitman, "Gino, you fool, you missed him again. How could this happen?" He was walking in a circle, raging, not sure where to turn. Tony Virgilio's efforts failed to kill Frederickson, once again.

***

Amy Harper sat in her hospital bed watching the news conference. When Detective Frederickson covered the details, Amy yelled, "What the hell!"

The nurse who was in the room helping her looked up, "Something wrong?"

"Sorry, I was commenting on the news conference." Harper knew her identity as the detective shot at Campus Martius was kept under wraps. She was in a special wing of the DMC so that news teams wouldn't find her, after all, according to the police chief's news conference close to a week ago, she had died. Harper watched Detective Frederickson giving the details of the ongoing investigation into the bombing at Detroit Public Safety headquarters. She wished she was better and could get back to work, something that wouldn't be possible for a few months after taking a bullet to the chest after all, she was lucky to be alive. The special news bulletin continued as Frederickson told Carole that the two dead had been identified. When she heard the name of Detective Robby Askew, tears began flowing down her cheeks. She looked down, "Could you please give me some time alone," she asked the nurse who was treating her. Grabbing her cell, she punched in a number. "Mindy, is Baker there?"

The SIU secretary was surprised to hear Amy's voice; it was shaking. "Harper, are you okay?"

"Getting better every day. What's this about Askew, is it true?"

"I better give you to Baker." Not wanting to be the one to give her the news, Mindy decided to let Tom handle it. She called out, "Detective Baker, I've got an important call for you."

Baker looked puzzled answering his phone. Harper immediately jumped on him, "What the hell's going on, Tom?" and before he could say anything, she continued, "Tom, is Askew dead?"

"Yeah, happened yesterday."

Baker didn't get much more out. "I've tried to call your cell phone, why aren't you answering? Why didn't you call and tell me?"

Tom had so many thing to tell her, how his cell phone was damaged in the blast. Should he tell her that he was hurt? "Amy, settle down, let me fill you in." He waited for her to slow down asking questions. "Okay honey, here's what we've got." He told her everything, as painful as it was for both of them. He knew he'd better give it all to her, because she'd be pissed if he lied.

"You sure you're okay, Tom?"

"Yes, the doctor said I was pretty lucky, just a few cuts and bruises. I'll get a new cell phone later today and text you the number. You know it takes close to a presidential order to get new equipment."

Harper had settled down now that she had the details and talked to Baker. "What can we do for Robby's family? His mom never wanted him to join the force."

Baker realized that she was closer than he was to Askew. "Mindy and the chief are taking up a special collection. I've heard that they will hold an event honoring him."

"Tom, too much has happened this week: I've been shot, Askew killed; we've got to find these guys." Now he thought she sounded like Frederickson, pissed off.

Baker knew she was ranting, but right, someone is out there targeting the team. It all started with the investigation of the stripper found under John Franklin's car, now it has possibly led to Councilman Perone, and the shooting at Campus Martius. The final blow was the car bomb. As he ran them across his mind he wondered—were they all connected? "Amy, maybe we've got only one case. It has to be the same people targeting us and the mayor. I've got to go."

"Okay, but keep me in the loop, Tom; I know where you live." The last comment made them both chuckle, after all, they had been living together for the past few months.

Baker hung up and walked over to where Spano and Johnson were running details from the case. Joe Spano looked up, "Guys, I think we have one group doing all of this: framing Franklin, shooting Harper, and the explosion."

Baker and Johnson stared at the computer screen. Spano said, "Look at this." All three men reread the details they found. It linked Councilman Perone's family to the owners of the Eastern Market drug ring that the team dismantled last year. As they scrolled down, that same group was involved in businesses located in Greektown. Johnson looked up, "It was Detective Frederickson and our unit that busted all of these cases. Perone is the key to it all." They knew this might break the case open.

EIGHTEEN

Gino was standing in line at the Detroit Metro Airport with a group of people. They were all watching the television. It was covering the news conference featuring Frederickson alongside the news reporter. Gino was shocked, knowing that he planted the bomb in the detective's vehicle. How did the he elude it? Mumbling to himself, *Christ, Virgilio must be going crazy; I'm glad I'm leaving town.* The gate agent in front of him called out, "Sir, you need to move forward; we're boarding." Gino quickly moved up and handed her his boarding pass. Once he entered the plane he was glad to be headed to sunny Miami. The first class seat was just what he needed. He didn't plan to return anytime soon, if ever.

Tony Virgilio was trying to call Gino. He only accomplished killing the stripper, but didn't kill the deputy mayor and missed Frederickson—again. Virgilio was livid, but couldn't get in touch with him.

When Tony couldn't get Gino on the phone, he called his son. "Lorenzo, did you see the news conference?" His son acknowledged that he had watched it, knowing that his father was on the edge. Tony continued, "Gino's not answering. I tried to call him, he's probably headed out of town."

"What can I do to help, Dad?"

Virgilio had already gotten his youngest son involved deeper than he wanted to, but he was the only person he could trust. Lorenzo was an excellent marksman, having developed sniper skills and proving it earlier by shooting Detective Harper. "I don't want you to do anything else right now. I'm getting in touch with my partners." After hanging up with Lorenzo, Tony made a call. The man on the other end didn't say anything. Tony led the conversation, "We've got problems. Yes, I saw the news conference, that's why I'm calling you."

His contact finally asked, "Who is this guy Frederickson? I can't believe you didn't get him."

Virgilio understood the implication that he was being blamed again for missing the detective. He wasn't completely pleased that his partner hung it all on him. "It was your guy Gino who said he killed him. The guy is a jackass. I paid him just as we agreed, now he's got my money and I can't get ahold of him." His partner didn't have an answer. Tony continued, "You need to call him, maybe he'll answer your calls." Tony didn't want to wait until the man decided what to do next. He was still outside pacing in the delivery area behind his market. He wanted to protect his son and their business, but Tony swore he wouldn't run like Vinnie La Russo did last year. No, he'd take care of everyone before he let anything or anyone hurt his family.

***

Back at headquarters Frederickson made his way up to the SIU office after the press conference. When he entered, he saw his team gathered around Johnson's computer screen. "What's up?"

Spano turned, "Baker's made an observation. We think he's right." Baker pointed to the chart that they had sketched out. All four of them were concentrating on the board as Spano went over what they had written down. "This whole thing started with Franklin being charged with vehicular homicide; however, the body ends up being a stripper, one who works for the club on Eight Mile. One of the owners is Councilman Perone, who is running against the mayor in the upcoming election. Perone's family is connected to the Eastern Market drug ring we busted last year."

Spano was talking so fast, Frederickson put his hand on the detective and said, "Slow down, Joe."

Joe was close to being out of breath as he continued, this time a little slower. "Okay, then someone shoots at either the mayor or chief and hits Amy. Where did he shoot from but Greektown. That's where we started our first big drug cases a couple years ago." Don Frederickson listened and knew this was making sense. Spano looked at Don, "Boss, you're connected to every one of these events and suddenly a car bomb is placed in your car, here, at headquarters. This is a personal vendetta against you. Someone is seeking revenge for your breaking up their drug ring. They have an ulterior motive for putting Perone into the mayor's seat." Looking back at Frederickson, "We've got one group doing all of this and Perone is the key. The three of us don't think the other owners of that strip club matter, it's all Perone."

Frederickson looked over at Baker and put his arm around his shoulders, "Good job, Tom! We've been running in circles thinking that these are connected, but we didn't know how or why. Christ, could Perone be involved in the drug business too? We need to talk to Franklin one more time." At least they had the deputy mayor in custody. Heading to the room where Franklin was being held, all four entered.

John Franklin stood, surprised when four men entered the room. "What's going on?"

"We need you to listen," Frederickson said. "How long have you been hanging out at the strip club on Eight Mile before this all happened?"

Franklin looked at the men standing in front of him. "Before all what happened? What's that got to do with anything?"

"All what happened! You've got a lot of nerve! I've got a dead detective and another one in the hospital lucky to be alive. Your car is on top of a stripper from the club and you're asking all what? We need to know and need it now." Spano was afraid that Frederickson was going to deck him.

Franklin was standing in the middle of the room and backed up, "I'm not sure, I've been going there for a while."

Spano moved past Frederickson, putting himself between Don and Franklin, "Sit down," placing his hand on Franklin's chest, pushing him into a chair. "Now, either give us straight answers or you're going to be charged as an accessory to murder." They could see fear on the guy's face. "Now, asshole!" Spano was as close as you could be to another human without sitting on them.

Franklin took a deep breath, "Maybe sometime late last year. My wife, Misty, and I were having issues. This guy, one of Councilman Perone's staff knew I was having family problems and invited me to join him. We went to the strip club and had a few drinks, then he introduced me to some of the girls."

"Who exactly introduced you to girls at the strip club. Think John, this is important, why didn't you didn't think to mention this before?"

"I'm not sure what you mean."

"What was the name of this guy from the councilman's staff?"

"His name is Gino, Gino Rossi, Perone introduced us."

Spano looked over at the others, "You're telling me that the councilman introduced you to this guy, Gino? Can you identify him?"

"Yes, I've actually got a photo on my phone of the two of us one night at the club."

"You've got a photo of this guy?"

"Yeah, we were getting a lap dance. Gino set it up. The girls did whatever he said. I thought the guy was one of the owners. When one of the girls was on him, I snapped the picture. He didn't know I took it. You've got my cell phone; if you get it I'll show you."

Johnson left the room and came back with the phone that was in Frederickson's desk.

Spano took the phone. They gathered closer looking at the photo that Franklin held up. Spano stopped when he saw it, "Hold on!" He turned and headed out of the room while the others waited with puzzled looks.

"Where did he go?" Johnson asked. The others shrugged.

Spano came rushing back in, "Look at this!" He held a copy of the photo he and Chief Mathews had seen when checking the surveillance earlier at the garage. "This is the man who entered the garage, attempting to hide his face. It's the same guy, although you only get a view of the right side of his face, actually his ear and neck. Look at that mole." They saw what Joe was referring to. "Same mole on his face as the one on Franklin's phone of this Gino guy." The mole was unusual, had a sort of hook at the bottom. Spano was right.

Frederickson immediately turned back to Franklin, "Tell us everything you know about this guy."

"Just that the councilman introduced us but never really said what this guy did on his staff. He always seemed pretty nice, always bought rounds at the club. I kinda thought he was either an owner of the place or managed it."

"Why?"

"Everyone knew him; he signed for drinks. The girls always hung around him. Heck, he introduced me to both Jasmine and Diamond." That's when Franklin stopped talking for a second. "Hey, Diamond, she was the stripper that was found dead under my vehicle. I didn't have anything to do with the club, just went there."

Frederickson held his hand up, "We've got to go over this. I might need to ask you more." The four detectives headed back to their office.

Spano and the team knew their case was coming together; they were all were talking at the same time. Johnson said "Don, this Gino guy is the link to Perone."

Joe jumped in, "We've got to put a new BOLO out on this guy with this photo," still holding Franklin's phone.

Baker wasn't going to be left out, "Could we check Perone's office records? Maybe this Gino is in a staff photo."

"Wait guys!" Frederickson held them all back, "More than likely, Perone never had this Gino on any actual payroll, or in a staff photo. He's a thug, one that people like Perone use without being linked in any public way. He used Gino to set up Franklin so they could get to the mayor." They knew he was right. "Our best hope is to find Gino Rossi, he'd be our proof, the key to proving Perone's involvement. Joe, get that new photo and BOLO out. Make sure you get it to the FBI. Who knows where the guy might head to. Johnson, how about you running an internet search to see if there is any way to link Gino to Perone. Baker, you need to head this whole thing up. I don't want you out there, we need you here, running this. Joe and Johnson will report everything they find to you; you keep us all advised on the case. I'll head downstairs and give Chief Mathews what we've found."

Before going to see the chief he returned to Franklin. He was still sitting in the middle of the room. "Detective what do you need from me?"

Frederickson looked back at him, "You're not out of the woods yet; for all we know you're involved with all of this." He turned, leaving and locking the door behind them.

***

Gino Rossi sat back smiling in his seat in the Boeing 747. After the plane took off from the airport, he looked out as the ground slowly disappeared. The flight attendant strolled down the aisle, "Miss, can I get a drink?" Gino asked. He was sitting in first class and the young lady smiled and nodded, returning with what he had ordered. Gino had plenty of money now that Virgilio wired him a bundle after the bomb blast. Perone had taken care of him after he handled framing Franklin, although he never finished the plan. He figured that nothing could stop him now. He planned on catching another flight from Miami after he landed. Maybe he'd head to a South American country that didn't have an extradition agreement with the United States. His money will go a long way down there. The pilot banked to the right and the seat belt light came back on, Gino asked the flight attendant that passed, "What's going on?"

"I'm not sure," the young lady answered, "Give me a few minutes and I'll find out for you."

There was an open seat in the row behind Gino. He was preoccupied getting a drink and didn't notice and a tall man who slid into it. The pilot's voice came on the speakers, "Folks, I'm sorry but we've got an electrical problem and have been ordered back to Detroit Metro. I'm being told that it is a minor issue but we must make sure that everything is okay. The delay should take just a short while, but we might have to all get off and re-board." There were groans heard throughout the plane but many people were just happy that the problem was spotted and would be taken care of quickly.

After the announcement, Gino looked around, hoping to get confirmation from a flight attendant. "Miss," he flagged the person down who had brought him a drink. "What's the problem?"

"The only thing I know is that it's an electrical problem. We always try to be extra careful. They need to make sure we're safe." She continued down the aisle making sure other passengers were okay.

Gino was a little uneasy at first, but when he watched the flight crew, he saw everyone acting normal so he relaxed. He flagged another attendant down, "Can I get another drink?"

"We'll be prepping for landing in fifteen minutes, I'll bring you a drink but we'll have to pick up your glass pretty quick."

"Sure, I understand. How about a Jack on the rocks." She returned with the glass and handed it to him.

"I'll be back to collect it; here's some peanuts to go with your drink."

Everything was good, Gino knew once he finished his drink he would soon be back on his way to Miami. The Boeing staff continued their normal preparations for the landing back in Detroit.

NINETEEN

The action at the airport was fast and furious as authorities helped move people away from Gate A38 in the McNamara terminal. Detective Spano along with agents from the FBI were all waiting for flight 1803 that was originally headed to Miami, now on its way back to Metro Airport. "I hope this works," Spano said to the agents working the scene.

"Take it easy, Joe," the special agent stated, "we're good at this. They'll get him off the plane and we'll arrest him. We are lucky that Rossi purchased his tickets under his own name." Brian Sikorski, the Eastern Area FBI Special Agent In Charge, stood at the gate with Spano. "I'm happy to help Chief Mathews, Joe. This guy could be the key to international drug issues as well as your two cases." Although this meant that the FBI would take most of the case over, the Detroit Police would still be involved in solving and closing the murder investigation. Working together was the best way to solve the events surrounding this case. "Just remember Detective, we're handling this capture." Sikorski looked at his cell phone and answered an incoming call. "Yes, we're all set here on the ground. You can get him off the plane first. That will work." Once he hung up he strolled over to some men who were standing near the gate area.

Spano walked to where they stood, "You going to let me know what's happening?"

Sikorski dropped an eye brow, giving the detective a frown to go along with the weird stare. He didn't answer but instead walked away toward where a young lady, who was most likely the airport gate agent, was standing. Spano wasn't happy and felt that he'd been slighted on purpose. He moved to where Sikorski now stood alone. "You know it was the chief who got you involved. It was our team that got all the details for you." Nodding, Sikorski didn't answer. That was a little more than Spano could handle, "I'm talking to you!"

Brian turned, "Joe, I'm just making sure everyone in play is aware of the plan. Right now you're supposed to stand down; this is ours to handle. I'll fill you in when it's appropriate." Crossing his arms, Sikorski directed his attention to the woman at the gate. She was unlocking the door and that's when Joe saw it, a small bulge on her right side—she had a weapon. He realized she was an FBI agent. Spano moved back away from the gate as the players took their places. The two men that Sikorski talked to earlier were in casual clothes. He thought, *must be under cover too.* The door to the gateway was now open and the gate agent moved into the opening. Two men stood at each side of the opening. Looking out of the large wall of glass, Joe saw a plane had moved into position at the gateway.

Sikorski made a hand motion to Detective Spano, advising him that everything was set. Joe smiled, wishing he hadn't acted like a jerk earlier. Spano wasn't used to being a spectator, but that was his assignment this time. He heard the sound of the plane's engines through the opened gate. The gate agent spoke to the first two men who came through, "Welcome back to Detroit; sorry for the inconvenience. Two members of our staff are here to help you so we can re-board quickly."

Gino Rossi smiled as he was followed by the man who was seated right behind him. He asked, "Miss, can we get a drink while we're waiting?"

"Not a problem." She turned to the guys walking behind Gino, "Please escort our guest to the bar area. Everything is on our tab, sir." She watched as the four men headed down the short hallway, surprised that the suspect never turned around. She walked back down the flyway and was gone for a few seconds, coming out and closing the gate. Spano followed Brian Sikorski as the two FBI agents along with the air marshal grabbed Gino, cuffing him before he had any idea what had happened.

"I wouldn't believe it, if I hadn't seen it for myself!" Joe said to Sikorski. The two of them walked behind the agents who escorted Gino Rossi to a waiting vehicle.

***

Detectives Johnson and Baker continued checking on the other owners of the strip club. Baker filled Frederickson in, "Boss, I contacted the Fort Wayne police and filled them in on our case. They were more than happy to run down anything on Buddy Swinton. Chief, he has a record; they're going to send us the details."

Frederickson asked, "Where's Johnson?"

"He left the office, headed to the east side checking on Alexander Ramos."

Frederickson hoped to hear from him once he got to where Ramos lived. "Baker, did Johnson take someone with him like I suggested?"

"Yeah, Boss, he talked to Chief Mathews and they assigned an officer to work with us until I'm off desk duty; the guy's name is Flowers."

"Benny Flowers?"

"Yeah, do you know him?"

"God, makes me feel pretty old. Must be the son. I partnered with his dad when I came out of the academy. I heard his kid joined the force."

Baker didn't know what to say, he was doing math in his head, finally asking, "Is his dad still on the job?"

Frederickson turned and gave Baker a funny look. "No, he retired a long time ago, and if you're wondering, Flowers' dad was a senior officer when they assigned me to work with him."

Baker laughed, "So you really didn't join the force when Judge Woodward was helping assign names to the streets downtown?" Baker laughed and looked over at Mindy who had been listening to the entire conversation.

Mindy had a smile on her face, "Baker, you sure the doctor said you didn't suffer brain damage?" Frederickson laughed at both of them.

When the call came into the SIU office, Mindy answered. "Lieutenant, it's Detective Spano for you." He grabbed the phone and Spano filled him in. "Don, I'm riding with the bureau guys. They've got Rossi; he's cuffed but isn't talking. They're taking him to their downtown headquarters. I'll stay with them; Sikorski said he'd let me sit in on the questioning." He gave Frederickson the details which were hard for him to believe too.

Don turned Baker, "They've got the guy. Hopefully the feds can crack him. Bet he'd give us Perone and who knows who and what else. Spano, you were right."

Spano described the event to Don. "Boss, the man was stunned when they grabbed him. The two agents walking next to him shoved him into the wall and cuffed him. Only thing he said was What the hell! That was the last thing that I heard him say. I watched the two agents put him into their waiting vehicle in front of the terminal. A small crowd started to gather, but the agents were able to shield Gino from anyone with a cell phone hoping to catch it with their cameras."

Frederickson smiled. "If I know Sikorski, he made sure his agents understood that they needed to do this as quickly as possible without getting this guy on the front page or on the six o'clock news."

"Well, his agents did their due diligence making sure they used an empty wing of the terminal and blocked off the exit so people wouldn't be hanging around. They know there are too many cell phones and people snapping photos of everything nowadays. Rossi struggled with the agents. The agents never said anything else, just swept him off to their headquarters."

Frederickson understood, "The bureau doesn't mess around. It was a good idea getting them involved."

Once he hung up, he again turned to Baker. "What did you find out about Singleton?"

"The guy owns a supply company, has contracts with all the major companies. He's using the strip club to entertain customers. Looks like his involvement is to get an advantage on his competition."

They laughed, "Same old crap: Strippers, booze and business. So what else do we do about Singleton?"

"I've got his address and made an appointment to see him later today. I'm not sure if he knows anything about his other partners but I'm going to check it out. We're making progress, now we're just waiting to see what the FBI can get from Gino Rossi."

***

Chief Mathews had filled the mayor in on the new events in the investigation. "We might have the key person involved in both

Franklin's incident and the explosion here at headquarters. The FBI has taken him into custody and are running that part of the case. If all goes well we will get those involved." Mathews didn't give the mayor the theory about the councilman's potential involvement. Because it would be a political coup, he didn't want to taint the situation. The chief had total confidence in both his SIU team and the bureau's involvement. After filling the mayor in, he buzzed Lieutenant Jackson. "I need you to come in here." She entered the office and he asked her to sit. "Lieutenant, I'm concerned." She moved to the edge of the seat. "We've put a lot of this case into the hands of Frederickson and his team; however, do you think I'm putting too much on them?"

Jackson didn't answer immediately. "Chief, when you think about it, they really have had a lot to handle. Harper is recovering from that chest wound." She stopped for a second, chocked up when she then said, " Robbie Askew was killed along with Officer Sowers in the awful bomb blast." She took a deep breath shaking her head, "I don't think Frederickson has fully recovered from last year's car crash." She waited a few seconds, "They also have Baker injured in the explosion."

Mathews knew she was right. "I'm thinking about bringing more officers into play."

Jackson appreciated him asking her opinion. "Chief, before you do that, how about asking Frederickson if he could use extra help. He did have Baker call for an additional officer to partner with Johnson earlier."

"That's your opening, Jackson. Let them feel it's their decision. You can tell Frederickson that you want him to help you select a couple more officers to join their team while they're shorthanded."

"Thanks, good idea."

I want you to do some research for me. I need the four best candidates to present to him. He can pick the two or three that he wants." She left his office to complete the assignment. She had been with the Police Chief for a long time and he knew she'd have some solid suggestions. He also knew that Frederickson would appreciate the help.

***

Nancy Frederickson wanted to ask her husband more questions about the explosion, but he must have left pretty early. She never saw him in the morning, just the pile of his clothes in the hamper. He got in so late they didn't discuss a lot of things. She thought again about the delivery guy that Olivia told her about, *Maybe I should tell Don. Oh well, probably nothing.* The phone rang, and she answered, "Nancy, it's Olivia, did you find out anything about that delivery guy?"

"Thanks for calling. No, I didn't want to bother my husband. They had a big explosion at headquarters and he's been buried in that case. Maybe now I should call and tell him what's going on."

"Okay, but you need to tell him that I saw the same guy again."

"The delivery guy, you saw the delivery guy again, at our office?"

"Yeah, not in the office but when I was leaving, he was sitting in a sports car talking on his phone. Nancy, I think this guy is trouble."

She started to panic. "Olivia, you better tell someone; make sure there's a deputy from the Macomb Sheriff's office who knows about this. I'll let Don know what you said. He'll probably call the sheriff and fill him in."

"I guess you're right. I'll call them now."

"Let me know everything that they tell you and let them know that the guy asked for me and that I'm a Detroit detective's wife."

"Nancy, good thing we got him on surveillance."

"Yes, they'll want that." Nancy felt a lot better now that Olivia was calling the cops. *I'm glad she's got the guy on tape.* Now she had to call Don.

TWENTY

Tony Virgilio was asked to a meeting with the councilman at the Eastern Market. Perone ordered that they'd meet at midnight in Shed 5. Although their other partner, Vinnie La Russo, the owner of the property, had been put out of business, their group still controlled the shed. Perone knew no one would be around at that time of night. Virgilio had Lorenzo join him, never wanting to be left alone, not even with his partner. They waited for close to a half hour, "Lorenzo, if he doesn't show we've got problems. I'm not going be to holding the bag on this." Tony remembered what previously happened to his two other partners, La Russo and Castellanos. Both of them were now serving life terms and the councilman out and now running for mayor. Suddenly headlights were headed their way. "Lorenzo, I want you to duck behind the pallets," pointing to the stacks near the back of the shed. "Stay low, don't do anything unless it looks like it's going to go bad."

The black Suburban slowly pulled toward the entrance, dimming it's headlights and stopping behind Virgilio's Cadillac. Tony watched as two men stepped out, scanning the area before the councilman exited. Perone was a tall, slender man, in his fifties, with a full head of dark hair, greying at the temples. He was the city's best looking version of George Clooney. Reaching out with his right hand, "Tony, glad you could meet me." Virgilio wondered, *Do I have a choice?* Perone scanned the shed, "You here alone?"

"Yeah, you said to come alone, why, do I need backup?"

"No, I just wanted to confirm that you're here by yourself. Hope you don't mind but Sam needs to check you."

Tony stepped back, "What the hell, you ain't touching me!"

"Tony, can't be too careful, just gotta make sure you're not wired." Lorenzo wasn't close enough to hear everything but didn't like what was taking place. He held the Glock 9mm in his right hand, ready to come to his father's aide if needed. "Tony, I'd expect you'd want to be extra careful too."

Sam, one of the men who accompanied the councilman moved forward. He said, "Tony, I just want to pat you down. Would you please raise your arms." Taking a deep breath, he raised his arms, as Sam ran his hands across his chest, around his back and reached up to the back of his neck. "He's clean."

Virgilio wasn't happy, "Maybe I need to pat you down, Councilman."

Perone let out a hardy laugh, "That's one thing I've always liked about you, a great sense of humor." He looked around and grabbed a wooden crate, sitting on it, He started the conversation, "Gino called me after you wired him the money, said he was sure he got that detective."

Virgilio was still pissed that Gino didn't carry out killing Frederickson. "Yeah, he's going to be living it up on my dime, but the detective is still alive." Tony still stood, looking over at Sam and the other man who seemed to keep scanning the interior of the shed.

"Tony, sit! We need to plan our next move. I saw that special report today too. How in the hell that detective got out of this is hard to believe." Virgilio was still standing. ""You need to sit down, you're making me nervous."

"I'm good. I sit too much, it's not good for you." Perone ran his fingers through his hair with his right hand. "Okay, have it your way. We've got to find the deputy mayor. The cops have him hidden somewhere. I've tried to find out but my sources haven't had any luck. He can hurt us."

Tony was feeling a little better about the meeting, "Your guy, Gino, failed at everything. He didn't kill the mayor's deputy, and worst of all, he missed Frederickson."

"Okay, are you done with past history? Now we got to find John Franklin."

"What're you thinking?"

Turning toward where Sam stood, Perone offered, "I've got a few officers who might be able to help. If we can locate him, I will get someone to do the job for us."

"How about Frederickson?"

"He isn't going to be a problem; he's probably laying low knowing that someone is still gunning for him, and if we get Franklin, they can't connect us to anything." Perone stood, "I'm guessing that you're responsible for the shooting at Campus Martius?"

Virgilio didn't want to address it. "Not my concern, your campaign against the mayor is your thing."

Perone stared at him. "Well, if you were trying to help me, you only brought people to the mayor's side." Virgilio didn't answer. "If you've got a hitman out there, he missed everyone. Frederickson and the mayor were both on the podium. Who was this detective he killed, Amy Harper?"

"My responsibility is Frederickson, you were supposed to handle Franklin. How did your guy, Gino, get him drunk, kill the stripper and plant the body under his car? He was supposed to set the frame up. Why didn't he kill the guy?"

Perone didn't like the lecture. "Okay, Gino screwed up, for both of us. How are we going to get Franklin so both of us can relax?'

Virgilio thought for a few seconds, "You need to handle that, I'm out."

When Perone was leaving, they did not shake hands like they did when he arrived, and as Perone headed back to the Suburban, followed by Sam and the driver, he turned, "I'll let you know when we find him." The partnership looked like it was getting a bit rocky to all involved.

Tony watched as they drove off. Once the Suburban disappeared from view, Lorenzo stepped out from the rack of pallets. He stood next to Tony who kept staring at the empty road. "So, what are you thinking, dad?"

"I think the councilman might want to eliminate anyone who can tie him to this. We might want to take out some insurance." His son nodded, not sure exactly what his dad meant by that.

"You know you can count on me doing anything you need me to do."

"Yeah, I know. Right now I'm glad that he doesn't know you've been involved in any of this." He put his hand on Zo's face, "I need you to lay low, you can't be involved in the next step."

"But, I ..."

"Lorenzo, listen to me, you need to let me handle this."

"But..."

"I love you son, but honest, I can handle it."

Lorenzo didn't like it but shook his head in agreement. "Dad, remember, I'm here for you." The two embraced, before heading back out of the Eastern Market.

***

Lieutenant Jackson entered the chief's office. "Sir, I've got four great officers for you to give to Frederickson for his consideration to add to the SIU squad." She handed him the short list and he looked it over.

Chief Mathews looked up at her with a smile on his face. "I like it; really, all four would be perfect for the team. They've all had outstanding careers, been part of critical investigations and I'm sure Frederickson would agree. I'll run it by him later when he gets back from Novi." Mathews said, "I hope to hear from Don soon. They're running down every lead on the other three owners of the strip club, making sure none of them are tied to the councilman. We've got to make sure this won't get tossed out of court on a technicality." The district attorney advised them that it was critical to uncover everything about all four of the club owners. With the potential charges they needed details. This wouldn't go anywhere without proof.

Detective Baker continued putting everything together that he learned from the Fort Wayne Police Department. Buddy Swinton owned a strip club near the airport there. Baker said, "Detectives in Indiana uncovered that Swinton bought the club in Fort Wayne ten years ago. Records show he joined the group that bought the Detroit club back in 2014. Guess what, Boss, both clubs are under an international company ownership. The whole thing is tangled up and finding all owners is almost impossible."

Frederickson questioned, "Can we untangle any of it?"

"Well, problem is, nothing links these guys to Perone other than the fact that they were all part of the international enterprise. The Fort Wayne police did a complete records search on Swinton. There's nothing connecting him in any way to Perone other than joint club ownership."

"Good job, Baker, but I'm afraid we've got problems. Without that manager, CK, who said these guys were the owners, we don't have much else. The D.A. approved our official arrest of CK, charging him as a material witness. At least we can hold him for the time being. Did Johnson find out anything on Ramos?"

"Looks like Ramos also bought into the conglomerate in 2014. Boss, something doesn't make sense. Both these guys came in at the same time; that's the same year Perone became president of the City Council. Maybe Perone was trying to cut ties with the club."   The case was becoming more entangled and Frederickson knew it. They needed John Franklin's statement that it was Perone who introduced him to Gino, and the feds had to get Gino talking. Baker was about to hang up when he remembered, "Hey, we've got that ledger from the club, can't we use that as ownership proof?"

"You'd hope so, but it took the manager to show us how those four names were listed." Frederickson was heading back from a meeting with Singleton, the last of the four club owners, "I think you've got something there on all of it happening the same year. Singleton said he was given the offer to join the organization in 2014. Of course he's saying it was a good write-off. We'll need to get the Securities Exchange involved in this. I wonder if Perone was sole owner before he sold off parts of the club."

The team was getting key details but it now seemed to lead them in a circle. Frederickson asked himself, *If Perone was selling off the strip club, most likely to run for mayor, why did he keep part ownership? It just didn't make sense.*

TWENTY-ONE

The news outlets were covering an important event downtown. It was seven a.m. and Councilman Perone knew that he'd have all the stations covering him during the highly watched morning news time slot. Perone stood on the corner of Woodward and Jefferson in front of the Spirit of Detroit statue, with cameras rolling. His publicist made sure every news station knew he'd be making a big announcement. Perone had a great speaking voice. "I'm standing here today, pledging to the citizens of Detroit that when I'm elected mayor, I'll clean up City Hall." Perone went on, "We've had a police detective murdered," turning and pointing up Woodward, "right down the street at Campus Martius and now the city's Public Safety building on Michigan Avenue had a bomb placed in the garage, killing two more police officers. We've heard nothing from the mayor or our police chief that they have a suspect in either event. The only thing we've gotten is a partial explanation from one of the detectives. The people of the city deserve and demand answers. What are the mayor and chief of police doing to solve these and stop this rash of killings?" Pausing for effect, "This week is just another example of the problems this administration hasn't solved." He paused again as the crowd applauded. "I'm running for mayor to clean up this mess. If elected, no, *when* elected, I'll get to the bottom of these and other unsolved crimes."   Cheers rang out from the couple hundred people in attendance, many holding "Perone for Mayor" signs. Although this was an obvious political move, he brought out questions, ones that the Free Press had covered in recent articles, especially since the last two incidents.

Carole Newton, the reporter from Channel 7, held a microphone near the podium and leaned in, "Councilman, do you have any idea who might be responsible for these crimes?"

Perone stood tall and stared into the cameras, "I'm calling a special meeting of the City Council today. I want to draft a motion to have the police chief answer questions on these investigations. If he can't have answers to satisfy us, we'll ask the mayor to fire him. Too many people have died on our streets, it has to end and end now!" That brought another round of cheers.

Carole smiled, having reported on this type of political event in the past. She knew that Perone was talking to the voters through the personal appearance, but more importantly, trying to show his strength as a leader. Once Perone left the podium, Carole continued standing in front of the Spirit of Detroit statue with the camera still rolling. She spoke into the camera, recapping the event, "We've just heard Council President Edward Perone asking questions about the two incidents that we've all witnessed this week. I plan to ask the mayor if he'd like to address these issues. Yesterday, I brought you Detective Donald Frederickson of the SIU department, and asked about the explosion at headquarters. He didn't have any leads on the bomber. Frederickson did tell us the names of the two officers who were killed in the bomb blast. Our prayers, as we know yours do too, go out to the families of Detective Robby Askew and Officer Angela Sowers. Both officers were assigned to headquarters. We'll let you know when the services will be held." She made her way into the Frank Murphy Hall of Justice, camera and microphone in hand. Two other reporters followed her along with their cameramen. She entered the building, telling the guard, "I'm here to see the mayor."

The guard standing at the hall's entrance, held his hand up, "I'm sorry, the mayor isn't here and you can't bring those cameras in here without an appointment."

"Can you tell us where he is?"

"You'll have to contact his office, they might be able to help you."

The reporters all left without a rebuttal to the charges leveled by the councilman. Carole contacted the Channel 7 on-air news team. "I'm headed back to the Public Safety building. Hopefully I'll have something for the noon news."

***

The mayor was meeting again with the police chief. While they were talking, Lieutenant Jackson entered, "I think you're both going to want to see this." She turned on the television in the office.

They saw Perone standing in front of the Spirit of Detroit statue. "Son of a bitch!" yelled the mayor, pounding on the chief's desk. "What's that asshole doing?"

"Calm down, Jerry," the chief suggested.

"Talk about piggybacking on other's misfortunes, that jackass! You know his team planted all those people waving signs."

"I know, trust me, people aren't buying that. The election is one month off and he's nowhere close to you in the polls."

The mayor looked back at the chief. "He's going after you too, Barry." The Chief nodded. They continued to watch as Carole Newton asked questions. "I thought you said Frederickson covered the bombing and Newton said she'd lay low until we could give her more."

"Yeah, we met with her and Frederickson covered the bombing, but she's a reporter and if there's a story, I'm sure she's going to cover it." Both men knew that the news media was just doing their job. The public had a right to know what was going on. Once the news coverage ended, the chief sat down. "Mayor, we've got to fill you in on a few more details."

The mayor gave Chief Mathews a questioning look, "Okay, what haven't you told me?"

"Why don't you sit down. I need to get Frederickson down here."

Once they were all together in the chief's office, Mathews gave the mayor the new details in their case. The mayor jumped up from his seat. "You're telling me that Perone owns a strip club on Eight Mile, and you think he's involved in both the frame-up of my deputy mayor and the bombing here?" He paced around the office. "We need to tell the press who this guy really is."

"Slow down, Jerry. The FBI is working on the case too. They've made progress with the suspect. We need to confirm what he told them first. If we act too soon, Perone might be able to avoid prosecution. There's a good chance that he's involved in all of this."

The mayor settled down. "I want to know everything you've got and what else you think he's involved in."

"I can't do that right now. The FBI is key in the whole thing, Jerry. If they get the proof on Perone, they can charge him with racketeering. One of the club partners, a guy named Buddy Swinton, is the owner of another strip joint in Fort Wayne." The mayor stared back at Chief Mathews who continued, "Perone screwed up; he owns the syndicate that owns the club on Eight Mile and the Fort Wayne club. They're both part of the group." Mathews saw the mayor relaxing, "Jerry, they might even have him for murder for hire."

Now the mayor was smiling. "When will you talk to the FBI again?"

"I talked to the FBI Chief, Brian Sikorski, earlier. He said they've made good progress and the key suspect was cooperating. He promised to update me later today."

Jerry stood, "Chief, I'm glad you and your detectives, along with the bureau, are handling this. You both have my full support. Frederickson nodded.

"Sir, my team is just doing our job. We're just going to continue protecting the city."

Mathews stood, "Jerry, you can't tell anyone what we just told you. If you even allude to it, Perone will start covering everything up that we've got. You know, no one's more connected in this city than Perone; we just need another day to put it together. The district attorney is aware of what we're doing and he's going to let the feds charge Perone first. We'll have him in court for years."

The mayor asked, "What if I inform Perone that we're getting close to arresting a potential suspect?"

Mathews thought about it for a second, "Yeah, that might work, but be careful, don't really tell him anything, just tease him."

The meeting ended with both men smiling and shaking hands.

***

Tony Virgilio knew the meeting with Perone the previous night wasn't a good sign. Why would his partner want to meet there. Perone seemed a bit paranoid. Tony called his son, wanting to make sure the kid didn't do something rash. He knew Lorenzo could be a bit impetuous. Tony walked around the back room of the market, waiting for Lorenzo to show up. When the Mustang pulled up in front, Sal spotted him and immediately went into the back to let

Tony know the kid had arrived, "Boss, Zo is here."

Virgilio was happy that his son got the message and came right away to the market. "Thanks, Sal." He walked to the front where a few customers milled around. Spotting some regulars, he said, "Hello Mrs. Cochran, how're the kids?" She smiled, appreciating that the owner recognized her. They talked for a second and when Lorenzo entered, Tony excused himself and said, "Lorenzo," hugging his son. The two of them talked to the customer before walking to the back room.

Lorenzo knew something was wrong, especially with his father calling him to head right on over. This was the second time in a week that his dad made that request. "Okay, Dad, what's up?"

"We've got problems. First Gino didn't get the target and our partner hasn't called since we meet late last night. That bothers me. He usually needs something from me by now. I didn't like that last meeting at the Eastern Market and I know you were concerned. Did you see the guy on television, big political speech, saying he'll get the City's Council to fire the police chief? Of course we've still got that damn Frederickson running around town giving news updates."

Lorenzo listened to his father, knowing that when they missed killing Frederickson again, that it was eating away at his dad. "You told me Perone had his eyes on a bigger prize and you knew he'd make a political play for power, maybe that's why he isn't calling." Lorenzo waited a second and decided to bring up the subject. "I think it's time to use the bipod that I planted on the rooftop."

Tony looked back at him. "I want to make sure I cause as much damage as possible with it."

"Of course we're not sure where they put it, but I put as much explosive as possible in the hollow tubes. With the trigger that is keyed to my cell phone, we'll kill anyone in the vicinity of where it's stored."

"Maybe another explosion will have all of them running for cover. I want to get as many of that special team as possible. Hopefully Frederickson will be near it." That brought a smile to his face. "Let me know when you're going to do it."

Lorenzo nodded, wishing he had a contact inside who knew where the team stored the bipod. "Do you know Perone's guy? He might try to find out for us."

"I don't know how to contact him; I'll try Perone, maybe he'll return my call." Virgilio was still mad when he thought about Gino, knowing he paid him a lot and Frederickson is still very much involved in the case. "I've tried to contact Gino, but he's not returning my calls. We paid him for the bomb blast but I wish I hadn't until it was clear that he got the job done."

"Dad, he'll probably call you later."

"Lorenzo, I've known too many of these guys. He'll protect himself first and foremost. You never know but he just might try to hang all of this on me and next thing I know he's having me hauled in for everything."

"Yeah, guys like him never leave you around to testify. If I know you dad, you got some shit on him too."

Tony looked at his kid, "I don't have enough to prove that he's behind everything we've done." Virgilio knew the shooting at Greektown was all his idea. He never ran it by Perone, just personal payback. Now his partner was shutting him out; that didn't bode well."

"What can I do for you, anything you want?"

"I appreciate that but right now, the best thing we can do is protect ourselves. I have some papers hidden that no one else knows about." He gave Lorenzo the secret location. "I want you to get the documents and keep them where you'll be able to get to them if we need 'em."

"Do you think we need to let Anthony know what's going on. Perone knows you have two sons; he'll need to be careful."

"Your brother is safe up at school, we don't need to bother him."

When Lorenzo left the market, he was concerned. He'd never seen his dad like that. He knew whatever was in those papers, they must be pretty important.

***

Chief Mathews left headquarters for his meeting at the FBI building. He was getting an update on the interrogation of Gino Rossi from Brian Sikorski. "Chief, we've had our guys grilling your suspect over the past day. We've got some surprising information. Although he didn't connect the councilman to the crimes, he did tell us that he knew the deputy mayor. The guy is pretty slick, the entire time, from picking him up at the airport to now, he's claiming that your John Franklin got a message to him hoping to escape your custody."

Mathews was stunned, "You mean he's saying that Franklin contacted him?"

"Oh yeah. He says not only did Franklin contact him, but when we showed him photos from your surveillance showing him sneaking in the building, that's when he said he was there to help Franklin escape." Both men paused, not sure what to believe. "He said he was caught in the explosion and crawled out of the basement with help from firefighters. We're checking with them now."

Mathews was puzzled. Could John Franklin be involved more than they thought? "I'm sure no one knew that we we're holding Franklin at headquarters. Our detectives removed all the phones from the room where we're holding him. How would he get a message to this guy?"

Sikorski shook his head, "I think you better run a check at your headquarters, something's not right."

TWENTY-TWO

John Franklin paced along one of the four walls of the room that had become smaller to him each day he'd been kept there. He was beginning to think that a prison cell might be better than this. With no windows to look out of, the room was closing in on him. He mumbled, "How long have I been here." The last time the detectives questioned him, he felt it didn't go well. Detective Spano was pretty aggressive and left Franklin thinking he'd be charged with murder regardless of what they found. When the door opened, Franklin jumped up, "It's about time one of you came to talk to me. I want to get out of here. Can you arrange that?" He stood in the middle of the room, hands on his hips and a frown on his face.

Baker looked at the man, "Okay, calm down!" holding his hands up in front of him. "I'm just bringing more groceries for you." Baker put the two bags on the counter and kept an eye on Franklin who looked pretty nervous. He had to make sure the man didn't charge him. Never take anything for granted. "I want you to move to the chair," pointing to one of the loungers. "I'll fill you in on the case, but you're going to have to sit down." Baker waited as Franklin walked in a circle then moved to the chair.

Franklin was apprehensive and suddenly realized that the officer had a bandage on the left side of his face, "What happened to you?"

"Car accident. You need to sit down."

Franklin sat and asked, "What was that loud noise yesterday? I thought I heard an explosion. Am I really safe here?" Before Baker could answer, Franklin stood back up. "That other detective," waving his arms, "he said you guys still think I killed that woman. What's going on? What was that noise?"

Baker only planned to keep Franklin calm, but the guy was very agitated. He had hoped by giving him some information on the case, the guy would chill out. "Sit down, I'll answer your questions, but you've got to sit." Once the man sat back down, Baker continued,

"The noise you heard was just a transformer outside the building, and yes, you're safer here than anywhere else." He waited making sure the guy bought that excuse. "Now, on the case, our chief and the mayor met earlier. They've got a plan, but it might take another day or two."

Franklin was shaking his head, "Another day or two, I'm going stir crazy!" He paused, "Hey, how are you keeping my name out of the news? I haven't seen a newspaper in days, can I get a paper? How about the television set that was in here? Your guys took it away."

"I'll try to get you a paper but no promise on a TV set. We've got the story under control. The mayor told the press a few days ago that you were taking time off for family issues. We've kept the investigation on the body under your car off the front page, at least so far, but that isn't going to last long if we can't give the press a suspect, someone besides you of course."

Franklin frowned when Baker said that, he jumped up again, "I didn't do it, you know that."

"Keep your shorts on. We've got to have proof and we're working on it. You've got to remain calm, our team is doing everything we can to solve this." Baker moved toward the door, "You better put those groceries away before they spoil." He walked out of the room and locked the door behind him.

Franklin was still puzzled: Where did this case stand? How long had he been kept there? Christ it had to be a week. He resumed pacing as he emptied the two bags, "Chips, beer. Thank God. I need a beer."

***

Detective Frederickson looked at his watch, "I need to call Nancy." He knew she'd have a lot of questions. He dialed, surprised that she answered on the first ring. "Honey, I'm so sorry, I should have told you what's going on."

She was so glad to hear his voice, a tear ran down her cheek. "I'm fine." She took a deep breath, "Can you please tell me now what happened?"

He knew he'd have to give her everything. "Okay, better sit

down." Don went over the events, everything from the shooting at Campus Martius to the explosion. When he said that it was his car that exploded, he stopped talking, waiting for her reaction. To his surprise she was pretty calm. "Nancy, you there?"

"Yes honey, I'm here. Just trying to think. I'm guessing what you're not telling me is that the bomb was meant for you."

"That's what we're thinking. Askew and Baker were headed out of town and I suggested using my vehicle."

"Don't blame yourself, it isn't your fault."

"I know, at least now I know. At first I was stunned." He paused, "Maybe I shouldn't have told them to take my car, but then I realized that I didn't do this, Nancy. I'm just pissed. We're going to get these guys."

"How can I help?"

"Just knowing you're always there for me, that's all I need."

Nancy Frederickson was happy that she knew all the details of what had happened; now she had to tell him her story. "Don, I've got to tell you something." Once she finished the story about the delivery guy, he wasn't exactly as calm as she was.

"What! Nancy, why didn't you tell me right away? Where are you now?"

"I'm okay. I'm sitting on our patio at home."

"I'm sending a squad car over right now. Get inside the house and lock all the doors and windows. I'll call you with the name of the officer; don't let anyone else in." Before she could answer he hung up. She knew she shouldn't have told him about the delivery guy, after all, it was probably nothing and he had a lot on his plate. Her phone rang again, it was her husband. "Nancy, I've got Officer Handle headed your way. He will have the lobby guard call you when he gets there. Make sure you get his name. Handle!"

"Don, take it easy, you're going to have a stroke! I'm sure Officer Handle will be more protection than I need."

He needed to reassure her. "I'm fine, just making sure the most important person in the world is safe. Nancy, I love you."

She smiled to herself, "I love you too. I'll wait for Officer Handle." She thought again about what Olivia told her that they might have the guy on the building's surveillance camera. She made another call, "Olivia, it's Nancy. What did the Macomb sheriff's office say?"

"They want me to meet them at the office. I hope we've got a good view of him on the camera."

"You can't go there by yourself. I'll meet you there."

"No! Nancy, I'll be okay. I won't get out of my car until I see the sheriff's car, I promise."

"Okay, but you call me when he gets there. Let me know once the sheriff checks out the surveillance. Don will want to see what they've got on film."

"Sure, I'm headed there now."

When she hung up the phone rang. "Mrs. Frederickson, this is Tommy downstairs at the desk. I've got an Officer Handle here, says you're expecting him."

"Thanks, Tommy, you can send him up." She waited at the door of their unit and when the elevator doors opened, she saw a tall, handsome Detroit Police Officer exit. He headed toward her unit and spotted her. "Hello Officer, may I see your badge please." He showed her the badge and introduced himself. Once she was sure he was who her husband sent, she let him in.

"Mrs. Frederickson, your husband wants me to escort you downtown to headquarters."

"Yes, I understand but we need to make one stop first." He wasn't sure that was okay. "I'm going to call him and let him know. You can talk to him if you need, Officer."

"That's not necessary. I'm doing what I'm told to."

She dialed Don's cell number, "Don, Officer Handle is here. We'll be leaving soon but I'd like to head to my office and get a copy of the video that Olivia thinks we got of the delivery guy for you."

"Nancy, I'm ahead of you After you gave me the details, I talked to the sheriff's office; they're sending a copy here once they've got it."

She chuckled, "I should have known you'd do that. I'll be headed to headquarters.

***

Tom Baker continued surfing the web, looking for anything tying Gino Rossi to their cases. He hoped that they'd find some evidence linking Rossi to Councilman Perone and any of the people at the Eight Mile club. They already had a case with Perone tied to Buddy Swinton, the owner of the Fort Wayne strip joint. Now, if they could link Rossi and Perone into the club on Eight Mile, it would let them tie Perone to the dead stripper under the deputy mayor's vehicle. Frederickson walked over, "You find anything Baker?"

"No, Perone kept himself pretty much out of the picture. None of the dancers or the manager ever saw him there. I tried checking every lead possible. I was hoping that Perone signed something, even a delivery receipt, but no luck."

Frederickson gave him the details that Nancy had given him regarding the delivery guy at her old office. "Maybe the video from the office will give us something." He looked up. Nancy had just entered with Officer Handle. Frederickson was happy to see her. "Thanks, Handle." He hugged his wife.

"Did you get the video from Macomb County?"

"No, not yet."

Nancy walked over to where Baker was sitting, "Tom, I'm glad you're doing okay; how's Amy?"

Baker was surprised that Nancy wanted to know how he was and about Amy, "I talked to her earlier; she's getting better but wished she could help with the case. I never told her I was in the same hospital after the blast as she is. That wouldn't be received very well."

Nancy nodded, "Be careful Tom, you don't want her to find out on her own. Women don't like that."

He knew she was right, "Yeah, I promise I'll tell her soon."

"You all are working so hard on this, it will turn out okay, I'm sure of it." Baker smiled. She turned back to her husband, "What can I do to help?"

Frederickson knew she wouldn't be happy just sitting around. "Maybe call Olivia and see if the sheriff's office found anything for us." She was glad he gave her something to do.

TWENTY-THREE

Lorenzo Virgilio wanted to help his father. He called his friend. "Bobby, I'm going to need that gun I asked you to hide. Can you bring it to me?"

"Sure, where should I meet you?"

"Get the gun and I'll call and let you know where to go." Once he hung up, he called his dad. "Dad, I've got an idea, how about I set that bomb off that I planted in the bipod at headquarters..."

Tony immediately stopped him, "I don't want you doing anything yet. Right now the cops have no idea we're involved. My concern right now is our political friend."

"I understand but let me finish." He waited a second, and when his dad didn't say anything, he continued, "After I trigger the blast, I'll be in position near the building and I can shoot anyone running out. If the blast doesn't get that detective, I'll get him." Lorenzo thought he had the perfect plan.

"I appreciate what you're doing, but we need to keep a low profile right now. That bomb you planted in the bipod will come in handy, but not yet. I promise as soon as I know what our next move is, I'll let you help."

Lorenzo was disappointed but would do whatever his dad wanted; however, he had to do something, anything to help his dad. "Dad, think about it for a little while, don't just say no."

"Figlio," Tony often called Lorenzo son in Italian, "I know you mean well but I need to handle something with my partner first. I might need your help after I meet with him again."

"Okay, Dad, but know that I'm ready to do anything for you."

"I know, figlio. I love you."

"Me too, Dad." Once he hung up, he called Bobby, "Hey, forget the gun for right now, but I'm coming by to pick you up. We need to take a ride downtown, maybe we can get a better handle on the situation for future plans." It was agreed they'd drive downtown, making plans in case Zo got approval from his dad to put things into action.

***

The Macomb sheriff's deputy arrived at the office building on Hall Road and was going over the surveillance video with Olivia, the office manager. She called out, "There, stop the video, that's the guy!" She was standing as the officer and the building security guy ran the video back. Pointing, "It's him," she shouted. "We got him on the tape." Olivia was pleased that they had caught the delivery guy on their surveillance system.

The deputy knew this was important. He told the security guy, "I need two copies of this, in fact, let it run a copy of the whole time he's captured on the tape. How long does your system keep the tapes?"

"It runs on a seven-day loop, it's taped over."

"Then I want the original too."

"Okay, I'll make two copies and give you the original."

Olivia was pleased. She hurried to call Nancy. "Hey Nancy, we got him, he's all over the surveillance tape."

Nancy was thrilled, "Olivia, is the deputy still there?"

"Yes."

"I'm sure Don will want to talk to the deputy, can you put him on the line?" She handed the phone to her husband, "Don, they got the delivery guy on the tape. I figured you'd want to talk to the deputy."

He smiled at her, "This is Detective Frederickson."

"Detective, we're happy to aid in your investigation. The surveillance tape at your wife's office has a pretty clear shot of the suspect. I'm having them make a copy for you and one for our office plus we'll get the original tape just in case it's needed."

"Great job, Deputy, we appreciate your help. I'll make sure to call the sheriff and fill him in on everything." Once he hung up, he turned to Nancy, "You got him, babe. I'm going to send an officer to the sheriff's department to get a copy for us. Once we see it, I'm sure we'll find this guy." She was happy that she finally told her husband about this. She smiled at him. "Now can I head back home?"

"No, not yet, I'll need you to check out the guy for us when the tape arrives. Maybe you've seen him before." She understood.

"Nancy, how about we send out for something to eat. The guys are hungry and I bet you are too."

"Sure, but I'm more interested in seeing this creep arrested than eating." That brought a chuckle from him. Nancy walked towards Mindy's desk. He knew that they would be able to talk about the case without interference from him.

Frederickson needed to inform the team about what was going on. "Guys, we may have the guy who was asking about Nancy on video. We're getting a copy from the sheriff's office."

Spano was pleased. "I know that makes it easier. It's pretty rough when our family gets threats."

Frederickson agreed. "Joe, I appreciate what you were trying to do before." The two men nodded, knowing the events of the past week had everyone on edge.

***

Chief Mathews was aware that the SIU team was getting a video with help from the sheriff's office. He called the sheriff to acknowledge their help. "I just called to thank you and your deputies for helping with our case," Mathews knew it was always good to keep solid relationships with the county officials.

"Glad we could help. I've put a copy of the video in our safe and given the original to the county district attorney. He'll hang onto it in case you need it for a trial." While the two men discussed the cooperation of their departments, the tape arrived upstairs.

The SIU team gathered around as the video played. "That's the guy!" Spano yelled.

"What guy?"

"It's the same guy, the guy from the casino hotel. He was in one of the rooms on the top floor of the Greektown Hotel. We questioned him. He said he and his buddy were at the Tigers game. We checked his alibi and he was there. Either him or his friend have something to do with the shooter, or was the shooter!"

Baker pressed in closer, thinking, *Was this the guy who shot Detective Harper?* "I want in on arresting him!"

Frederickson held his hand up, "Hold on guys." Calling his wife over, "Nancy, think, have you ever seen this guy before?"

She was now standing in the group watching the video play, "No, I don't think so. Can you play it again?" They played it through one more time. "No, I'm sure I've never seen him; who is it?"

Frederickson turned back to Detective Spano, "Joe, you already know his name?"

"Oh yes." He had grabbed his note pad as soon as he saw the video, "Lorenzo Virgilio." He looked puzzled.

"What is it Joe?"

"When I ran everyone's alibi, this guy looked pretty legit. He has season tickets for the Tigers and is a regular at the hotel and casino. I've even got the names of the people who sat next to him at the ball game. We checked into his whereabouts the night before. He was playing blackjack until three in the morning."

Frederickson didn't remember him. "Joe, did I talk to this guy?"

"Maybe, I'm not sure. You were on the roof checking out the situation up there."

Baker had run Lorenzo Virgilio's name through their data base. "Hey, our records show that the guy's clean, no record, no arrests." They moved to his desk. Baker scrolled down as he read aloud, "Lorenzo Virgilio, twenty-two, adopted son of Tony and Rosa Virgilio of St. Clair Shores. The kid is a high school graduate, no college, maybe he works for a furniture company?"

Spano shook his head, "Could this be a coincidence?" He looked up at Frederickson.

"Joe, you know I don't believe in coincidences. We've got the same guy staying in a room at Greektown on the top floor where we found evidence leading to where Harper was shot. Now he shows up at my wife's workplace, looking for her with a supposed delivery that she didn't order. He's the guy. Not sure how he fits in, but he's the guy. I want a full court press on this."

Spano said, "Baker, run data on his dad. Also check on the other guy that was with Lorenzo at the hotel. He's got to be involved."

Nancy was confused. "Who is this guy; why not bring him in?"

Frederickson knew she wanted to be involved. "Nancy, let us run some checks first. You hadn't seen him before so we need to check it out further." He hoped she'd accept that for now. "We can't just start bringing people in without something incriminating. Besides, if he's involved, I don't want to tip them off that we're on to them." When he thought she understood his points, he hoped to move her away from the investigation. "Nancy, please get with Mindy and see if our food has arrived yet."

She looked at her husband, knowing it was his way of telling her that she needed to let them handle this. "Sure, I'll let you know when it gets here." Nancy moved back to Mindy's desk and the two of them checked on the food order first, then discussed the events without interference from the team.

Baker had Tony Virgilio and his wife's information on his computer screen. Everyone was crowded around. Baker read what he found, "Tony Virgilio, owner of a meat market in St. Clair Shores, been there for over twenty-five years. They have two kids, Lorenzo, and Anthony who attends the University of Michigan." Baker was shaking his head. "I'm confused, these guys look pretty normal. What in the hell was this kid doing at Nancy's office?"

Spano thought, *There had to be more to this than the information they're showing.* "Don, what do you want us to do?"

"I'm thinking we might have stumbled onto a bigger picture. Joe, how about running his alibi again and the details on his roommate from that day." He looked over at Baker, "Tom, I know you want to be involved; maybe run more background on this family. They seem too perfect." He turned his attention to Spano and Johnson, "I want a twenty-four hour team following both the father and son."

"Boss, who do you want involved in the surveillance?"

"The chief said he and Lieutenant Jackson have candidates for us to help in the case. Joe, go get those names and choose a few people to work with us on it."

"How much do we tell these people?"

"Everything, Joe. If they pan out, I'm sure we'd need to add people to our team." Spano seemed puzzled; was someone leaving the unit? He knew they'd have to replace Askew.

TWENTY-FOUR

Tony Virgilio made the call that would help him decide what his options should be. He never called the councilman directly in the past; always going through a contact. When the person picked up, he asked, "Is he in?" Perone made sure that he and Virgilio never left a trace of them being in direct contact.

"Right now he's planning to call a special meeting of council members. He'll call you later."

The person who delivered the answer, hung up. Virgilio wasn't happy. He wanted to confer with the councilman before making a move. Tony walked to where Sal was waiting on customers. There were a few people standing at the counter. "Hello, Mrs. Russell, how can I help you?"

She pointed at the display of steaks. "I'd like three strip steaks, a pound of lean ground beef and a couple of pork chops."

He slid open the glass door and pointed at the steaks so she could choose. Once she did that he started to package everything up for her. Tony wanted to keep busy, he was concerned about his partner. What was he up to? Once she left, the shop was empty. "Sal, can you handle the rest of the day?"

"Sure, it's getting late, things will be slow." Sal knew Tony had been troubled, but not sure what was going on.

Tony went into the back room and hang up his apron. He thought about Lorenzo's suggestion, knowing the bipod held an option that would cause havoc when it was triggered. Maybe he needed to re-think his son's proposal. The police must still be scrambling after the bombing; maybe it was time to strike again.

***

Councilman Eddie Perone was calling the other members of the City Council, hoping to get them to agree to a special meeting to discuss the current events and what they should do. They agreed that the morning meeting with the news media went better than expected. Perone had his key man with him. He turned to him and said, "I've got to follow up with action." He continued, "Convincing other members of the council should be pretty easy; they're all up for re-election in a few months and none of them want to be seen as holding up an internal investigation into the police department." After calls to council members, Perone quickly had agreement from everyone. They'd call a special meeting for tomorrow afternoon. The councilman was making a move, one that would have positive effects on his race to win the mayoral election. Although he had been behind in recent polls, he had been gaining momentum and he wanted to capitalize on that. Perone knew he had three members in his pocket and knew it would be easy to sway others. Once the meeting was set he needed to handle other pressing issues.

The aide informed him, "Sir, you've had two calls from Mr. Virgilio." Standing with his bodyguard, he replied, "What did Tony want?"

"He didn't say, just needed you to call him. He seemed pretty nervous to me."

Perone shook his head, not willing to talk to him again, not until he met with the council. "We explained everything the other night, what in the hell didn't he understand?" He started to pace. "I'm concerned; we've come too far to have him screw this up." He looked back at the big man standing across from him. "Maybe it's time to clean this relationship up."

The bodyguard knew what he meant. "I can handle it, sir, but how about that kid of his. He's become a real problem. He's always at the club and pushing himself on the girls."

Perone nodded, "I've wondered if it was Virgilio and his kid who orchestrated the shooting at Campus Martius."

The bodyguard looked over at him, "I found out that the kid is a sharp shooter. One of my buddies spotted him at the shooting range."

Perone shook his head, concerned and wanting to handle this as quickly as possible. "I agree. We were fine until that kid of his grew up and got involved. If we plan something, we'd need to have both of them disappear."

"When do you want to do this?"

Thinking about his council meeting tomorrow, "Let's hang on until I get to talk to him. Maybe after we talk, we'll see what he wants." Perone was concerned about what the news would say about the popular market owner, especially if he and his son both came up missing. "Maybe we'll arrange another midnight visit."

The secretary buzzed the councilman, "Sir, the mayor is on line one."

Perone had a big grin, his fist was clenched. "He's feeling the heat." Turning to the bodyguard, "I want to beat him and do it big." Picking up the office phone, he smiled back at those in the room, "Mayor, what can I do for you?"

"Councilman, I thought you'd like me to update you on what the police chief has on the bombing at headquarters."

Perone was puzzled. "Yes, the other members of the City Council plan to meet tomorrow to discuss this, we need to be kept in the loop." Holding his hands up, he was surprised that any progress was made in the case.

"I just came from the Public Safety building. Chief Mathews and his team have new leads on both the shooting at Campus Martius and the bombing at headquarters. They're thinking both incidents are related."

The councilman gritted his teeth, *Can they really have a suspect?* After taking a deep breath, he gave the mayor a quick answer. "Great, it's about time they knew something. Christ it's been a few days since the shooting downtown." He waited, hoping for more details.

"Looks like Mathews and his SIU team have a suspect in custody."

That statement made Perone shudder, "Suspect?"

"Yeah, they said the guy has given them specifics on both events. I can't give you the details yet, but I expect that we'll all know something in the next twenty-four hours. Guess they have the FBI involved."

Perone was waving frantically to his men as they stood there waiting for orders. He pounded on the desk, holding his hand up, signaling for them to stop everything. "Mayor, that's great news; you need to fill me in. I told you the council wants to meet tomorrow. They should have everything you know so we can be of assistance." Once he made that statement, he pointed to the big bodyguard, having the man come closer. He whispered, "Call Virgilio. We need to meet as soon as possible."

The mayor sensed confusion on the other end of the line and he asked, "You okay, Councilman?"

"Yes, ah, just making a note so I have everything straight."

The mayor concluded, "I'd like to fill you in on the details but after your condemnation earlier of the police chief, I think he'd rather not tell you until he completes the pending arrest."

Perone was pissed. "That's bullshit, I'm a representative of the people and the people want to know what the police department is doing to protect them and our police force."

"I'd like to help but it looks like you're on your own right now. If you want to call Chief Mathews, that's okay with me, but I doubt he'll want to fill you in." The mayor hung up, knowing he did exactly want he and the chief had discussed: Give the councilman just enough rope and have him fill in the details, making sure he's in the dark as to what they actually had, and maybe he'd hang himself.

Perone slammed the phone down, yelling something neither understandable or barely understandable. The yells turned to mumbling, then pacing. "What is it?" The bodyguard, now standing across the desk, asked.

"What is it, are you kidding me? The mayor and police chief are playing games. They think they can keep me from finding out what they've got. Call our man in the Twelfth Precinct."

The man pulled his cell phone from the jacket pocket, dialed and waited for an answer. "We got word that the cops have a suspect in the bombing. You're to find out what the police chief knows. We need to know now." He turned to Perone, "I've got my nephew checking for us."

Andrew Perry, the rookie officer from the Twelfth, was standing next to his squad car, holding his phone when his uncle hung up. He wondered, *How can they have a suspect?* The young officer decided to call one of the officers he graduated with from the academy. "Hey, it's Andy, just heard that the chief has news on the bombing downtown, you know anything?"

"Not much, there is a shitload of work going on down here, construction people everywhere. Haven't heard that they got any leads. How about you?"

Andrew continued, hoping to get something for his uncle. "Oh, you know, same old crap. My captain is pushing everyone to help break the case on who planted the bomb at headquarters. Can you help me? It would be nice to get off of parking detail."

His friend laughed. "That might be better than standing guard on guys with jack hammers and saws. I'm stuck outside, can't wear ear protection and covered in concrete dust. I'll trade with you."

Andrew needed to give his friend a little more, "Hey, we're hearing that the chief has a suspect. Can you poke around? If I can give my captain something maybe he'll bring me inside. You know I'd help you if I could."

"Okay, but no promises."

Andrew called back, "Uncle, my friend is stationed at headquarters. He's going to see what he can get. Right now he hasn't heard anything, but give me a couple hours."

"Thanks kid, but I'm not sure we've got a couple hours. The councilman needs to break this to the news. You'll be a hero. I know he'll get you a sweet job when he wins the election."

"I'm on it."

***

The mayor called Chief Mathews after his conversation with Perone, "I think he bought it, I could hear a lot of shuffling in his office. I bet he'll be snooping around pretty soon."

"You sure you didn't give him any actual facts?"

"I did exactly what you and I talked about. Told him you had a suspect. Bet he'll have someone call you."

"Really, after what he said about me at the news conference?"

"The guy has guts."

Chief Mathews needed to fill Detective Frederickson and the team in on the events from the mayor's call. Once he informed Frederickson, he answered. "Thanks Chief, we're waiting to hear from the bureau on the interrogation of Gino Rossi. I've got everyone working on the guy we've got on video at Nancy's workplace. Chief, I think he's involved in the Campus Martius shooting and probably more."

Mathews knew that finding the person who shot Amy Harper was important to his SIU team, as well as who placed the bomb at headquarters. "Okay, I understand. Let me know if you come up with something."

Frederickson moved across the room where Detective Spano was meeting with four young officers. He listened to what Joe was telling them. "We're here handling special missions. Each one of you will be considered for a position with the SIU team once this investigation is completed. Anything we discover must be protected, you cannot discuss anything with anyone outside of this office." Frederickson stepped forward. "We are working on many fronts; several of you will be working with Detective Johnson, he's heading up the case on the bombing. The others will be assigned to Detective Spano or Baker. They are working twofold on the shooting of Detective Harper at Campus Martius, as well as the bombing."

The four officers, two men and two women, were receptive to the assignment. One stood and she asked, "Why haven't we seen a memorial for Detective Harper?"

Frederickson was quick to answer, "This is a highly secretive department. Detective Harper and her family knew this. We'll have a memorial for both her and Detective Askew when the time is right."

She nodded. "Thank you, sir."

"Okay, let's get started."

TWENTY-FIVE

Tony Virgilio had waited for the councilman to return his call. When he finally got a message from Perone's assistant, he listened to the caller, not pleased that they didn't answer his pressing issue. Sal was working on an order. He heard him talking in the backroom, knowing that Virgilio was alone. "That's bullshit, he's playing me again."

Sal peeked into the room, "You okay, Boss?"

Virgilio realized he had been talking too loud. "Sorry Sal, yeah, everything's fine. I just wanted to get an answer that hasn't come in yet." After talking to Sal, he decided to call his son. "Lorenzo, I just got off the phone with Perone's guy, they're wanting to meet tonight."

Lorenzo didn't trust these guys. "At the Eastern Market again?"

"He didn't say, just that Perone got my message. They'd let me know later where to meet. Lorenzo, his man said they think the police have a lead on the shooting downtown. They got a witness!"

Lorenzo knew that couldn't be right. "Witness! That's impossible! Just me and Bobby know about it except for you. It's a bluff, Dad."

"Okay, but why is he saying that. I know Perone has someone in the police department giving him inside information. Are you sure you didn't leave any prints—maybe on the bipod?"

"I wore gloves the whole time." Lorenzo paced while talking to his dad on his cell phone. "Dad, don't agree to meet where they tell you, make another location suggestion."

"Lorenzo, why would I do that?"

"If these guys plan the location, who knows what else they have in mind. They could have something going on," he paused, "maybe like eliminating you."

"I understand. I'd never put myself in that position."

"Dad, you've always been able to keep yourself out of the limelight with these people, but if Perone is running for mayor, maybe he doesn't need any loose ends."

Tony knew his son was right. "Lorenzo, I'd never go to a meeting without you as backup."

"Good, how about I head to the market; we can make our own plans."

"Thanks, son." After hanging up with Lorenzo, Tony walked into the front of the store. Sal had just completed an order. "Sal, what can I do to help?" Tony knew keeping busy was the best thing he could do right now. He wondered, *What is Perone up to?*

While he was cutting a slab of beef for the display shelf, Sal walked over to him. "Boss, what's going on?"

Tony looked up at him, "Sal, you've been with me a long time. Things are just a little rough right now. Lorenzo is on his way. If we need you, I promise I'll let you know." Sal smiled and Tony patted him on the back. "Sal, you're like a brother to me." The two men embraced.

Lorenzo walked into the market. "Hey, you guys need me to turn on some music for that dance?"

He laughed, as both men turned. Sal pointed to him, "Yeah, you got a waltz, you can play for us, kid?"

Lorenzo made his way over to them, "Uncle Sal, I've seen you dance before and it ain't pretty." The three of them had a good laugh.

***

Chief Mathews was pleased with the plan that he, Detective Frederickson and the mayor devised. "Don, the mayor filled me in on his conversation with Perone. He thinks we're on to something." He paused, "Don, we need to keep on the lookout for any of our people asking too many questions. If we've got a mole working for Perone, it's going to show soon."

Don understood. "I agree. We've got everyone up here listening for any questions that seem too interested in our case."

"Good. I've got Lieutenant Jackson in the loop too. She often gets calls from the field or even a reporter trying to pry proprietary information from her. If either of us hears anything, call. We've got to stop this."

Frederickson made his way over to the team's secretary's desk after talking to the chief, "Mindy, this is very important. I want to know the name of anyone, and I mean anyone, police officer, reporter, even if it's one of our City Council representatives, looking for information on any of our cases." She felt this was a little unusual but given the current situation with Harper shot, Askew killed and Baker still recovering, she understood the order. After talking to Mindy, he walked to Tom Baker's desk. "Find anything else out on our other club owners?"

"No, the only one who has anything that seems similar to Perone is Buddy Swinton."

"The guy that owns the club in Fort Wayne?"

"Yeah, but what we didn't know is Swinton owns a condo here." He motioned to the computer screen. "See, it shows Buddy Swinton as the owner of a condo unit downtown off of St. Aubin. Don, it's the same complex that John Franklin lives in."

Frederickson was stunned. "Swinton lives in Detroit? Why didn't we know that?"

"I'm not sure how often he's here but the records show that he bought the unit four years ago, the same year he bought into the strip club with Perone." Baker opened another screen. He pulled up more details as he read them aloud, "We knew Swinton spent five years in prison, what we didn't know is it was for bribery. Looks like he attempted to bribe an Indiana congressman. He was sentenced to five to ten years and got out after five years."

Frederickson sat down next to Baker. "Tom, can you contact this congressman for us?"

"Sure, he's still in the Indiana house. What do you want me to ask him?"

"The guy may be able to tell us what Swinton offered him, or more importantly, what he wanted the guy to do."

Baker looked at Frederickson, "I'll call him right away. Do you want to listen in?"

"Yeah." He pulled his seat closer as Baker dialed. They both waited and were pleased when a man answered.

"You've reached the office of Congressman Farley. Please leave a message, we'll return the call as soon as possible."

"Shit," Frederickson yelled.

Baker was quick to leave a message, "This is Detective Tom

Baker, Special Investigations, Detroit Police. Congressman, we need some information to help us with a murder case. Please call me as soon as you can." He left Farley his cell phone number.

Don said to Baker, "Good job, Tom. I'm sorry if I lost it for a second."

"I understand. If he returns the call, what do you want me to ask him?"

Frederickson thought for a minute. He started to write down some notes. "I've got three important questions. I'm going to write them all down for you." He continued writing in the note pad. "Tom, if he gives you an answer that you think could lead us in another direction or you think of a better question, ask it."

Baker was pleased that the Frederickson had so much confidence in him. "Thanks, Don, that means a lot to me." He looked at the list, "Oh, I like this question, *How much money did he offer you to do what he wanted?*

"Tom, maybe we'll find out a little about Perone and how much money it takes to swing you to do what he wants."

"Good point but who do we think is bribing who?"

"That's a key question but if this Swinton is involved in this whole thing, maybe he's key to Perone and a money grab." Frederickson stood, "Tom, right now I'm not sure who's the top dog in this show; is it Perone, Swinton or do they have someone else in the loop?" They both knew he was on to something. Who knows who else or how many people are involved. "Tom, our mission is to find out who's responsible for shooting Amy and ..." he stopped. Frederickson cleared his throat, "Sorry Tom, I want to find the asshole who killed Askew."

***

Lorenzo and Tony Virgilio planned to counter Perone with a meeting place of their own. Lorenzo had a map of St. Clair Shores open on the table in the back room. "Dad, the park on Twelve-and-a-half Mile Road is perfect. There's always people around, and even if they want to meet late at night, I know the maintenance people. I can get us in there."

Tony asked, "Why that park?"

"I told you, I know the maintenance guys, I can get in and set up cameras. If they plan something, maybe like sending someone in early, I'll know it."

Tony smiled at his son, "Okay, I like this. If they plan to surprise us, we'll know in advance." Tony mulled it over for a second or two. "What if they don't agree to meet there?"

"Dad, we're going to make sure they understand—it's there or we're not going to meet with them. " Lorenzo was determined that the plan would work. "We've got to watch our back. Perone might be getting desperate, after all, he's still behind in the mayoral race and he did seem determined to make something happen on television earlier."

"Okay, Lorenzo, I'm going to call back and set it up before they come up with a location."

"Great idea." The plan was set. Zo listened as his dad called Perone's office.

The assistant answered. "Tell Mr. Perone it's Tony Virgilio, I need to talk to him, it's important."

Perone came on the line, "Tony, glad you called. I thought that my guy said we were going to meet later today. What can I do for you?"

Virgilio was surprised that Perone answered. More importantly, he thought that Perone's tone was strange—he never talked to him like that. He turned to Lorenzo and whispered, "Must have a guest in his office." He answered Perone, "Councilman, I did get a call from your people but we've been very busy at the market, so I was hoping to set something up with you now."

He waited for a response, "Sure, where do you want to meet?"

"I'd like to do it close to my store. How about Memorial Park here in St. Clair Shores? It's on Jefferson and Twelve-and-a-half Mile. You can pick the time."

"Tony, that's okay with me. Let me have my assistant look at my schedule and he'll call you back and set it up."

"Thanks, see you then." When Tony hung up, he looked at Lorenzo. "He said okay. Call your friend and get it all set up."

"I'm on it."

Once the councilman got off the phone with Tony Virgilio, he turned to his bodyguard. "Virgilio's up to something. What's this shit about meeting at a park in the St. Clair Shores. I want you to help arrange it. I've got another idea for our friend.

TWENTY-SIX

The return call from Councilman Perone's office to Tony Virgilio came pretty quick. The assistant making the call stated, "Mr. Virgilio, the councilman said he'd be happy to make it as easy as possible for you and him to meet. He told me to have you name the time and he's okay with meeting tomorrow at Memorial Park."

Tony wasn't exactly sure what to say. He and Lorenzo were sure that this was going to be the first point of contention. He danced around an answer. "Great, I'm glad he's okay with the meeting place. It's close to home since things have been pretty busy here."

"Mr. Virgilio, I understand what you want, so does the councilman. I really have a lot to do, can you just give me a time and spot in the park to meet, please."

He wished Lorenzo was there with him. "Sure, let's meet at seven o'clock down by the covered picnic areas. I'll get there a little early and choose one that is away from most everyone else."

"Thanks, I'll give the councilman your message. He'll see you tomorrow night at seven."

The assistant hung up and Tony was left holding the phone, not sure what that was all about. He dialed Lorenzo. "Zo, just got a call from Perone's assistant. They're okay with meeting at Memorial Park tomorrow at seven."

"What, they went along with your choice?"

"Yeah, the guy said that Perone was fine with the location and I chose the time. You need to get in touch with your friend and set up cameras. I told them we'd meet at one of the covered picnic areas, one that was secluded."

"Dad, this doesn't sound right. The first time they wanted to meet at midnight at the Eastern Market, and now this time they're okay with meeting in the middle of Memorial Park during daylight. Something is fishy, dad."

"I thought so too, but Lorenzo, I've got a lot on him and he has the same evidence on me. Maybe he understands we need each other, so get it done and I'll meet with him tomorrow."

"I hope you know that I'm planning on being there too. I'm not leaving you alone with these guys. We can't trust people who seem desperate in one moment and so agreeable the next."

"Okay, Lorenzo, get the cameras handled. I'll make sure Sal will close up and we'll see what Perone has to offer. Maybe it's nothing, but we're better off talking together, making sure we're all on the same page. If this goes well we'll both be in a better position going forward."

"Okay, but I still don't like this. It was way too easy." Once he concluded talking to his father, Lorenzo called his friend who worked maintenance at Memorial Park. "Hey, it's Zo. I need a big favor." They covered the plan and how it would work. "I'll head over first thing in the morning. Get me a park vest so I don't appear too obvious." Lorenzo was going to use the new cameras that operated from his cell phone. Today's electronics made all of this so much easier.

***

Detective Baker was concentrating on the information he found on Buddy Swinton. The SIU team wanted to know why they didn't know that the guy had a place here in the city. They ran a search history on the condos on St. Aubin Place. Baker wrote down the information and gave it to Frederickson. "Don, I've got the address of the condo that Swinton owns. We didn't know about it because it's in his corporation's name. The condo is on the second level of the building and facing the river."

"Where's Franklin's unit?"

"It's on the lower level midway along the building, not near Swinton's place."

Frederickson stood by Baker, who kept searching on the computer. He stated, "Tom, this isn't a coincidence, Swinton didn't just end up buying a place there. He's there for a reason." They both nodded, knowing Frederickson was right.

Baker looked up, "So where do we go next?"

"You need to hang in here, I'm hoping that the Indiana congressmen calls you. I'm going to take one of the new officers with me; I want to check out those condos on St. Aubin." Frederickson told Mindy where he was headed. Waving to one of the two new officers, Sandy Michaels, he said, "I need you to come with me, we've got an assignment." Michaels, a ten-year veteran of the force who graduated at the top of her academy class was happy to be involved. She quickly jumped up and followed him. Frederickson was glad that the chief had Lieutenant Jackson send them extra help.

"Where are we headed?"

"I'll fill you in as we head there." He tossed her the key, "You can drive."

She was surprised; she'd heard that the detective was tough on people outside his team, "Where did you park?"

"I'm at the DTE building. They gave us some spots after the fire. It's great that so many of the companies close by have offered help." They walked across Michigan Avenue to the parking garage. When they got to his vehicle, Frederickson turned to the officer. "We're going to do a little surveillance—take Jefferson east to St. Aubin."

"I know it well," she said.

He turned toward her, "You do?"

"Yeah, great little bar and restaurant down there."

He smiled, knowing that he's been a little out of touch with new places in the city. They headed east on Jefferson, past a few car dealerships then she turned on St. Aubin. He saw the restaurant she described. "Head to the condos at the end of the street." The sign on the left side showed that the Stroh's River Place units were ahead. "Slow down a little." Frederickson thought that maybe they'd head to the rental office. "Pull in there," pointing to the main office sign. Once they stopped, he went over the details, "Michaels, I'm sure you've been updated on our case," he stopped.

"Yes, sir, Detectives Johnson and Spano filled us in."

"Okay, we've got one of the suspects who owns a condo here and possibly another guy we're looking at living here too."

She looked over at him, "That can't be a coincidence."

He was pleased with her assessment, "You're right, that didn't just happen. I'd like to know why they both live here." Getting out of the vehicle, they walked to the office entrance. "Just go along with me."

They entered and Frederickson addressed the woman at the desk. "Hi, my daughter and I are interested in one of the units along the river." Sandy went along with his story.

"Sure. Glad you're here. We've got two units open right now and one is on the river side." She handed them a brochure, pointing out the open unit's location. "It's on the second level, one bedroom, bath and half. I can show it to you."

"We'd like that."

The woman asked them to register. Officer Michaels took the pen, she filled out the form for both of them and handed it back to the realtor. "We're all set, Dad." Frederickson smiled, glad she picked up on what to do.

The realtor then led them outside. "Sandy, I'm happy that you and your father chose our place." As they walked down the outside of the complex, she pointed out the amenities including covered parking, pool and gym. When they got to the river, she stopped. "This is a premium unit that we're headed to, great views of both Belle Isle and Canada."

Frederickson asked, "Like many dads, I want to make sure my daughter is safe. Can you tell me about the neighbors she'd have?"

"That's one of the great things about this unit, the man that has the connecting unit is hardly ever here."

This was exactly what he hoped to hear. "Wow, surprising. If I had this great view, I'd be here all the time."

"Well I understand the guy also lives in Indiana. He's got business interests here."

After getting the information he hoped for, they continued with the guise of condo shopping. After leaving Stroh Place, they headed back downtown to headquarters. She looked back at Frederickson, "Thanks for including me in this."

"You did great. We kind of made it up along the way. Glad you're here. Now you can give this information to Detective Baker when we get back. Maybe you can help him with his research." This was great news to her; it was nice to be involved. More importantly, she thought, *People really were wrong about Frederickson, he's a pretty cool guy.*

When they returned to the squad room, Baker waved to both of them. "I got the call from the Indiana congressman; he gave me a lot of information. Looks like our guy, Swinton, wanted the congressman to push through legislation that would help buy up land that the owner had failed to pay taxes on and that the city now owned. Don, he offered the congressman a bundle." He showed them his note pad.

"A hundred grand! Why would he be willing to pay a bribe that big? Any idea what he planned to do with the property?"

"The congressman said he reported it to the local police. They ran a sting on Swinton. That's how they got him and why he spent five years in prison."

Frederickson looked at the note pad again as he mumbled, "One hundred grand. "Guess Swinton might be playing the same game here with Perone."

Baker nodded, "Don, when the congressman asked why I was inquiring, I had to tell him at least part of the reason. Hope that was okay?"

"Sure, good job Baker. We know the Indiana congressman was on the level, after all, he turned Swinton in."

Since Sandy had been to Swinton's building, she joined the conversation, "Detective Baker, we found that this Swinton guy has a condo, just like your research said. The woman we talked to said he's not there most of the time. Is there a benefit to him in having a Detroit address?"

Frederickson and Baker looked at each other, "That's got to be it! Swinton needed to appear like a normal city businessman. Once Perone wins the mayoral election, he could toss Swinton business and tell voters that he's keeping it all in the city!" Frederickson looked back at her, "Thanks, we wondered what benefit Swinton would have by having an address here. Nice job, officer."

She smiled. "I have one more suggestion." They both looked at her. "If Perone is head of City Council, he's probably already thrown his friend some business. We could check our records and see if Swinton or a company he's involved with has won city contracts."

Baker shook his head, "I should have thought about that."

"Hey, that's why we're a team," Don said, "it takes all of us to make it work." He smiled at Officer Michaels.

***

Lorenzo stood with his friend at Memorial Park on Jefferson. "I appreciate you letting me do this."

"No problem, Zo. Your dad has always been good to us here at the park. Last year he donated a case of hot dogs and a box of hamburgers for our employee event. If it wasn't for him, we'd have a pretty crappy time."

Lorenzo smiled, "Hand me that camera." He continued with the installation of the final camera into the pavilion at the park. "Thanks for giving me these supports, they make it pretty easy to hide the camera up here."

"We've used them before, they are solid and will cover the entire pavilion. Your dad won't have to worry where they stand to capture everyone."

"This is important to him, he said that the people he's meeting with might be able to assist the community and park next year. Guess he wanted to make sure that he got everything they discussed without taking notes." He climbed down from the ladder, holding his cell phone and punching in some information. The park employee peered over Lorenzo's shoulder as they watched the screen. The interior of the pavilion came into view and Lorenzo smiled, happy that it worked as he had hoped.

"Hey Zo, that's great. Can you turn it on and off from your phone?"

"Yeah, the guy at the computer store said it was the newest model. Many people are now using this in their business for surveillance."

"Big brother at work."

They both chuckled. "I'll help you put the ladders and other items back in the storage shed."

"Thanks, Zo. Make sure you let your dad know if he needs anything else to just let me know."

"I'll tell him." They walked toward the storage building. Once Lorenzo got to his car, he called his father. "Dad, everything is set. I placed the camera in the back corner of the pavilion. It won't matter where you stand, it will capture everything."

"Great, I'm going to call you when I see Perone approaching. You can turn the camera on then."

TWENTY-SEVEN

Mathews and Frederickson sat in the chief's office meeting with the Macomb County Sheriff and Chief Glass from St. Clair Shores. Mathews opened the meeting, "Gentlemen, I appreciate both of your teams and assistance with this case." Turning toward Chief Glass, "Can you fill us in about the Virgilio business?"

Glass had worked with Chief Mathews and his team before and knew how they handled their cases. "I had my team do a lot of research into Tony Virgilio and his business. I've got to tell you, it's hard to believe this guy or any of his family members are involved in anything criminal. The market has been in the Shores for over twenty-five years without issues. He always donates food for any events that are held in our area, including the yearly police picnics at Memorial Park. The only surprising information we found was that his uncle, Vinnie La Russo, owned a business at Eastern Market. Vinnie, as you know, was involved in a major drug business that you busted last year."

"How about his son, Lorenzo?"

"The kid is kind of a self-proclaimed playboy. He's gotten a few tickets for speeding, but nothing else. I did check and there's no record of him working for a furniture company or anywhere else."

Mathews turned to Frederickson, "Will you please play the video that the sheriff brought for us." They all watched as Lorenzo was shown with the furniture cart asking about Nancy Frederickson.

Glass nodded, "Yeah, that's Lorenzo. His friends call him Zo. I don't know if he was just helping out but we contacted the furniture company, as I said, and they don't have him listed as an employee."

Mathews turned it over to Frederickson. He covered the incident at the Greektown Hotel the day Harper was shot. "Our team checked out his story; looks like he accounted for his time the afternoon that Detective Harper was shot. We needed to do more research on his friend, Bobby Flynn. The only thing we've found on him is that he has an apartment in mid-town and is unemployed. He attended Wayne State for one year and people remembered him as a computer geek. These two are each other's alibi for the day in question. Everyone that Lorenzo gave us has confirmed they were on the shuttle and at the ballpark. The shuttle ride is crucial because it had to be within minutes after the shooting. It's almost impossible for them to be on the shuttle and rooftop in that short of a period."

Chief Glass turned toward to Frederickson, "Given that he's got an alibi for the shooting, that's a heck of a coincidence, Lorenzo at the hotel when your detective was shot and then at Frederickson's wife's business."

Frederickson nodded, "I don't believe in coincidences, there has to be more."

Glass nodded and said, "I'm willing to put an officer on both Lorenzo and the market. We can follow the kid for the next few days and see if he's up to something. It won't look odd if we place an officer along Little Mack. We're always checking on the businesses making sure everyone is safe."

Mathews was quick to answer, "That's greatly appreciated, Chief. We're at a stalemate on the shooting and Lorenzo and his friend might be our only lead. We're also putting a man on Bobby Flynn." The meeting broke up with everyone knowing the next step in the investigation. Frederickson shook Chief Glass's hand, as the two men stood. The chief walked with the Don to the SIU squad room. "Don, maybe you and Nancy need to think about staying somewhere other than your place for a while."

"No, Spano suggested that too. I'm not hiding from these people. Last year we sold our home and moved downtown. It's about the safest building in the city."

"At least let me assign an officer to help with security."

Don wanted to refuse, but knew that the chief meant well. "Sure, but I can't tell Nancy. She's already upset after the incident here and then someone showing up at the office on Hall Road, asking for her."

"I understand. My wife and I have been married for twenty years and I try to keep her out of everything that we do." Mathews said,

"I'd like to talk to your team for a few minutes, if that's okay with you."

Absolutely, Chief."

***

Chief Glass held a meeting with his officers. It was critical that they operated as instructed; there couldn't be any deviation. "This is an important assignment. Starting now," pointing to Jake, a five-year officer on the force, "You're going to stake out Virgilio's Market on Little Mack." Turning to the other officer, an officer who knew the younger Virgilio, he said, "Sue, I know you're familiar with Lorenzo since you've written a few speeding tickets on his Mustang, so I want you to keep an eye on him. Follow him but don't let him know what you're doing. Use one of the unmarked vehicles."

"Got it, what's going on?"

"It appears that Tony's kid might be involved in an important case in Detroit. I meet with their chief and my idea was to follow him for the next week or so. Just in case his dad is involved, it makes sense to keep an eye on the market too."

Sue asked, "What do they think he's involved in?"

"We're not sure, but Lorenzo was downtown in the hotel when the Detroit detective, Harper, was shot. Now he has been captured on video at the detective's wife's workplace."

"Isn't that just speculation? Is there any evidence that goes with this?"

"If we figure it's just a coincidence, it does seem odd that Lorenzo was in both places. I've checked, he doesn't work for the furniture company that he said he was delivering a desk for. Why was he there? I can't let one of our citizens be involved in this crime and we're not aware."

That made sense to both officers; It would look bad if the Detroit problem exploded into the Shores and the chief and his team knew nothing about it. "We're on it, sir."

"Keep a record of everything whether it appears odd or not to you." Turning to the officer assigned to watch the busy market. "Jake, it would be best to park behind the stores, you know, in the area where the market and pub patrons often enter the two businesses. If anyone asks, let them know we're operating a safety watch." They both nodded and headed out to their assignments. Once he completed talking to his men, Chief Glass phoned Mathews, letting him know what his team will be doing.

***

Two men sat in the black Suburban, watching the front of the market. "What time did the councilman say he was going to meet Virgilio?"

"Seven. The park is four miles north of here. The market closes at seven. The guy that works with Tony usually closes up."

"Let's pull around back, I want to sneak into the place before they lock up." Pulling around the back of the stores, they watched the back of the market. The passenger said, "I'm going to stroll over to the pub just past the market; they have an entrance in the back. I'll stand outside and grab a smoke. I'll call you if the coast is clear. Bring me the bag from the back." He was dressed like a repairman as he got out of the Suburban and started to walk in the direction of the bar. Just then, Tony walked out the back door of the market. The two passed each other as Tony headed to his vehicle. It was six-thirty and he planned to arrive at the park a little before the meeting time. The guy turned and watched Tony get into his vehicle. The back door of the market was open with just a screen on the rear entrance. Once Tony passed, the guy grabbed his cell phone, "Bring me the bag, the coast is clear." Tony never paid attention to either guy as he pulled out of the lot.

The second man handed his partner the black bag, "What do you need from me?"

"I'm going to slip through the screen door. I can fray the wires here in the back. It will take an hour or so for sparks to fly. I know it's where they keep all the cardboard. Saw it piled up last time I was there. It's going to set a major blaze." He opened the screen door and slipped into the back room. This door was about ten feet from the rear customer entrance. Sal was still up front waiting on the few customers left in the building to leave. It only took about five minutes for the guy to complete his plan, sliding the boxes close to the frayed wires, making sure they'd ignite once it sparked. He knew if someone saw him the uniform it would be a great cover.

They knew the place didn't have any sprinklers. By the time the fire department arrived, it would be hard to put out. By creating a short circuit in the positive and negative terminals, it would cause a large amount of energy in a short period. It's the same thing that happened down the street last year at a restaurant. These places go up pretty fast. The two guys were pleased that they were all set to handle the assignment that Perone gave them. "I'll call the councilman once we're done."

Perone sat in the back of his vehicle as he listened to the information that the driver gave him.

"He's in there, Boss, shouldn't be too long."

"When do you think it will go up in flames?"

"With the spike in electricity, I'd say two to three hours from now."

"Great." Perone hung up and told the driver, "Let's stay here a few minutes. I'd rather be a little late to meet with Tony."

"No problem, sir. Just let me know when you want me to head there." They were parked down the street, about a block away from the park.

***

Tony pulled into the parking lot across from Memorial Park, got out of his vehicle and crossed Jefferson. He nodded at the man sitting at the gate. "How's it going?"

The man recognized him. "Great Mr. Virgilio, they told me you were having a meeting here tonight. I kept everyone away from that the last pavilion like Zo asked. I told them it was reserved. Is there anything else I can do for you?"

"No, you've taken care of everything we need. I'm expecting a couple men to meet me; if they ask, let them know where I'll be."

"Sure."

Tony waved to a few people having a picnic as he made his way to the pavilion where Lorenzo had set the camera up. He knew that if he had the councilman on video, it would help in case there was a double-cross in the works. It was a nice summer evening, close to seventy-five degrees. Memorial Park was always teeming with picnickers and boaters this time of the year. Tony loved the location and often brought his family here as the boys were growing up. Rosa would pack a picnic lunch and they'd meet after the market closed. He sat on a table in the pavilion, waiting for his guest to arrive. Looking at his watch, it was ten minutes after seven when he spotted Perone walking down the path toward him. He was surprised the man was alone. Virgilio stood, waiting for the man to arrive. "Councilman, glad you found the place."

Perone was looking very casual, he wasn't wearing a tie or jacket. "I've been here many times as a kid. My parents used to bring us to this park. Although we didn't live in the Shores, my cousins did and we'd use their passes."

Virgilio hadn't seen this side of the councilman. "I didn't know that."

"So, Tony, what's so important?"

The councilman was quick to the point, Tony wanted to keep him facing the camera to record their meeting. "You and I have been partners for a long time, but lately it appears that you are distancing yourself from me."

"I'm not sure what you mean." Perone and Tony sat down at the table.

"We're both equally involved in this business."

Perone stopped him. "I'm not sure what you're talking about."

Tony knew the guy was slippery. "I'm talking about the drug business we've both profited from and I don't want you to get into power by winning the mayoral election and hanging it all on me."

Perone stood. "What in the hell are you talking about? I don't know anything about drugs or the business you're referring to!"

Now both Perone and Tony were standing, face to face. Tony raised his voice, "I've got documents, you, me and Vinnie, we're all on them. Ever since Vinnie went down in the drug raid, you've distanced yourself from the business. I'm not going to take the fall for it."

"Listen, Tony, I've always appreciated your support for me and my message for the citizens of Detroit. This drug business you're talking about is all news to me. If you're involved in any illegal activity, that's on you."

This had gone like Tony feared. The man would set him up

eventually for all of it. He wondered if Perone knew he was on camera.

"Tony, you're wired. If you're trying to hang a crime on someone, it won't be me. If you planned to incriminate me in something you're involved in, your very wrong. When you called I thought you wanted to meet about helping one of my charities. I'm leaving." The councilman turned and walked away. Tony was left standing by himself, wondering what had just happened.

TWENTY-EIGHT

The surveillance records were approved by the court and the team of detectives had everything they needed to check the alibis one more time. Videos were coming in on Lorenzo and his friend Bobby from their stay at Greektown. The hotel and casino sent the surveillance photos that were listed on the court orders. The hotel's security cameras had both men walking through the hallway and at the front desk earlier that day. The casino only showed them on the date in question after the baseball game. They didn't have anything the afternoon of the shooting. The detectives that reviewed the hotel video over and over only saw what would confirm the suspects story. The time stamp showed Lorenzo walking out the front entrance at twelve-ten, but Bobby wasn't with him. That was just minutes after the shooting. One of the men watching the video said, "Run that back again." They watched and confirmed the timing. "Okay, let's check the street camera." They had videos from three views that they checked out. The camera from Old St. Mary's Church showed Lorenzo walking down Monroe, but Bobby wasn't with him. "Hey, where is Bobby Flynn?" They ran it back again; Flynn wasn't with Lorenzo. They checked another camera further down the street. It showed Lorenzo, again walking alone to the Old Shillelagh bar, but no Bobby Flynn. Looking at one another, "This is important. Didn't the chief say that the two suspects said they rode to the stadium together on the shuttle?" They checked the report. If Bobby Flynn wasn't with Lorenzo, he didn't have an alibi for the time around the shooting, just Lorenzo. "He must be the shooter. We need to call the chief and Detective Frederickson."

***

Sikorski and the FBI were once again interrogating Gino Rossi.

The man hadn't said anything, but they pressed on, "Gino, you're pretty cool. You don't have to talk to us. You can save it all for your attorney. I'm sure you got one. The murder trials will be a real event in the city. You and your pal, Perone, will fry for all three of them."

He sneered, "Murder, that's a laugh."

The two agents chuckled along with him. "Glad you think it's funny." They stood, "Better tell Sikorski that one, maybe it's more than a federal crime, could be terrorism."

Rossi looked startled, "What the hell are you talking about, terrorism?" He shook his head, but this time his laugh was tempered a little.

"You don't know? They passed that new law that the president wanted. Any crime that crosses borders could be considered terrorism. I know he didn't consider drug trafficking from Canada at the time, figuring it would most likely refer to Mexico."

"I don't have anything to do with Canada; I don't know what you're talking about."

"You go with that, Gino. Maybe your friend Perone didn't tell you about his connections in Windsor. Now Deputy Mayor Franklin has given us those details and Perone is under investigation. Who will be there for you? They'll hang it all on you: The bombing at headquarters, the drugs coming across the bridge and the murders at the strip club. We've got you on camera downtown planting the bomb. You're not as slick as you thought."

The two agents walked out as Gino yelled back, "Wait, I didn't do anything. You got nothin' on me!"

Sikorski watched from the one-way glass, "Nice job. We'll let him stew in there for a while."

The silence was too much for the man. "I want out of here," Gino yelled. "I want my attorney, now!"

Brian Sikorski smiled. "Now it's time." He opened the door to the interrogation room. "You've got to stop yelling. If you want to talk to me, I'm here; if not, shut the hell up!."

He turned, opening the door to leave.

Sikorski stood in the doorway. "Unless you're going to tell me about the councilman's part in this, I'd just as soon put it all on you."

"Wait, I've got details that you couldn't know about, but I want a deal and I want it in writing."

The agents listened, but Sikorski wasn't ready to deal, not yet.

"Before we offer you anything, Gino, we'll need proof."

"I got proof. Get the district attorney. I ain't talking, not until it's all in writing."

"We'll see." Sikorski walked out of the room. He told one of the agents, "Better call Chief Mathews, we just might have what he needs."

***

Detective Baker continued searching city records. There it was— two months ago the City Council approved a contract for demolition of sixteen abandoned homes on the lower east side to a new company. Searching the company's records, he found that the ownership was listed as Wayne Demolition, a Detroit business, address 17444 Gratiot. He turned to Officer Michaels. She had given him and Frederickson the idea that Buddy Swinton was already doing business in Detroit. "Michaels, you got a minute?"

"Sure, Detective." She moved to where he was working on the computer screen.

"What do you know about doing a reverse search on the internet?"

Sandy smiled, "I'm pretty good at using the web."

He pointed to the screen. "This was your lead. Maybe Wayne Demolition is what we're looking for. Can you take this information and check out this business and the ownership? I tried everything I know but couldn't find anything."

"Slide over." Officer Michaels moved behind the computer and started punching keys. Baker watched in amazement. She had flipped through a dozen pages. She was at it for about ten minutes when she stopped. "Look at this."

He leaned over her shoulder. "Christ, how did you do that?"

"A lot of these guys use the same tactics. Multinational businesses always try to cover up the individuals who own the place, but they still have to pay taxes. The IRS has names and locations in case tax fraud exists." She looked at Baker. "I'm not sure what I did is legal." They were looking at the tax records from the past year and right on page two of ownership, Buddy Swinton was listed as sole proprietor.

"This is it! Frederickson is going to really be happy!" Realizing that if she hadn't discovered the details, he'd be punching information into the computer for hours. "Sandy, you need to tell him."

"No, you had it all there, all I did was punch in a few searches."

Laughing, he pointed to his graying temples. "Sandy, look at this hair; it would take me days to accomplish what you did in a few minutes. Go get Frederickson. You did a nice job." She smiled, getting up and walking across the office. "Sir, Detective Baker needs you to come see what we found regarding possible ownership of a company here by your suspect."

Frederickson quickly followed her, "What've you got there Baker?"

"Looks like Michaels here," pointing at Sandy, "found a company that Buddy Swinton owns that's doing business with the city— demolition of abandoned homes. The City Council has to approve these contracts."

Frederickson looked at the details. "Michaels, walk me through this."

She looked a little sheepish, peering down at the computer screen above her glasses. "Actually Baker found the important part, I just ran a back trace through the IRS."

"Is that legal?"

"I'm not sure, but we've got the proof you wanted." He laughed when she said she wasn't sure if it was legal.

***

Chief Mathews was pleased that Brian Sikorski of the FBI was calling, hoping that they made progress with Gino. "Chief, Gino Rossi is willing to give us details about Perone's involvement.

Mathews was happy. "I knew you'd break him."

Sikorski knew how to pedal the information softly. "Chief, we've got one problem," taking a breath, "he wants a deal."

"A deal! He blew up headquarters, killed two police officers and most likely the woman under Franklin's car. He wants a deal? Hell no, he's going to pay for what he did!"

"Wait Chief, we haven't given him anything yet. Maybe we can offer him something."

"Like a lesser charge? Did you hear me, he killed two of our police officers. He can go to hell; we'll get Perone, with or without him!"

Sikorski knew the chief wouldn't be happy, but hoped to get some concession. "Okay, I just had to run it by you. We're going to charge him in the bombing."

"We've got him on video getting into the building here. I want our people to know that we protect and defend our own." Once Mathews hung up, he paced around the office and grabbing the intercom, he hollered, "Lieutenant Jackson, come in here!"

The lieutenant was surprised that he was so loud, she knew something was wrong, but what? Hurrying in, she asked, "Chief, you okay?"

He was still walking in a circle. "The bureau has the guy who blew up our building. He wants a deal to give us a bigger fish." He looked at Jackson. "Am I wrong in demanding that he pay for what he did?"

"No sir, the safety and integrity of our officers is too important. Your standing up for them, even after one of our own has been killed, is why we all go the extra mile for you." She moved closer to the front of his desk, "Chief, we'll all stand behind you, whatever decision you make."

Mathews appreciated her support. "I can't wait to tell Frederickson what the man wants. Christ, I can't believe anyone would think we'd accept an offer like that." He smiled at Jackson. "I'm going to call Sikorski back, maybe I was too tough on him."

"I think he understands."

"You're probably right. I'll wait, maybe he'll have an update after talking to the suspect."

***

Sal finished locking up and walked to the rear exit, as he normally did. He turned the lock and started to close the door. He stopped, spotting cartons stacked in the wrong place. He thought, *How did they get there?* He turned and went back in moving the boxes. Walking to his car, he spotted a St. Clair Shores police vehicle. "Evening officer," Sal said and waved as he was getting into his car and heading home.

TWENTY-NINE

Two officers stood outside Bobby Flynn's apartment door, knocking. They waited for an answer. "Do you hear the television playing? It's pretty loud." One of them knocked again and called out, "Mr. Bobby Flynn, Detroit Police, we need to talk to you." They stood there for another few seconds, rapping at the door harder. "Flynn, either let us in or we'll break down the door." Still no response. "Bullshit." Officer Tanner brought his foot up. Crash! the door cracked and swung open. Tanner moved into the room, holding his weapon in his right hand. He called out again, "Detroit Police, we have a warrant for your arrest." Both officers were slowly searching through the apartment. The television blared but no one was in sight. A room-to-room search proved the place was empty. Tanner yelled, "There's a back door here and it's unlocked." Opening it, he and his partner hurried down the hallway that led to a rear stairwell. "He's on the move, call it in."

Tanner issued an APB for Bobby Flynn. "Suspect on the run in the murder of Detective Amy Harper. Bobby Flynn, twenty-three, brown hair, six foot tall." A second team of detectives were called in to do a thorough search of the apartment building. Tanner and his partner searched the neighborhood with no sign of the suspect. He needed to handle the search of the apartment, hoping the APB netted the suspect.

When the second team arrived, Tanner directed them, "We need to go through everything; the guy is on the run but our job is the apartment."

As the team searched the rooms, one officer called out, "I've got some loose boards on this side of the bed in here." Pushing the full-size bed out of the way, they pulled up one board, then another and another, then a third. The floor under where the bed sat was now open close to three feet wide. Tanner entered the room. "Stop, we need to document this." One man recorded it while Tanner was on his knees. "I've got a long bag hidden under the floor of the apartment of our suspect, Bobby Flynn." Pulling the bag to the surface, he opened it. "We've discovered a box with a long-range scope," holding it up for the video to capture. "There is a rifle under the scope. It fits the description of a sniper's rifle. I'm bagging it all for evidence." They found what they were looking for, now to find the suspect.

***

Bobby Flynn ran down Lafayette, looking back a few times, headed to the Central Parking garage on St. Aubin. He pulled out of the lot, headed east on Jefferson, grabbing his cell. Although Lorenzo didn't answer, he left a message. "Zo, I need help, there were cops at my door!" Bobby kept driving. He passed the entrance to Belle Isle when he spotted a police car coming up behind his Dodge Charger. He panicked, making an illegal left on East Grand Boulevard; that was a mistake. The Charger spun in front of the Coney Island, making another illegal turn. The officers in the squad car following turned on their lights and gave chase. Bobby saw the lights in his rear view mirror and gunned it, doing close to eighty and climbing on the Boulevard.

The car giving chase hadn't gotten the APB yet. Officer Anderson, a two-year veteran called it in. "We've got a 10-42, a black late-model Dodge Charger heading west on E. Grand Boulevard; requesting backup. I've got a code 3, lights and sirens in use." Anderson's hands were shaking; it was his first chase. The radio message was clear, "Anderson, it could be our APB, possible dangerous suspect, may be a cop killer." He kept an eye on the Charger as it sped past E. Vernor Highway, bouncing, now getting close to one-hundred miles per hour. A second squad car joined the pursuit as they passed Mack Avenue, gaining on the suspect.

Bobby had both hands on the wheel, holding tight as he swerved to miss slow-moving or parked cars. He punched the call button on the steering wheel, "Zo, help, the cops are chasing me, I need you!" Lorenzo still hadn't answered and Bobby was losing it. He didn't see a third police car entering Grand Boulevard. It spun in front of his Charger, kissing the front fender and sending the speeding car over a curb, through the grass and into a fire hydrant. Water shot up twenty feet into the air as officers jumped out of their vehicles, guns drawn.

Anderson slid into position. He called out, "Get out of the car with your hands up in the air." The other officers surrounded the Charger. Water was spraying over the hood but no one was getting out of the vehicle. Anderson again called out, "You've got one choice, get out of the vehicle or we're going to start shooting." The last thing Officer Anderson wanted was a shootout. His wife just gave birth to their first child. He continued toward the suspects' car.

A hand emerged from the driver's side. "I'm hurt, I can't move."

One of the officers who was involved in the chase circled around the other side of the Charger, crouching. He spotted a figure behind the steering wheel. It wasn't moving. He called out to Anderson, "Do you see any movement?" He didn't see anyone else in the vehicle. He radioed back to the responding officer, "I've got a clear view, one suspect, the driver, looks to be pinned behind the steering wheel. I'm moving in closer." Anderson crouched down as he made it within a few feet of the Charger. The suspect still wasn't moving. "Police, I want to see both of your hands."

One hand still hung out of the driver's side window, but the suspect wasn't answering either of the requests. Anderson, along with the other officer, moved in and found the driver slumped over the wheel, blood coming from a gash to his forehead. Anderson took a deep breath, glad it was over, "Call it in. We need a bus; driver unconscious and bleeding."

***

Lorenzo walked back from his hiding spot at Memorial Park. He had watched the meeting but couldn't hear the discussion. He had waited until Perone left. "What did he say, Dad?"

"Nothing. He asked if I was recording him. He must have known something, Lorenzo, he kept saying that he thought I had called him to donate to his charity. We're going to have to go this alone."

"I'm here for you; what do you want me to do?"

"I think we're going to have to take care of this ourselves. Call your friend; you're going to need that rifle."

Lorenzo pulled his cell phone from his pocket. He had turned it off while he hid during the meeting between his father and Perone. He saw that he had two missed calls, both from Bobby. Listening, he panicked. "Dad, it's Bobby. He says the cops are chasing him down Grand Boulevard!"

"Why, what's going on?"

"I don't know!" He started to call Bobby's cell but stopped before completing the call. "Shit, if they get him, I don't want my cell number shown calling him back." They agreed.

"You told him to hide the gun, didn't you?"

"Yeah, no one's going to find it. Bobby can't be linked to any of this."

"Okay, you know what you have to do." They walked out of the park together. Lorenzo didn't like that last option.

***

The St. Clair Shores officer watched as another man walked out of the back of the market. He knew Sal left ten minutes ago; why did this guy come out of the market? He got out of the squad car and walked toward the guy. "Sir, stop right there." The man stood in the parking lot, holding a black bag. The officer said, "I want to see your hands."

The man looked back at the officer. "I'm just finishing a repair job, Officer."

The officer walked within a few feet of the guy, then stopped. He spotted a gun handle protruding from the waistband of the man in front of him. "Stop right there, drop the bag on the ground and hold your arms out at your sides." The man looked to the parking lot, than did as he was asked. The officer had his weapon drawn. "I want you to lay down on the ground, right there." The officer kept an eye on the man as he moved closer.

The guy was kneeling as requested, looking up at the approaching police officer. "I just finished a repair call at Virgilio Market. They had a problem with the A/C unit. You can call the owner."

The man's partner watched from the Suburban, waiting for a

signal. There it was, his partner making a circling motion with his right hand. Starting the vehicle and slowly moving into position, he gunned the motor. The thud of the front fender hitting the officer was sickening, sending him flying into the fence. Blood gushed over the pavement. Then the vehicle ran the officer over, crushing him. The driver yelled, "Get in!"

Grabbing the bag off the pavement, the first man jumped into the Suburban as they sped away. A man standing at the rear of the restaurant jumped out of the way, as more people ran out of the bar. The patron smoking outside had seen all the action. He gathered his wits then he ran inside yelling "Call 911, someone just ran over a cop!"

THIRTY

The St. Clair Shores Police Department sent every available car to the scene on Mack. Reports of an officer down came in from multiple sources. The first team arrived. "Oh no," a young officer covered his face, "How could this happen here?" he mumbled. The arriving EMS team covered the mangled body. The news of the incident spread as crowds gathered. After arriving, Glass moved into the center of the area. Officers stepped back as he knelt on one knee. Putting his left hand on the pavement he lifted the corner of the cover with his right hand. Tears ran down his face. He took his hat off and wiping his face, he stood, yelling orders to those around. "Do we have a description of the car?"

An officer standing near grabbed his pad. "The caller said a black Suburban or maybe Chevy. We've got a partial plate, Michigan, first part looked like 5LL, but when the vehicle swerved, the guy said he didn't see the rest of it."

Chief Glass listened. "That's a Macomb County plate. Put an APB out on all vehicles like that with those plate numbers." Glass was now standing. "I want to talk to our witness." Making their way to the man standing at the back of the restaurant, Glass saw that he was talking to a news reporter. Chief Glass leaned in, "You'll need to back up, this is a working crime scene. Give us a minute, please." He turned to the officer with him, "How did someone from the press get here already?"

"Believe it or not, she was here eating at the restaurant with her cameraman."

She backed up but motioned to the cameraman to keep filming.

Glass shook the witness's hand. "Thanks for everything you did. I need to ask you a few questions. Did you see the driver?"

"Not very good but I'm sure it was a man. He was big, dark hair, but it all happened so fast. I gave all of this to your officers."

"Would you mind going over it one more time?"

The man nodded. "I came out here for a smoke. The officer was in the parking lot; he was talking to a guy."

"Is that guy still here?"

"No, he got into the SUV."

"He got into the SUV? You're saying the guy our officer talked to got in the getaway vehicle."

"Yeah, he jumped in after the cop was hit."

"What did that guy look like?"

"Not sure, normal height, dark hair." He paused, then finished, "He was wearing a uniform."

"Uniform?"

"Yeah, he looked like a repairman of some sort."

"Did you recognize the uniform, maybe it had logos or writing?"

"No, too far from me to see," pointing to where he saw the guy. "Anyway, your officer seemed to be talking to him, when out of nowhere, a black vehicle, SUV, like I told the other officer, maybe a Suburban or Chevy came flying across the lot. I couldn't believe it! He hit the officer, then turned around and ran over him. The other guy, the one in the uniform, jumped into the vehicle and they took off. I was frozen for a second; I just got a look at the back of the vehicle."

Glass was puzzled; this didn't make sense. He repeated it. "So the SUV hit the officer and the workman got into it?"

"Yeah, I wish I had thought about taking a photo, but I got some of the numbers on the plate when they sped past me."

"We appreciate that; it will be a great help. We might contact you when we catch these guys. Maybe we'll need you to look at a lineup."

Glass again shook the man's hand. As he walked away, the reporter stepped back in. "You heard that, Chief Glass from St. Clair Shores and his team are searching for a black SUV. If you have any information that can help call our hotline." She gave the number as the cameraman continued filming.

Chief Glass was hoping that they'd find something with the numbers on the plate. He started walking away and stopped. Turning to the officer following, "Why would the guy in the uniform get into the SUV? Did anyone check the back of the restaurant or market? What was the guy in the uniform doing?" Before the officer could answer, Glass was hurrying back to the scene. Grabbing a couple of officers, he said, "I want each one of you checking the buildings. What was the uniformed guy doing back here?" They fanned out, following his orders.

"Chief," one of the officers asked, "should we call Tony Virgilio? The witness said it looked like the repair guy came out of his business. I checked, the doors to his place are locked."

Glass shook his head, "Son-of-a-bitch, Virgilio's Market. Yeah, call now."

Councilman Perone was sitting in the back seat, wondering what Virgilio had been planning at the park. The driver was heading back to the councilman's office downtown. His cell phone rang. "Yeah," He listened and grumbled, "What, you ran over a cop? What in the holy hell is wrong with both of you? I wanted to burn his place down, not alert the entire Shores Police Department to get involved! Where in the hell are you now?" The caller tried explaining. Perone yelled, "Go to the warehouse at the Eastern Market, both of you, meet me there." After hanging up he told the driver, "Head down Gratiot to the market. I've got to make another call."

***

Frederickson was listening to the call from Detective Johnson regarding the interview with the fourth man listed as owner of the Eight Mile club. "Singleton checks out; no connection to Perone or Buddy Swinton."

"Okay, you and your partner need to head back. We've got to concentrate on Lorenzo Virgilio and Bobby Flynn." He walked where Baker was still on the computer with the new officer. Sandy looked up as he approached, "Buddy Swinton is in town, what do you want us to do?"

"Nothing yet, not until the FBI gets Gino Rossi talking. We need rock solid evidence before we take the next step."

Baker smiled, "Don, Officer Sandy Michaels has been a great help." She stood off to the side as Baker continued. We've got a lot on this Swinton character. We just need more of a connection to Perone. If the FBI gets Rossi talking, we might have everything we need."

Mindy was waving to them. Getting up from her desk, she moved pretty fast to where they stood. "Detectives, officers that you sent to bring Bobby Flynn in had a problem. He tried to run. There was a car chase. Flynn drove down Grand Boulevard, hit a hydrant and they're taking him to the hospital."

Frederickson was stunned. "He tried to get away?"

Mindy nodded, "I've got Officer Tanner on the line."

Frederickson grabbed the phone off Baker's desk. "What's going on, Tanner?"

"Sir, we did what you said, tried to arrest Flynn and search his apartment. The guy took off."

"Are you and your partner okay?"

"Yes, we're fine."

"How's the suspect?"

"A little banged up after driving into a hydrant on the Boulevard. We're at the DMC right now. Lieutenant, the forensic team found the rifle and scope in his apartment."

"Make sure you document everything; can't have a lawyer get any of this thrown out."

"It's all on video. The team is bringing it all in. We followed the letter of the two pronged warrant, for his arrest and search of the apartment."

"Great job." Once Frederickson hung up, he covered the conversation with Baker and Sandy, there was a cheer. "Yeah!" With high fives all around.

Baker stood, "If this is the guy who shot Amy, I want him."

"I understand, Tom. Let's take this one step at a time. Hopefully this is the weapon and the shooter. Now, we've got some key questions, who is he connected to is number one."

THIRTY-ONE

The phone call must have been serious as Lorenzo watched his father who had a look of panic. He was wondering, *What's it about?* He heard him say, "Okay, Officer, I'm headed there right now. How much damage is there to my store?"

Once Tony hung up, Lorenzo asked, "What is it?"

"I'm not sure. That was the police department; someone killed an officer behind our store. They ran him over."

"What?"

"The officer said someone coming out of our store was involved."

"Sal?"

"No, a witness said it was a repair guy. I didn't have a repair call in. Lorenzo, I'm heading to the store. You need to find out what's going on with Bobby." Both of them got into their vehicles and Tony headed down Jefferson to the market, hoping his son could find out what was going on with his friend.

When Tony turned onto Mack from Nine Mile Road, traffic was at a standstill. The police had the street blocked off. Tony pulled into a spot in front of the car dealership. He got out of his vehicle and approached the officer on the corner. "I need to get through, I own the store that was involved in a crime. I got the call from your department."

The officer immediately let him through. "Chief, the owner of the market is here, he's headed your way."

Chief Glass knew Tony; they had participated in many events. "Tony, sorry we needed you here," Glass said as he walked with him, pointing to a roped-off area. "Someone killed one of my deputies; a witness said they might have tried to break into your store."

Tony wanted to check his store out, but understood the aspect of an officer killed being most important. "I appreciate your call. What can I do to help?"

"Our officer who was killed may have been trying to stop a break-in at your place." Virgilio didn't know what to say, there hadn't been a murder in the area for years.

"I'm so sorry, who was it?"

"Jake Patterson. He was in the parking lot. It appears that he must have seen a suspicious man behind your store. A witness said it looked like a repair guy. Did you have a repair call at the market?"

"No, nothing. Sal was closing up, just like always." They both walked to the back of the store and Tony opened the screen and unlocked the rear door.

Chief Glass told him to stand back as he and an officer entered. The officer had his gun drawn, calling out, "You need to come out, hands up."

Tony followed behind, stopping, wondering why boxes were piled up to the right side of the back door. "Chief, I'm going to call Sal, he would have been closing up."

"Good idea."

Tony moved a few feet from Chief Glass. "Sal, I'm at the store with the police, looks like we had a problem. They think someone might have tried to break into our place; the guy killed a police officer."

Sal was puzzled, "Tony, I didn't see anything," then he thought back, "the only thing that seemed out of place was that some boxes were piled up on the shelf next to the rear door. They're not supposed to be there."

Tony walked back to the rear door and Chief Glass followed him. "Sal, I'm standing back here, the boxes are on the other side, not where they belong."

"Yeah, I moved them. Tony, they were piled up on the table against the electrical box."

Tony opened the cover to the box. As soon as he pulled the cover open, it sparked, sending an electrical impulse across the wires and flames went shooting up the wall. "Shit!" Tony ran, grabbing an extinguisher. "Look out Chief!"

Glass stepped back. "I'm calling the fire department." Tony was spraying the wall of flames shooting up five feet high. It was under control, but Tony continued spraying a second layer of foam on the area. Sounds of sirens blared out as the fire department headed to the scene.

***

Frederickson and Baker entered the emergency entrance of the Detroit Medical Center. Officers were standing guard on the suspect who was still being treated by the staff. Baker thought about how ironic it was, Harper was in a hospital room upstairs and her suspected shooter was here in the emergency room being treated for injuries. He turned to Frederickson, "I want to see this asshole."

"Tom, let's wait, he isn't going anywhere. Why don't you go upstairs and let Amy know we might have the guy."

Baker nodded, "She'll be happy to hear that. I'll only be a minute." Frederickson knew Baker had a lot of personal reasons to question Bobby Flynn. It would be better to make sure if there was any connection to the other parts of the case that they'd be able to uncover with specific questions. The doctor walked out of the room, "How's he look, Doc?"

"A broken left arm is the worst of his injuries other than a few cuts, bruises and a cracked right rib. You can see him now. We set his arm and ran x-rays, making sure there weren't any internal injuries."

"Thanks." Frederickson went into the room. He saw the suspect cuffed by his right hand to the gurney. The officer standing guard nodded to him. "Were you one of the cars responding in the chase?"

"No." He pointing to two officers who were at the desk filling out a report.

Don looked at the suspect; he wanted to jerk him off the gurney. Taking a deep breath, he moved to his right side. "What's your name?"

The young man looked up with tears in his eyes, "My name, you want to know my name? I'm hurt, I'm going to sue your department." Frederickson laughed as he leaned hard on Bobby's right side. "Hey, get off of me, shit I have a broken rib!"

"That's going to be the least of your problems. I'm going to break your other arm and rib if you don't answer my questions." Bobby looked up with fear in his eyes. "Now I'm going to ask you one more time, what's your name?"

"Bobby Flynn. Why did your people run me off the road?"

"I'm asking the questions. Where do you live?" Bobby gave him the address. The officer watched, appreciating Frederickson's methods.

"How do you know Lorenzo Virgilio?"

"He's my friend, we've been friends since high school, why?"

"When you took the shot from the hotel rooftop, who was your target?"

"I don't know what you're talking about." Frederickson leaned back on the suspects side. "Ow! get off me!"

"Not until you answer my questions."

Flynn was crying. "I want a lawyer."

Frederickson turned to the officer, "I think you need to go check on your team out at the desk." He knew what Frederickson meant.

"I'm not going to give you anything and no one is going to be here to be your witness. I want answers and I want 'em now!"

"I didn't shoot anyone."

"Then who did?"

"I don't know what you're talking about. I want a lawyer." Bobby yelled out, "Help, he's trying to kill me!"

A nurse came into the room. "What's going on?"

Before Bobby could answer, Frederickson said, "I'm not sure, he's been yelling the whole time. Maybe he needs something to calm him down."

Bobby cried out again, "Get him out of here, I want a lawyer!"

The nurse didn't quite know what to do. Frederickson smiled. "Sure, we'll get you one." He looked back at the nurse. "He's a suspect in the killing of one of my detectives. We'll be taking him downtown once he's released."

Bobby was sure he'd be killed if he didn't give the cops what they wanted.

Tom Baker was upstairs with Detective Harper. "We got the guy, Amy." She smiled, "They got the rifle and scope that he used. No doubt about it, he's involved but even if he isn't the guy, he knows who it is."

She was sitting up and leaning forward she hugged him. "That's great Tom; I want to see him."

"No, you don't want to see him, both of us want to kick his ass."

"Can you blame me? Where is he?"

"In the emergency area; they got him in a car chase."

"Car chase?"

"We got a warrant for his arrest and to search the address on file. We had questioned him before and although he appeared to have an alibi, we found that just his friend had an alibi."

"Go downstairs and make sure we've got everything we need to put him away for good."

Baker hugged her. "You get better; I'll take care of him."

***

The fire inspector was looking at the fuse box inside Virgilio's market. Chief Glass along with Tony remained at the scene watching him work. "Here's the problem, Chief. These wires are what caused the short and sparks." He was pointing to a charred bank of wires inside the metal box.

Glass bent down, taking a closer look. "How would that happen?"

The inspector turned toward both of them. "Someone tampered with these. There isn't any insulation on these wires. It's been stripped off."

Glass looked back at Tony. "Any idea who might have it in for you or your business."

Tony shrugged. "No, I don't know why anyone would want to do this."

The fire inspector stuck a red notice over the box, "You must have this repaired before you can turn on your power."

"Christ, all my meat will spoil."

"Sorry, but the whole block will go up in flames if it isn't repaired. Once you get it fixed, we'll re-inspect it for you; just give us a call."

THIRTY-TWO

Lorenzo pulled up in front of the Lafayette apartment building. He spotted two squad cars parked along the side of the place. He wondered, *What happened?* Pulling into the parking garage down the street, he saw that Bobby's car wasn't there. He listened to the message from his friend again.

As he sat there, his phone rang, he saw it was his dad calling. "Lorenzo, where are you?"

"Dad, I'm outside Bobby's place, it's surrounded by cops. Bobby's car isn't here."

"We've got other problems. Someone tried to burn our store down."

"What, is everything okay?"

"I've got a call into an electrician and he's coming to the market. Someone was here; looks like they stripped wires causing a fire."

"Are you and Sal okay?"

"Yeah, the fire was caught by Sal right away, it burnt the electrical box shorting everything out. The fire was put out but we got to get the electricity fixed. We can't turn anything on."

"What do you want me to do?"

"Zo, this wasn't an accident. We've got real problems. You better get back here."

Lorenzo was puzzled, *Did Perone have his guys try to burn the market down? Could he be planning to kill his dad?*

Tony Virgilio walked around the back of the market. He knew that Chief Glass and the police were still in the rear lot. They'd be there a while investigating the murder as well as the possible break-in. Sal arrived, walking in the back door, "Tony, what's going on?"

"I'm glad you're here," Tony waved him to the front of the market. "Someone tried to burn the place down. Think back, did you see anyone when you were leaving?"

Sal looked at him, "No, I locked up, closed the customer door and then went out the back door." Sal paused, "I saw a squad car in the back lot. One officer was in it, nothing odd."

As they were discussing the events, there was a knock on the back door. Tony walked to the back. He said, "Hello Bill, I'm glad you're able to help me. We had a fire." He walked him to the electrical box. "Right here. The fire department turned off all my power. The meat will spoil; I need it fixed as quick as you can."

"Tony, this is a big job. I'll need to call in some help."

"Okay, I don't care how much it costs, it has to get done or the loss will be catastrophic." The electrician made some calls and went back to his truck for tools. Tony and Sal headed back to the front of the market. "Sal, I called Lorenzo. We need to protect ourselves and the business." Sal knew exactly what he meant.

***

Chief Mathews had been apprised of the recent events. He had Detectives Frederickson and Baker in his office. He asked, "So you're pretty sure this Bobby Flynn is the man who shot Harper?"

Frederickson answered, "We've got the rifle and the forensic team is checking it for fingerprints. They are hoping to match the bullet to the one they took out of Harper. Chief, he sure looks and acts guilty. If he's not the shooter, he knows who is."

"That's not going to be good enough unless we can get him to talk."

They knew the chief was right. "Once he's patched up, we'll bring him in. I'm sure we can break him, Chief."

"Where are we on Councilman Perone?"

Frederickson looked at Baker. "Chief, we're running a search of the business that the council awarded to Buddy Swinton in the city. We've got to show that the two of them are in this together."

Mathews shook his head. "So we're nowhere yet." He stood, walking around to the front of the desk, "Can we connect these two events together, Harper being shot and Perone and this Swinton guy in business?"

"Unless the Bureau can break Gino Rossi or we get a confession from Bobby Flynn, no, we can't connect them."

"Okay, let's take another shot at Flynn and tell Sikorski to hold the other suspect, Gino Rossi. We've got to break one of these guys." The meeting broke up with the SIU team on a mission. When they got upstairs Frederickson turned to Baker, "Let's talk to Franklin one more time."

"Good idea, he's right here, maybe we'll get lucky." They grabbed some photos of the suspects in both investigations. Heading to the area where Franklin had been held, they unlocked the door. Franklin jumped up.

"Good news, John." He was startled and Frederickson chuckled. "You're going home tomorrow."

"Oh my god, thank you, thank you." He was so thrilled. "So what happened?"

"We solved the case, just need to finalize a few things."

"Like what?"

Frederickson reached into his pocket. He pulled out an array of photos. "John, we need to make sure we've got it all together. I need you to look at these, it will only take a minute."

"Sure." They sat at the table.

Frederickson laid out the photos. Baker pointed to the first one. "This is Gino Rossi, you said Councilman Perone introduced you."

"Yeah, I've already said that."

"Okay, John, we're actually putting the case together." Pointing to the next photo, "We all know this is Perone, and this is his friend, Buddy Swinton." Franklin nodded, Baker looked up at him. "Where and when did you meet Swinton?"

"I met him at the club."

"Did Perone introduce you to him too?"

"No, Rossi introduced us, he said that this Swinton was a local businessman."

Baker and Frederickson smiled, this was new information. It would help connect the two men along with Rossi. "John, we don't know who these two guys are, do you?"

Franklin picked up the photos of Bobby Flynn and Lorenzo Virgilio. "I don't know this guy," handing the photo of Flynn back to Baker, "but I've seen this guy at the strip club many times," pointing to Lorenzo.

"So did this Lorenzo guy know Perone?"

"I'm not sure but he was a friend of Gino Rossi."

Frederickson repeated what Franklin said, "Rossi and Lorenzo Virgilio were friends?'

"I didn't know Lorenzo's last name, but Rossi usually called him Zo. I'm thinking it was short for something or his nickname. That Lorenzo was always in the strip club."

Frederickson wanted to jump up. He again asked, "John, this is critical, think before you answer. Gino Rossi knew Perone, Perone introduced you to Rossi. Did you ever see Perone with Buddy Swinton and Lorenzo Virgilio?" He pointed to the two photos one more time.

"Yeah, I met Rossi and Swinton at the strip club, Councilman Perone introduced me to Rossi, and Rossi introduced me to Swinton. I never met this guy Lorenzo, but I saw both Rossi and Perone at the bar talking to him. I asked and they said his name was Zo. Does that help?"

"You just don't know how much. Do you need anything?"

"No, I just want out of here."

"Tomorrow, John, tomorrow." As the two detectives walked out of the room, Frederickson turned to Baker. "Tom, we've got them. These are all connected. I'm not sure if this Lorenzo or his friend Flynn shot Harper, but I still think the goal was to kill the mayor."

Baker agreed, "I can't think of any reason they would shoot Amy The bullet had to be meant for the mayor."

Frederickson said, "We'll need to go over all of this with the chief. I'm glad we've still got the club manager in custody along with Flynn and that the D.A. gave us something to charge him with. If we have a conspiracy, they can't alert the others involved."

THIRTY-THREE

Bobby Flynn had been patched up at the DMC and happy that the cops stopped asking him questions. The officer guarding him cuffed both of his hands together. "I'm doing this in front because of your broken arm."

"Thanks but I wish they'd give me some pain killers."

"Well maybe they'll give you some downtown at police headquarters."

"Police headquarters! I need to be in the hospital!"

"You're lucky they even set your broken arm. Cop killers usually don't get any medical treatment until you've been arraigned." The officer put Bobby Flynn into the back of his squad car. "You better hold on kid, I'm not a great driver." Flynn feared that he'd be tossed around. When they arrived, Bobby was happy to get out of the car. He was handed over to Detective Johnson.

Johnson smiled at Flynn. "So you're Bobby Flynn. I can't wait to get you upstairs. We've got a lot to talk about."

He moved Bobby into the elevator, holding him against the wall.

"Where are you taking me?"

Johnson laughed, "You're in for some serious questioning. Wait until Detective Harper's partner gets ahold of you."

Flynn was in a sheer panic. Why hadn't his friend Lorenzo tried to help him? "I need some pain killers, I have a broken arm and ribs. I think one of your cops busted another rib in the emergency room."

"Anyone see that?"

Bobby hung his head, "No, but I assure you that my attorney will know what to do."

They entered the interrogation room on the first floor. Johnson cuffed his suspect to the table. "This isn't going to be pretty kid, you better think about talking to the detectives. Good luck."

Bobby sat alone in the room, looking around. On the wall in front of him was a large mirror. He didn't like what he saw in his reflection, it didn't look good. His one arm was in a cast, his face bruised and he looked so small. The other three walls were stripped of everything, just cold cinder blocks. The plan was to leave him in there alone because maybe if he was by himself, once he was questioned he'd give up the details they needed. He was there for close to an hour.

Chief Mathews and Detective Frederickson stood on the other side of the one-way mirror. "What's the plan?" Mathews asked.

Frederickson turned, "I'm going to let Baker talk to him first."

"No, no, you can't do that."

"Take it easy, I made him promise to only scare the guy, I told him he cannot touch him."

"I hope you're right."

Baker walked into the interrogation room a few minutes later holding a folder in his right hand. He sat across from Bobby Flynn, never saying anything for close to a minute. "Hey! I want to see my attorney." Baker kept reading the papers in the file. He didn't even look at the suspect. Flynn yelled, "I'm talking to you!"

Baker put the file down. The look on his face even scared Frederickson as he watched from the other room. "You're talking to me, you want me to talk to you," Baker stood. You asked for a lawyer, I can't talk to you, but I'm not leaving."

"Forget the lawyer, take me back to the hospital!"

Pushing a pad in front of Flynn. "First, sign this saying you said you didn't need a lawyer." He watched Bobby fill out what Baker told him to do.

"Okay, now take me back to the hospital."

Baker pounded on the table, "When I get my chance with you, you won't know what's coming." He turned and slammed the door on the way out of the room.

Mathews looked back at Frederickson, "Don, remind me not to piss Baker off."

"He did good, just what we might need. This kid will need a friend."

It was close to ten minutes before Johnson entered the room. "Guess you met Detective Harper's partner." Flynn didn't answer, just nodded. Johnson sat down and starting to read aloud. "Bobby Flynn, birthdate February 4, 1995. Attended three schools, graduated from South Lake High School." He kept going through a litany of information just to show Bobby that they knew a heck of a lot about him. He stopped after reading the details of computer training, "I wouldn't have thought you were a computer nerd."

"Why, do I look stupid?"

"No, this says you're outstanding at programming." Bobby smiled. Johnson said, "Who'd think someone who had this skill was a killer."

"I didn't kill anyone."

"We've got your gun and the scope you used; your fingerprints are all over them. They were in your apartment."

"They're not mine."

"Yeah, I'm sure that's what you want us to think. Once you're arraigned for murder, the weapon will be entered into evidence and it'll be a sure thing. Too bad we don't have the death penalty in Michigan."

"I told you, it's not mine! I just hid it for a friend!"

"Sure, I guess I'd say that too if I were in your place."

Bobby clenched his fist, "I'm telling you the truth. It's not mine!"

"Okay, then who does it belong to?" This was where they wanted to get to. Johnson waited, holding his breath.

"It belongs to my friend. I don't even know how to put it together. I can't even shoot a gun!" Johnson gave him a doubtful look. "I'm telling you the truth, you can call him."

"I'd be happy to, maybe we can clear all this up." Johnson held his pen in hand, "Okay, what's his name?"

Everyone held their breath. "Lorenzo Virgilio, it's his gun." There it was, Frederickson and Mathews were thrilled that their plan worked; fear and confinement took its toll on Flynn.

Johnson played it cool. "Good, do you know his phone number?"

Bobby shook his head, "It's in my cell phone. I know the home number but he has a new cell number."

"Okay, you can give me the home number." Bobby gave it to the detective. "Bobby, you said the gun belongs to Lorenzo; why do you have it?"

Just that minute Bobby realized that he'd been tricked. "I ain't saying anything else." He was running everything back in his mind,

What exactly did I tell him?

"Bobby, I'm just trying to help you. We'll get a public defender to come in here, but you've got to help yourself. Did your friend Lorenzo shoot the detective?"

"I'm not saying anything."

"Okay, I'll see if we can get a lawyer in here for you."

When Johnson walked out both Mathews and Frederickson shook his hand. "Great job, you did it." Mathews said, "I'll get the district attorney to issue a warrant for Lorenzo Virgilio.

When Johnson and Frederickson got upstairs Baker rushed over, "So?"

"Lorenzo Virgilio, he gave us Lorenzo. Flynn is just the patsy who had the weapon. Virgilio had to be the shooter." Baker breathed a sigh of relief as tears ran down his face. He nodded as he walked back to his desk.

Johnson and Frederickson knew they needed to leave Baker alone for a little while as he picked up the phone. Frederickson turned to Johnson, "He's calling Harper." They smiled.

THIRTY-FOUR

Lorenzo and his father stood in the market, hoping the electricians would be able to repair the wiring and save their freezer full of fresh meat. "Mr. Virgilio, I'm pretty sure we've got it repaired. We called the inspector, but I can turn it on without his approval. He just has to inspect it so you're able to open back up." It was now close to five in the morning and the power had been off for close to ten hours.

"Throw the switch," Tony said. They watched as the electrician pulled the lever in the main fuse box. When they heard the hum of the small freezer in the back room, Tony pumped his fist. "Thank you."

"Mr. Virgilio, we need to check it all out. I'm glad you didn't open anything. It should have remained cold enough to keep the food safe." He watched as they put testers on all the wires in the box, checking the new casings and grounds that were installed. The lead repairman turned to Tony, "This wiring is old and needed some updates, but this was a deliberate act. Someone shorted out the main wires. This whole place could have gone up in flames pretty quick if this hadn't happened."

Virgilio looked over at his son. "I don't know anyone who would have done that. Thanks for everything."

"We called the inspector's office and left a message. He will probably be here early this morning. I'm going to leave the power on, but we will have to keep a man here until we get the final approval."

"Don't worry, I'll pay anything to save my store and its contents."

The man nodded, looking at his watch. "It's close to six; the office will call you tomorrow afternoon with a total cost."

Tony shook his hand, "I hope you'll come by next week. I'd like to send a gift for the men in your office."

"Thanks, not necessary. My wife always shops here; can't beat your meats." They smiled as the rest of the men were packing up their tools. "I'll stop by later to make sure everything is running good."

Tony motioned to Lorenzo and as they walked into the front of the market, Sal followed. "This is Perone, that's why he met me alone at the park. He probably had his guys here trying to burn the place down." Both of them agreed with him. The question was what would they do now?

***

The district attorney walked into the SIU office. Frederickson saw him enter. "Brandon, you slumming?"

"The chief said this was critical to your solving the shooting at Campus Martius. So, I'm guessing that you've got a lead?"

"Yeah, we've got the weapon and an accomplice. He's given us the name of the gun owner. The suspect Lorenzo Virgilio was at the hotel at the time of the shooting. He gave us some alibis that checked out, but now we have the guy who helped him and most likely hid the weapon for him. We want to surprise Virgilio." As Frederickson read the warrant, he smiled. "Thanks, this gives us a lot of leeway."

District Attorney Hanson nodded, "I want this as bad as you do Don."

"I know, thanks for bringing it right over."

Brandon shifted from one foot two the other. "Can we go over a few things before you take him into custody?"

"Sure."

"We're looking at a major criminal prosecution, I need to make sure my team is prepared for this." Frederickson listened, knowing that Brandon Hanson was a thorough investigator as well as attorney. "You're building quite a list of suspects, Don. There are so many people involved in these two cases. We almost need a score card."

"I understand it's just in the past twenty-four hours that we've connected the two events and participants."

Hanson continued, "Gino Rossi is being held by the FBI. He planted the bomb here, killing two officers and he's responsible for the woman under Franklin's car. I want to prosecute him, he's not getting any deal." That pleased Frederickson. "This new guy, Bobby Flynn, he has the weapon that was used in Harper's shooting. But he's not the shooter. Now you're saying that he's implicated Lorenzo Virgilio?"

"Yes, that's why we need to bring Lorenzo in. Brandon, we've also found out that this Virgilio guy is also known to both Rossi and Councilman Perone."

Hanson shook his head, "Christ, how far does this go?"

"That's what we need to figure out."

"Where's the deputy mayor, how does he fit into this?"

"He's just a patsy. We're pretty sure he's been framed for the killing of the woman he supposedly ran over. He has furnished us with information; he is a witness that can tie most of these people together."

Brandon looked back at Don, "Okay, Detective. Make sure your team follows procedures, I don't want any evidence or questioning tossed out."

"We've got it handled, promise." Frederickson looked at the warrant. "I'm glad it gives us some leeway, never know what we'll find when we arrest Lorenzo. At least we can search both his apartment and his dad's store."

***

Tony and his son, Lorenzo, knew that their partner, Perone, was no longer was protecting them. They were sure when Tony was meeting with Perone at Memorial Park that he ordered his men to destroy Virgilio's Market. "Lorenzo, I need to retaliate."

Sal was standing nearby, listening. "You better be careful, Perone is in a position of strength, you can't just take him out."

Tony nodded. "I've got details that will take him down. I've made copies of everything he's signed."

Lorenzo looked at his father. "First, I need to find out where Bobby is."

Tony agreed. "I've got everything handled here son, you better take care of that now."

Lorenzo walked out front punching in Bobby's cell number one more time as his father waited for the city inspector to show up.

Holding his cell phone, he watched two St. Clair Shores police cars pull up in front of the market. He figured, *They must be checking up on the fire*. Chief Glass stepped out of one of the cars as another vehicle pulled up behind the Shores police cars. More officers were now moving to the front of the market but Glass was the first to speak. "Lorenzo Virgilio, you're under arrest." He spun the young man around, cuffing him.

One of the officers was holding a warrant in his right hand. Detective Baker got out of one vehicle had a smile on his face. Baker watched as Glass held onto Lorenzo. "We've got a warrant to search your home and business."

Lorenzo was stunned "What the hell!"

Tony saw the action outside and he rushed out to stop it. "You can't do that," he yelled. That's when he spotted Detective Frederickson standing in the group. "You!"

Frederickson stepped forward "We're assisting the St. Clair Shores Police Department. He handed another piece of paper to Tony. "This is a warrant for a search of your home and business. I've got officers outside your home right now. Cuff him."

"You can't do this. I haven't done anything." Tony moved away from him but the Shores officer pushed him against the front of the market.

"Tony Virgilio, you're resisting arrest." Chief Glass said as his officer held onto Tony. "Take him in." Sal was standing inside, puzzled, wondering what should he do.

Officers moved into the building. "What's your name," pointing to Sal who was in front of the meat case.

"Sal Francisco."

"You need to move outside." Sal followed the directions.

Tony was yelling. "I can't leave, we had a fire here last night," pointing to Chief Glass, "Ask the Chief."

Glass immediately said, "Everything is okay now. Take Tony in, we'll handle this here. Your employee, Sal, can take care of the fire issue." Two officers put Tony in a squad car and drove away. Glass gave Frederickson all the details that happened at the market.

As Frederickson stepped out the back door, he saw an area cordoned off with yellow tape. How did this fit into their case?

THIRTY-FIVE

The councilman stood in the Eastern Market, He was at Shed five waiting for his two men to show up that screwed up the situation at Virgilio's market. They had to get rid of the Suburban, knowing that someone most likely saw them speeding away from the market. Perone paced, *What in the hell is wrong with these guys?* he was complaining to no one in particular. They were both known members on the councilman's staff. "Boss, here they come," pointing to a dark Ford headed their way.

"It's about time." Perone let them exit the vehicle. "Over here," he called out. The two men looked at each other, knowing that the boss wasn't happy. Neither one said anything, just walked to where Perone stood. The councilman had a frown on his face. "Either of you numb nuts have any idea what happened after you hit the cop?" They just shook their heads. "Well jackasses, the place didn't burn down for one thing and someone got your description and plate number, that's why you had to ditch the vehicle. Where did you put it?"

Looking at each other, the smaller guy, who was the driver spoke up. "We didn't have a choice, the cop drew his gun on Freddie."

"Hey, asshole, where did you put the Suburban?"

"Torched it, took the plates and everything out of it first."

Perone hung his head. "Torched it, brilliant. I'm sure no one noticed a vehicle on fire, exploding in a vacant lot."

"We hid it good, no one saw, promise. Poured a couple gallons of gas on it in a gravel pit."

Perone said, "Okay where are the plates and 'everything' else?"

"Put it in a bag, it's in the car."

Perone turned to Bubba who stood near, "Get the bag, I want to check it out." The man moved into the Ford and found the bag on the floor of the back seat. He handed it to Perone. "Okay." They were happy thinking he accepted what they did. Perone said, "We've got another job for you." They were pleased and did as they were told. Getting into their vehicle they followed Bubba who pulled out of the shed's back parking lot. Perone turned toward his driver. "Take me home, Bubba knows what to do. We can't leave any loose ends."

***

Lorenzo was cuffed in the back seat of Detective Baker's car, yelling at the top of his lungs, "Lawyer, I want a lawyer! I ain't done nothing."

Frederickson turned, "I've got to warn you, anything you say, including all this yelling can and will be used against you in the murder trial."

"Murder, you've lost your mind old man, I ain't done nothing!"

Frederickson smiled. "Your English teacher at South Lake wouldn't like that. It should be, you haven't done anything." Both of the detectives laughed. Lorenzo kept trying to get loose from the cuffs. "By the way, your friend Bobby Flynn has been a great help. We appreciate him giving us your gun and scope. That was about all we'll need to put you away for a long time."

Lorenzo was now breathing deeply. *Bobby, what the hell did you do?*

While Lorenzo was being taken downtown, Tony was taken into the St. Clair Shores Police Department. "Why am I here, Chief? You saw someone set me up. They broke into my place, tried to burn it down. They must have set my son up too."

Chief Glass locked the cell door. "If you're innocent, why push my officer? You're going to have to cool off, Tony."

"My market, I've got to take care of my market."

"Sal is there, he can do whatever is needed." Glass slammed the outer door to the bank of cells, leaving Tony alone, wondering what was going on.

The squad car arrived at the downtown headquarters and Baker and Frederickson escorted the suspect into an interview room, just down the hall from where Bobby Flynn was being held. "You can't do this! I ain't done nothing!" When neither of them answered him he yelled one more time, "I want my attorney!"

"Sure you do." When they walked out, Baker turned toward Frederickson. "Now what?"

"Now we talk to Bobby Flynn. I think he's the weak link in this group. We'll try to turn him upside down." Baker nodded. "I think we'll let them stew in there a while."

Once Chief Glass secured Tony in a cell, his team, along with Detective Johnson and his new partner, Benny Flowers, were searching Lorenzo's apartment. Because both the market and Lorenzo's apartment were in St. Clair Shores, Frederickson wanted to make sure that the Shores police were involved. The apartment was off of Nine Mile and Jefferson, not far from the market. Detective Johnson told Flowers, "You and the officer that Chief Glass sent need to go through everything upstairs, I'll cover the first floor." Another team was searching the market and Glass sent a third team to Tony Virgilio's house. Both teams knew finding something was rare, but you'd never know for sure.

***

Chief Mathews and District Attorney Hanson joined Frederickson downstairs. They planned to question Bobby Flynn together. Frederickson entered the room where Flynn was wringing his hands, "It's about time you came back." When Mathews and Hanson followed he looked from one to the other. "What's this all about?"

"Sorry to tell you, Bobby but we just brought your friend Lorenzo and his father in for questioning. Looks like you lied to us. Lorenzo said the rifle is yours, he said you shot Detective Harper."

Flynn jumped up, the chain on the cuffs pulled his hands to the table. "No, he'd never tell you that!"

"Oh, but he did, that's why I've brought the district attorney and our police chief along with me. Bobby, this is Brandon Hanson. He's the D.A. He said we could turn you over to the FBI. Killing a police officer is a federal crime. You could get the death penalty for that."

"I'm telling you, I didn't kill anyone! I can't even put that damn gun together! I told you it belongs to Lorenzo. He shot the detective, not me!"

"Funny, that's exactly what Lorenzo said. He told us that while he was at the bar setting up your alibi, you took the shot from the rooftop and he went to the ballpark to keep your cover."

Bobby was shaking as tears ran down his face. "No! He shot the detective! I took the gun from him to hide it while he went to the bar and ball game. I came there after I hid the gun."

Frederickson knew Bobby was about to crack and spill everything so he asked, "Wasn't your boss upset when you missed shooting the mayor?"

"The mayor, no, Lorenzo was supposed to kill the female detective."

"That doesn't make any sense, why kill a cop?"

"His dad said she put their uncle Vinny La Russo in jail last year." Frederickson was surprised, he didn't expect that, thinking the whole time that the mayor was the target.

The D.A. stepped forward. handing Bobby a pad and pencil. "Write it all down, everything you and Lorenzo did. If this checks out, you'll have to tell all of this in court. Someone's going to jail for the rest of his life."

Bobby was still shaking. All he could say was, "Why did Lorenzo say I did it?" Hanson stayed while he wrote everything down.

Once the Chief and Frederickson left Bobby Flynn with Hanson, Mathews stopped them, "Okay, now how about Perone?"

"We flipped Bobby to tell us about Lorenzo, now let's see if we can get Lorenzo to tell us about Perone." The chief laughed. They headed to the cell that held Lorenzo. Frederickson stepped in first. "Lorenzo, I want you to meet Chief Mathews."

Lorenzo didn't even look up. "I want my attorney, I'm not talking until he gets here."

Mathews answered, "You don't have to say anything, we got all the evidence we needed from Councilman Perone."

They knew Lorenzo was smarter than Bobby Flynn, but when the chief referred to the councilman he perked up. "Perone? Who is this Perone? What the hell are you talking about?"

Instead of answering Lorenzo, the chief turned to Frederickson. "The councilman was better than you said, he promised he'd get us the leader of the drug ring. It's a shame about the kid's father. Did the medics say Mr. Virgilio will recover?"

Lorenzo was stunned. "What? Recover from what?" Lorenzo tried to stand but his hands were so tightly hooked to the table he couldn't. "What happened to my father?"

Chief Mathews looked at him without answering for at least a minute. "What happened to him? You should know, with everything you've put him through. He's having chest pains!"

Lorenzo was shaking. "Chest pains, he was fine when you brought me in, I want to talk to him!"

"He's been transported to St. John Hospital on Seven Mile."

Lorenzo had tears streaming down his face and yelled, "This is bullshit! I want to know what's going on with my dad, now!"

Mathews slammed his fist on the table. "We owe you nothing. You're both responsible for killing hundreds with your drug running in this city; you don't get to tell us what you want." Turning to Frederickson, he said. "Put him in a cell downstairs, I'm done with him. Detective, let's find that warehouse that the councilman said they own. We've got our suspects in this investigation."

Lorenzo was falling apart. "Perone, he's the head of all of this! He can't put it on me and my father! It's him and his pal, Buddy Swinton."

Mathews turned to Frederickson, "Don, it's up to you, it's your case. The councilman gave us a lot of evidence on Tony Virgilio and his son."

Lorenzo was still yelling. "Perone is the key to the whole damn operation! He owns the warehouse where the drugs are kept; him and his friend Buddy Swinton are in this together!"

Frederickson looked at him, shaking his head. "Why should we believe you? The councilman has proof. He gave us the address of the drug warehouse, he showed us payments to you and your father and it all fit with what Gino Rossi told us."

"Gino Rossi! Are you nuts? He works for Perone and I can prove it!" Lorenzo was thrashing with the cuffs. Give me a pen, "I'll write it all down, I'll give you everything, they're not hanging it on my dad. Now I want to know how my dad is?"

"Okay, let's say you're right. If you can prove it, I'll call and check on your dad for you."

"I told you, I'll give you the warehouse address. I'll even give you Perone's partner, Buddy Swinton, and how they've been working on this for the past year. They're in it together."

Frederickson looked at him, "Right now you'd say anything to get off. By the way Lorenzo, you and your pals aren't that slick, we discovered the explosives in that bipod. Our team made sure it's not going to hurt anyone."

Lorenzo hung his head. "I don't know what you're talking about, I'm telling you everything I know, I'm not lying about Perone."

Frederickson smiled, "Okay write down what you say you know and we'll check it out."

Chief Mathews knew they'd have to come up with more evidence to get the councilman. The idea of telling Lorenzo that his dad had chest pains may have been a shot in the dark, but it worked. Mathews said, "Let's see what you wrote down." He read it aloud, "Councilman Perone has paid my father close to fifty thousand every month." After reading that, Mathews had more questions, "What's he paying your dad for?"

Lorenzo looked up. "Distribution of drugs. The warehouse is a cover, it's listed as a meat packing building off of Gratiot."

"That's a convenient story. What proof do you have, right now it's just your word against his."

"My dad copies every check. It comes from Perone himself. He's got all of them. I can take you to the warehouse, but only after I know about my dad."

Mathews turned to Don, they knew if they had checks written by Perone they'd have what they needed. He didn't want to let Lorenzo know but hoped to get more. "Is that all you've got?"

"No, I've got a video on my phone of Perone and Buddy Swinton talking about a shipment at the strip club."

"You've got Perone and Swinton on video? Does this video have voice recording?"

"Yeah, they didn't know I was taping them. Your guys took my phone, I can show you."

"I want to see it first," Frederickson said, turning to one of the officers. "Get me his cell phone."

Both men watched the video that Lorenzo had on his cell phone. They knew they had enough on the councilman. "Chief, he's asking for a deal. If he truly shot Harper I don't want any deals."

"I agree, Don. Maybe we can work something out for his dad

depending on how deep he's involved."

Don thought for a second, "Maybe we allow the family to keep the market. I'm thinking both the son and father are too deep in this drug business."

"You're probably right. We'll let the D.A. handle that."

"Chief, that was genius saying his dad had a heart issue. How did you come up with that?"

"I knew he was smarter than Bobby Flynn and he seemed very concerned about his family; just lucky, I guess."

Frederickson laughed, "Yeah, just lucky."

Mathews smiled, "I've already called Chief Glass. He's keeping Lorenzo thinking his dad had a health scare. Christ, if my son was that deep in all of this, I'd have a heart attack." Don nodded.

THIRTY-SIX

Chief Glass was brought in to continue questioning Lorenzo. Mathews wanted to make sure the St. Clair Shores team was involved. Glass liked the idea that Lorenzo was made to think his dad had a health scare. Glass sat across from the young man. "Lorenzo, your dad is stable right now. He had chest pains but we made sure he's okay. It looks like both of you are in for a lot of problems. He's being locked up now."

"What do you mean, both of us? Why is he locked up?"

"Lorenzo, you're not stupid. Once the FBI raids that warehouse of yours and finds all those drugs, I think you'll both be going away for a long time."

Lorenzo immediately had an answer, "I told the detectives, it's not our warehouse. It belongs to Perone."

Glass stayed with the case that Mathews and Frederickson pushed. "You better be convincing because the FBI is closing your father's market. It would be sold if you're both in jail."

"They can't do that, it belongs to our family. Mom and Anthony can run it along with Sal."

The Chief said, "I'm afraid it's not going to work like that." He heard Lorenzo stammering, "I've got to go, you better handle it with the FBI."

Lorenzo began yelling, "I want to talk to the head man with the FBI!" When no one answered he yelled louder, "I want to talk to someone from the FBI, now!"

This was the plan, get Lorenzo knowing that the market was also in danger of being lost. The teams wanted to be able to have a deal they could live with. Letting the Virgilio family keep the market was their best option. Glass stood at the door, "Let me propose something like that to the FBI. No promise."

***

The teams had the information they were seeking. Sikorski and his agents, along with Frederickson and his officers, organized their next move. Don turned to the FBI agents, "I want to find Buddy Swinton first. We know he's involved, his information is critical. If we can get him to talk, it would give us the final piece of evidence to put the councilman away."

"Okay, how to you plan to do it?"

"I've got his local address. My team will search it while you're raiding the warehouse."

"Good plan." The FBI and Mathews team had the address of the building in the Eastern Market. Time was of the essence before Perone got news of their actions. Three cars from FBI headquarters headed down Russell Street, turning east on Alfred to Orleans. There wasn't any signage on the building. Sikorski directed his people, "Okay," pointing to two agents, "Cover the large front doors." Pointing to another group, "I want you to cover the back. We'll all go in at the same time. I don't know if anyone is here. Proceed slowly."

The warehouse was now surrounded and the FBI had Chief Mathews team send in two squad cars for backup. The agents at the front doors radioed in, "All locked up, should we break it down?"

Sikorski told both groups, "Let's go on the count of three, break in both doors." Crack! The sounds echoed through the massive building. Once agents entered the front door, shots rang out. The first agent in was hit. They pulled him to safety. Sikorski leading the group yelled out, "FBI, drop your weapons." That was met with a second volley of bullets. He told his agents, "Has to be a semi-automatic rifle. Everyone take cover." Gunfire was returned by the agents, hoping the second group coming in from the back had a better view of the shooters.

Officer Flowers, who joined Detective Johnson outside, ran to the opening. "Flowers," Johnson called out, "stay outside, cover the street in case someone tries to escape." Flowers was on one knee, guarding the front of the building.

Sikorski called out a second time, "You're surrounded, drop your weapons." Again that was met by a burst of gunfire. He radioed to the agents covering the rear, "Stay in place, I don't want anyone else hurt and we can't have anyone escape." Once they had the entire place covered, he called it in. "Chief, we've run into a buzz saw here. Both your people and mine are being held down by at least two shooters with rapid-fire weapons."

Mathews answered, "I'm sending in additional units." The streets around Russell and Orleans were soon alive with the sound of sirens. Police cars roared into position around the building as officers jumped into action. Chief Mathews arrived with Lieutenant Jackson. He got a message to the FBI Special Agent in Charge, "Brian, I've got three teams out here. Jackson and I will coordinate everything outside."

Sikorski appreciated the help. "Thanks Chief, we still haven't got a count on how many men they have, but we know they have at least two positions pretty well covered."

"Jackson brought additional help, we'll get the assault rifle in to you."

"Appreciate that, Chief. Have her get it to my men covering the back door."

The battle continued with the suspects inside holding their position, firing anytime one of the agents moved.

Sikorski radioed to the team at the back of the warehouse, "They have to be running out of bullets. Move closer and when you're in position, use the assault weapons."

Armed now with the Colt AR-15, the team along the back of the warehouse moved into position. Sikorski had his men purposely draw fire, that's when the second team let out a barrage of bullets into the nest the suspects had built on the second level. Shards of wood filled the air as men yelled, "Stop shooting, we'll come out.!"

"Toss out your weapons first." Guns came down from behind the barricade, one gun first, then two long range rifles and an AR 33 hit the ground. Sikorski yelled out, "Come on down with your hands in the air."

It was over. One man stood. "Don't shoot, I'm coming down." A second man called out, "I'm wounded, I need help."

Although it all seemed to be going according to plan, Sikorski cautioned, "No one move yet." The first man made it downstairs. The agents yelled, "Down on the ground, spread your hands out to your sides." Sikorski motioned the men from under the platform to cuff the guy on the ground. He called out to the remaining individual, "You need to come down, now."

"I can't, I'm hit!"

He'd seen this ploy before. "We'll send a man up." Chief Mathews heard what had transpired. He sent two more men into the front of the warehouse. Although they hoped it was over, until the last man was in custody, they just didn't know for sure. All of this depended that only two men were shooting at them. Two agents found the stairway up and moved into position, waiting for their orders. Sikorski already had one agent wounded and didn't want to lose anyone else. "This is your last chance, we need to see you or I'm going to fire on your position." There wasn't an answer. He called out again, still no answer. He gave his men the order, "Proceed with caution."

Moving up the wooden stairs, they could see where the original shooters were located. "One man was on the ground bleeding."

The agents called out, "We've got one man down, he's wounded." Sikorski radioed to everyone, "Search the premises, we've got two men but not sure anyone else was in here. Hold your positions."

The two officers who had arrived late to cover the rear of the building spotted a man heading out of the back of the warehouse and jumping in a van. Radioing in, "We've got a suspicious individual in a late model black Chevy van heading out from the rear of the warehouse. We're giving chase."

Just what the FBI feared, a third individual from the warehouse involved. "I'm sending another team to join the chase."

The van spun out of the alleyway onto Orleans Street. It was speeding toward Wilkens and turned east. The officers were gaining in the chase, calling it in to the FBI car following. The van spun after crossing St. Aubin and the Dequindre Cut Greenway. It was now out of control and crashing into parked vehicles. The driver didn't know that the old pathway was once a railroad crossing and pretty rough. Officers pulled up and jumped out of their cars with guns drawn, "Come on out with your hands up." The suspect climbed out of the van's passenger side, and began to run. They gave chase. "Shawn, you go left, I'll follow him." Now two officers and two agents were in a foot chase. Shawn took the short cut and caught up with the man, tackling him twenty-five feet from the crash scene. Cuffing him, happy that the man didn't get away. They all returned to the warehouse, happy that the final suspect was in custody.

The FBI along with help from local authorities had both the men cuffed and the third person being treated at the scene for gunshot wounds. They were searching the building. "We've got what we were looking for, Chief," Sikorski said. His men had identified wooden crates of un-cut heroine, "Must be valued in the millions of dollars," Sikorski said. Now all they needed was to find Buddy Swinton. The FBI knew someone like Perone would try to hang it all on anyone but himself.

THIRTY-SEVEN

Frederickson along with Officer Michaels made their way into the realtor's office at the Stroh's River Place condo units on St. Aubin. "Sandy, our way in here is that the lady thinks you're still looking for a place to rent. I'll let you talk to her, see if she'll show you that unit again on the waterfront, the one near Swinton's."

"I've got it, sir" She smiled as she entered the office, Frederickson followed.

Looking up, she smiled, "Oh, I'm so glad you're back. Have you decided on a unit?"

"I'd like to look at the one you showed me on the water one more time."

The realtor turned to Don, "You going to follow us?"

Frederickson said, "No, I'll wait here if that's okay."

"Sure." The woman walked with Sandy, holding a brochure, going over all the amenities of the complex.

Once they were out of sight, Frederickson called in to his back up unit, "Okay, Baker, you and Spano park, I'll meet both of you. We can head up to Swinton's place." Frederickson had gone through the realtor's desk, grabbing a worker's badge, hoping to use it to get into the unit. The three of them moved along the condos that sat on shoreline, to the unit owned by Buddy Swinton. They had confirmed that Swinton's vehicle was parked outside. Frederickson stood at the door with Spano and Baker out of sight. He knocked, "Mr. Swinton, I'm with building maintenance, we have a problem on your floor."

After knocking several times, there was an answer from inside, "Can you come back?"

"Sorry, but it could be dangerous. We'll only be a minute, but I've got to check for a gas leak."

He stood outside for a few more minutes. Spano whispered, "Is there a rear exit?"

"No, when Michaels and I checked these places out, we noticed only one way in and out." Then he heard the door unlock, "I'm so sorry, Mr. Swinton, but the unit downstairs has a gas leak and we've got to make sure the gas isn't leaking up here too."

Swinton stood studying the man in the doorway. He saw the badge and work shirt, sure the guy was from the condo office. "I don't smell anything. I'm just getting ready to go out. Do you need me here?"

"No, but we'd appreciate it if you stayed while we check it out. The office doesn't like to be in any unit without the owner's permission."

"That's okay, I give you permission."

"Great, would you mind signing this; we just have to protect everyone."

"Sure." Frederickson handed him the clipboard with the papers on top. "Just sign and date it for me. I'll need to bring the DTE men up here with us." Swinton didn't even look at the form as he signed it. He handed it back to Frederickson. Don looked at the form, "You have to date it and put the time down too, it's the fifteenth at two-thirty."

"I know." Swinton did as Frederickson asked. "Can I leave now?" Frederickson looked at the form. "Sure."

Swinton put his jacket over his arm. Leaving the open doorway, he moved onto the balcony. Baker moved around the corner, grabbing him. "Buddy Swinton, you're under arrest."

"What, you can't do this!" He tried to squirm free. "I haven't done anything!"

Baker and Spano were now both holding him. "Mr. Swinton, you're being charged with drug possession and interstate drug sales."

The realtor and Sandy Michaels came out of the unit next door. The realtor, startled, asked, "What's going on out here?"

Frederickson showed her his badge. "We're arresting one of your tenants; he's given us permission to search his place."

"No, I haven't," .Swinton yelled

Frederickson held up the clipboard. "This says you did, dated and signed by you." The realtor was stunned, she had no idea what was happening.

Swinton was still trying to get free, "You tricked me, you can't do this!"

"Just watch us. The FBI raided the warehouse you own and confiscated a boatload of drugs."

"It's not my place, I don't own any warehouse here!"

"We've got proof that you're one of the owners. Guess you're a partner with a man that owns a meat market."

"Meat market, what are you talking about? I don't know anyone who owns a meat market!"

"You don't know Tony Virgilio?"

"Tony who? I don't know who that is."

"Virgilio says he knows you."

"Virgilio, I know a kid with that name, he's a friend of Gino Rossi. I met the guy at a club. I don't know this Tony. Think the kids name is Zo or something like that."

"We've got you as the sole owner of a warehouse on Orleans. It's full of drugs and you're the owner of record. Guess you've been in jail before only this time you won't be getting out, pal."

Swinton tried getting loose the entire time Baker and Spano walked him to their car. "Guys, it's not me, the warehouse belongs to another guy."

"Sure, we've heard that before."

"Maybe we can make a deal."

"That's something you need to cover with the FBI and the D.A., they're waiting to talk to you." Frederickson and his team knew that Swinton was already a candidate to give up Perone and their joint ownership of the warehouse. They'd turn Swinton over the the bureau, knowing they'd have a better shot of getting the guy to give up Perone.

***

The FBI had now all the key suspects in custody. Sikorski told Chief Mathews, "Gino Rossi and Buddy Swinton are critical to getting the proof you'll needed to arrest Councilman Perone."

Mathews said, "Remember we've got Lorenzo Virgilio and Chief Glass has his father."

Sikorski acknowledged him. "Chief, I know you want to charge Lorenzo Virgilio and his friend Bobby Flynn for the shooting of

Detective Harper. We'll have federal charges of terrorism against Gino Rossi for the bombing of your building and killing two police officers."

The last piece of the puzzle was to link Perone to all of them. The FBI and Detroit Police were working together on the critical case. Mathews suggested, "I think we need to bring the mayor and councilman in together so we can spring what we have. I'd like to see Perone's reaction, especially when we arrest him right on the spot."

Sikorski laughed, "You really want theatrics. Planning on selling tickets?" They all laughed at this remark.

"No theatrics, just pinning it on him once he sees all the cards starting to fall. He'll hear about, Rossi, Virgilio and Swinton, then we'll hit him with the warehouse. Yeah, I want him squirming in his seat.

Sikorski nodded. "I'd like to do that for you Chief, but I'd rather put it all together and then we can arrest Perone. We've got to do it soon, he's going to know we've got all his partners."

Mathews knew the FBI chief was right. "Okay, we'll do it your way. But my team gets to charge Lorenzo and Bobby for the shooting at Campus Martius and I want my detectives to have a shot at Gino Rossi. He killed two officers and the stripper."

"Agreed." The two men shook hands, happy they got their suspects in custody, now they just needed to arrest Perone.

***

Councilman Perone paged his secretary, "Millie, please try Mr. Swinton again for me." This would be the third time she'd called Swinton.

Millie knocked on the councilman's door, "Come in Millie."

She walked in shaking her head, "Sir, I've tried his cell phone again, he's not answering." She stood in the doorway waiting for him to give her another suggestion.

"How about his office in Ft. Wayne?"

"I called that first. His secretary said he was here in town and would be here the rest of the week."

Perone didn't want to show his concern, but he was getting very nervous. "Maybe he's in a meeting, we'll try him later on." Millie started walking back to her desk. "Millie, did I get a call from Gino Rossi?"

"No, did you want me to call him for you?"

"That's okay, I'm sure he'll call later." Once she closed his door, he got up from his desk and stalked to the window overlooking Woodward Avenue. *Where is everyone?* Perone paced his well-decorated office. Moving over to the bookcase, he pulled a knob displaying a well-stocked bar. Pouring a glass of Jack Daniels, he turned back toward his desk. Grabbing the intercom, he said, "Millie, get Bubba for me."

She dialed his driver, Bubba. "The Councilman needs you, hang on while I put you through."

Perone wanted to make sure that the men from the botched job at Virgilio's had been taken care of. "Bubba, did you handle the two idiots who were supposed to handle the assignment in St. Clair Shores?"

"All done, just as you wanted."

"Thanks, I need you to pick me up in an hour; I want to visit someone." Once he hung up, he went through his desk and put documents into a leather briefcase. Paging Millie, "I'm heading out for a while. If either Gino or Buddy call, put them through to me."

"Yes sir. Are you coming back?"

"No, I've got to take care of a few things. I'll be in tomorrow morning." Grabbing the briefcase, Perone stepped out of the Coleman A. Young Municipal Center on Woodward Avenue. Walking down the street, he made his way to where he knew his driver would be waiting for him. Bubba always picked Perone up around the block on West Larned Street. Turning the corner, he spotted Bubba. As he headed toward the vehicle, two men approached and flashed their badges. "Councilman Perone, we're with the FBI, you need to come with us."

Pulling his arms back, "Bullshit! I'm not going anywhere with you!"

Bubba saw what was happening and he got out of the vehicle, another agent immediately grabbed him from behind. "Don't move, I'm with the FBI." As he showed the man his badge, Bubba just stood still outside the vehicle.

Perone saw what was happening ahead with Bubba. He took a different tone, "Gentlemen, I've got an appointment that I need to get to. Can I schedule something at another time?"

"Councilman, you're going to come with us."

"What the hell for!"

"Our chief will give you the full details." Perone stepped back, until he saw a crowd gathering. People had their cell phones out, recording the incident. The ultimate politician, Perone stopped struggling.

"Okay, but this is all bullshit! I'll want to call my attorney to meet me. Where are you taking me?"

"Tell him you'll be at the Federal Building on Michigan Avenue." They escorted Perone to the waiting vehicle parked ahead.

THIRTY-EIGHT

Chief Mathews sat in his office with Frederickson and Baker. He was holding the morning Free Press with the headlines ringing out the news, "Council President Perone Under Arrest." The first two pages detailed the raid at the warehouse that Perone and his partner Buddy Swinton owned. "Mathews smiled, "Detectives, you both have a lot to be proud of."

Frederickson nodded. "Thanks Chief. The team is happy that together with the FBI we have been able to put these people out of business."

Mathews turned to Baker, "Tom, I'm sure Detective Harper was pleased when you told her the news."

"Yes sir, the best part is the doctors said she'll be able to go home tomorrow." They all agreed that was great news. Baker had a smile on his face that would have been hard to miss. "Chief, Amy and I plan to announce that we've set a date; we're getting married September seventeenth. Harper wants to be able to walk down the aisle without a limp."

Both the chief and Frederickson stood, shaking Baker's hand. The chief smiled, "Detective, I'm very happy for both of you."

Turning toward Frederickson, "Don, I'd be very proud if you'd agree to be my best man."

Although it was a surprise, Don nodded his head. "It would be my pleasure, Tom."

Baker looked at the chief. "Amy and I know that we can't be in the same squad, so one of us will resign before the wedding."

Chief Mathews immediately held his hands up. "No Tom, Don and I also have news for both of you. When Harper is ready to return to work, she'll be appointed special liaison between the police department and the FBI. We know that we need someone in that important position. I plan to tell her when Don and I visit her later today."

Baker pumped his fist, "Sir, she'll be so happy."

"Detectives, we've still got a lot of work on this case. Trials for Councilman Perone and his partner Buddy Swinton will take close to a couple of years." Looking at Frederickson, "Don, you have to put together your case against Lorenzo Virgilio. We now know that he shot Harper as revenge for last year's cases against his uncle, Vinnie La Russo. I think it's going to be easy to put him and his father in prison for conspiracy in the shooting, thanks to everything we got from Bobby Flynn."

Frederickson said, "I want Lorenzo to get life for the shooting, but I also want Gino Rossi to pay for killing Askew and Sowers in the bombing."

"The FBI promised that he'd pay for that." Lieutenant Jackson knocked. "Come on in, Lieutenant."

"Chief, I've got FBI Special Agent Sikorski here."

"Show him in."

Frederickson and Baker stood. "We'll go and let you talk to him."

"No, both of you stay, we're all in this together." Sikorski entered and everyone remained standing. "Brian, I hope it's okay, I'd like them to stay with us."

"Actually I'm glad they're here. I wanted to let you know that Buddy Swinton has given us everything we'll need to put Perone in prison for a long time."

"That's great!" Mathews was pleased with the news. "We have one more detail, Don," looking back to Frederickson. "You probably need to tell John Franklin the news, I bet he'd like to go home."

Sikorski asked, "Who is John Franklin?"

That brought laughter from all three of the men. "He's been under our protection upstairs for a while. I'm sure he wants to be out of here."

The two detectives went upstairs to the SIU office, happy that the team succeeded. Baker asked, "Can I update the team?"

"Absolutely!"

He then said, "I'm going to call Amy on the conference room phone; I fixed it so it can use facetime. I'd like her to be in on the news."

Frederickson said, "Great idea, I'm not sure what facetime is but I'm in."

Baker laughed, "Come on, I'll bring you into 2017."

***

Nancy Frederickson was happy to hear from her husband. "Don, I know this has been tough on everyone. I'm so glad Amy is okay and happy to hear her and Baker's news."

"I thought you'd like that."

"Did you tell the chief your plans?"

"No, he has a lot on his plate. I will let him know soon that I'm planning to retire."

"You know, I'm looking forward to that cruise you've been promising me."

"I owe you more than that, but it will be a good start."

Tony Aued

Acknowledgements

To my friend, Carl Virgilio. Your work on the cover is outstand, as it has been with my other novels. You've worked hard helping me and all the members of our writing group.

Thanks to the members of the Shelby Writers group. Your input and suggestions helped me develop this mystery and created a clear story for my readers.

Thanks to those friends who played a part in this story. I hope all of you enjoyed you time on the pages in here.

To my wife, Kathy. You have helped me when I've needed your input and always supporting me when I spent untold hours working on my novels, and for being my best friend and the best partner ever. I love you.

ABOUT THE AUTHOR

Tony Aued is a retired teacher and lives in Michigan with his wife, Kathy, of 47 years. They have two children and he loves writing mysteries. This is his eighth novel and the fourth in the Motor City Murder Mystery series. Detective Don Frederickson is the main character and appeared in the first book of the series as well as the other three books.

The action in all four novels takes place in the Metro Detroit area and Canada. Murder in Greektown is the first book in the series and is followed by three more local mysteries. Mr. Aued has been interviewed on local television and in many newspaper reviews. You can read about and order all his novels on his web site, www.Tonyaued.com.

Made in the USA
Middletown, DE
08 November 2019